UNDENIABLY YOURS

For a moment both Kaitlin and Matt stood frozen and stunned. She managed to breath one word: "Matt." Unwanted tears burned her eyes as she held on to Matt for dear life. Kaitlin blinked rapidly. She could hardly believe that he had found her. For two and a half years she'd dreamed of this. The feel of Matt's arms around her. Those ice green eyes staring hungrily at her. Without uttering a word, Matt leaned over and kissed her. His lips crashed into hers as he pressed his tongue in between. The kiss was surprisingly gentle, but it left her blood fired with hot desire. Kaitlin could feel it sizzling through her veins, causing her knees to weaken.

BOOK YOUR PLACE ON OUR WEBSITE AND MAKE THE ARABESQUE ROMANCE CONNECTION!

We've created a customized website just for our very special Arabesque readers, where you can get the inside scoop on everything that's going on with Arabesque romance novels.

When you come online, you'll have the exciting opportunity to:

- View covers of upcoming books

- Learn about our future publishing schedule (listed by publication month and author)

- Find out when your favorite authors will be visiting a city near you

- Search for and order backlist books

- Check out author bios and background information

- Send e-mail to your favorite authors

- Join us in weekly chats with authors, readers and other guests

- Get writing guidelines

- AND MUCH MORE!

Visit our website at
http://www.arabesquebooks.com

UNDENIABLY YOURS

JACQUELIN THOMAS

ARABESQUE
BET
BOOKS

BET Publications, LLC
www.bet.com
www.arabesquebooks.com

ARABESQUE BOOKS are published by

BET Publications, LLC
c/o BET BOOKS
One BET Plaza
1900 W Place NE
Washington, D.C. 20018-1211

All Kensington Titles, Imprints, and Distributed Lines are available at special quantity discounts for bulk purchases for sales promotions, premiums, fund-raising, and educational or institutional use. Special book excerpts or customized printings can also be created to fit specific needs. For details, write or phone the office of the Kensington special sales manager: Kensington Publishing Corp., 850 Third Avenue, New York, NY 10022, attn: Special Sales Department, Phone: 1-800-221-2647.

BET Books is a trademark of Black Entertainment Television, Inc. ARABESQUE, the ARABESQUE logo, and the BET BOOKS logo are trademarks and registered trademarks.

First Printing: June 2001
10 9 8 7 6 5 4 3 2 1

Printed in the United States of America

To Jeanette Cogdell

PROLOGUE

Love had been kind to her after all, Kaitlin Ransom decided as she strolled happily along the wide corridor of the Los Angeles Airport, heading to gate 31B. There, she would board a plane to Phoenix. While she walked, Kaitlin wondered if her sister-in-law had given Matt St. Charles the message to contact her. Throughout the months they'd been apart, Kaitlin missed him terribly, and she could hardly wait to see him again. Just the very thought made her giddy.

A low whining buzz commanded her attention. Kaitlin ripped the pager off her purse strap and glanced down. It was Sara Mendelssohn, her boss. She sought the nearest pay phone and dialed the number from memory. "Hello, Sara. I just got your page."

"Kaitlin. Hello, dear," she responded before pausing. "Hold on a minute."

"Sara? Are you there?" Kaitlin asked.

"Yes, I'm here. I couldn't quite catch my breath, that's all. Where are you, dear?"

"I'm here at LAX. On my way back to Phoenix."

"Then I'm glad I caught you. Marta Rosales called. She said she's a friend of yours."

"She is. We attended college together."

"She's getting married in a few weeks."

"Really? That's wonderful!"

"I'm pleased you think so. Because she wants you to take care of all the details. The gown, the wedding . . . everything." Sara took several deep breaths.

Kaitlin's concern for her employer overshadowed her excitement about Marta's wedding. It wasn't anything she could really put her finger on. Sara just didn't sound like herself. "Are you okay?"

"I'm fine, dear. Been having some chest pains lately. And a hard time breathing. It comes and goes."

"Why don't you go on home?"

"I'm the only one here in the store right now. Lily won't be here until later."

"Well, as soon as she comes in, you should leave," Kaitlin advised. "You may want to think about seeing a doctor."

"Kaitlin, you know how I feel about doctors. I'll go when I'm sick. Now back to Miss Rosales. She wants you to come to Mexico immediately. She's reserved a ticket for you. You should be able to pick it up at the Delta ticket counter. The flight's leaving at ten-thirty this morning."

Checking her watch, Kaitlin announced, "That's about thirty minutes from now."

"Well, you have your passport with you, right?"

"I have everything, but I'm not really prepared to go to Mexico."

"She was adamant about you coming. And we could really use the business. Sales were down last quarter. Do you think you could just go down for about three or four days?"

Kaitlin laughed. "I guess."

"So you'll do it?"

"Sure. I'll do it, Sara." She checked her watch once more. "Well, if I'm going to Mexico, I'd better go pick up my ticket. Thank goodness I didn't check my luggage. Before I go, though, I want you to promise to see a doctor. You really don't sound well."

"I'll be fine. Now go on and have fun in Mexico. I'll see you when you get back."

Kaitlin hung up and started walking briskly through the airport. She needed to hurry if she intended to make that flight to Mexico City.

Sara had barely hung up the phone when she was seized by a great pain that held her captive in its concrete grip. Frantically, she glanced around the store, looking, searching for someone—anyone to help her. Relief swept through her when Lily strolled into the store. Sara wanted to cry out but no sound would come. Darkness closed in on her swiftly, wrapping her in a heavy cloak. She tried in vain to reach out. Sara felt no more pain as she floated toward a luminous light.

The turbulence caused the airplane to shake, and Kaitlin for once paid it no mind. Her body rippled with excitement as she fantasized about her reunion with Matt. Her sudden trip to Mexico City would now delay it by a few days. But then what was another three or four days when you had a lifetime together, she mused.

Three and a half hours later, Kaitlin arrived safely and was met by Marta. She immediately embraced her friend, whom she hadn't seen or spoken to in a couple of years.

"Girl, I hope you know that I'd only do this for a real good friend. Even one who never writes or calls unless she needs something."

Marta laughed. "I know. I know. I've been very bad, but, Kaitlin, I really appreciate this."

"You owe me big time, but I'm so happy for you."

"I still pinch myself every now and then to make sure I'm not dreaming. Did you check any luggage?"

Kaitlin gestured down at the small black suitcase on wheels. "No, this is all I have."

Marta looped her arm through Kaitlin's. "Let's get you to the car. On the way, I'll tell you all about Armando."

Kaitlin took note of a very pretty young woman standing nearby, watching them. Despite her mixed race, her African-American heritage paraded itself for all the world to see in her creamy mocha complexion, her full lips, and her ever-observant dark eyes. Her long, raven-black hair was pulled back into a ponytail. Meeting Kaitlin's gaze, she gave the barest hint of a smile.

As soon as they started to walk, the woman followed close behind. Marta didn't seem at all bothered by it, prompting Kaitlin to ask, "Is she with you?"

Nodding, Marta replied, "That's A.C. She travels almost everywhere with me."

Kaitlin gave the woman a quick once-over. There was nothing about her that indicated she was a bodyguard.

"There are many people who hate my father and would destroy anyone who is close to him," Marta said.

Kaitlin was careful to keep her voice low. "Doesn't that scare you, Marta? I mean, your father . . ."

"Don't believe what you've read or seen on TV. You've met him, Kaitlin. He's a good man. He really is."

Throughout the ride, Marta told Kaitlin all about her fiancé. A.C. remained silent through the entire ride. It was almost as if she were invisible. Almost.

". . . Armando actually proposed the first time he ever laid eyes on you?"

Marta grinned prettily. "Of course I didn't take him seriously at the time. He was very persistent."

"How did you meet him?"

"He was here to see my father. I had been taking a

walk on the grounds, and we ran into each other on the terrace."

"He works for your father then?"

"Yes. Armando is his attorney." Pointing outside the car, Marta said, "This is my home. It's pretty here, no?"

The totally secluded estate was secured behind a huge iron gate guarded by several well-dressed men. A few of them wore their guns like jewelry, prompting an uneasy feeling in Kaitlin. She knew it had to do with everything she'd heard about Marta's father, Hector Rosales, whom she'd met years ago when she and Marta were attending college.

Shortly after their meeting, she'd heard accusations of his heading one of the two largest drug cartels in Mexico. Hector had taken out both newspaper and magazine ads to declare his innocence. Embarrassed, Marta left college and returned to Mexico.

As they neared the house, Kaitlin spotted more men with guns. She regarded Marta uneasily, the corners of her eyes twitching ever so slightly.

Covering Kaitlin's hand with one of her own, Marta whispered, "It's just for our protection. They're harmless and very loyal to my father."

Kaitlin bit her lip but said nothing.

One of the men approached the black Mercedes as it rolled to a stop. He opened the door and held out his hand. Placing her hand in his, Marta climbed out first, then Kaitlin.

The man seemed to hold on to her hand longer than necessary. Raising her eyes, Kaitlin said, "Thank you," and pulled her hand away. As she walked away, she heard the man's soft laughter. She cast him a look of disapproval, which only seemed to further amuse him.

Kaitlin made a point of staying beside Marta and keeping her eyes averted. These men were dangerous, and they scared her. While she walked, she admired the three-story, twenty-seven-thousand-square-foot mansion. Kaitlin had to admit the place was breathtaking.

Behind them, Kaitlin heard A.C.'s footsteps. Marta came to a halt just before they entered the foyer. She quickly dismissed A.C.

Leading the way into the huge drawing room, Marta stated, "I'm sure you want to get settled. I'll get one of the maids to show you to your room. I'd do it myself but I need to speak with the cook about dinner."

"Marta, take care of whatever you need. If you'd just tell me where it is, I'm sure I can find the room on my own."

"It's the third room on the left in the west wing. This house can be confusing," Marta warned. "But I'll be right back, so just wait here for me."

As soon as Marta walked away, Kaitlin strolled through striking French doors that opened onto a one-hundred-foot terrace overlooking Lake Avándaro. While she admired the view, she heard voices. Two men were arguing nearby. From where she was standing, Kaitlin could see the long jagged scar on the face of the taller of the two. In his anger, he looked almost sinister. He glanced over and caught her watching them. Glaring, he gestured to his companion and the two men rushed off.

Kaitlin had just stepped back inside when Marta returned, followed by a maid carrying a tray of sandwiches and a pitcher of iced tea. She set it down on the coffee table.

The two women sat down side by side on a Victorian-style sofa. Marta turned on the television.

"Where is your father?" Kaitlin asked, picking up a plate and a knife.

"He's away on business. He should be back in a day or two," Marta responded, but Kaitlin didn't hear her. Something on television held her attention. A news reporter was talking about a recent plane crash in Phoenix. She gestured impatiently for Marta to turn up the volume.

"If you've just tuned in, we are reporting the crash of Phoenix Air flight 805 . . ."

Flight 805. Kaitlin dropped the knife she was holding.

"What's wrong, Kaitlin?"

She stared in horror at her friend. "Dear Lord, I was supposed to be on that plane, Marta. But you called . . ." Kaitlin couldn't stop trembling. She could have easily been . . . She didn't want to finish the thought. "I've got to call my family. I don't know if they've spoken to Sara yet. If not, they probably think I'm dead." Putting the plate back on the tray, Kaitlin rushed to her feet.

Marta stood up, too. "Of course, you need to call them."

Before they could leave the room, Marta was detained by one of the maids.

"*Sí.*" Sighing, Marta turned back around, facing Kaitlin. "You go on, Kaitlin, and make your call. I'll meet you in your room shortly."

"Okay." Kaitlin rushed off in search of her room. She veered to the right. "This house is much too big," she muttered as she turned around in confusion. "Now which way am I supposed to go?" Kaitlin turned and headed in the other direction. "This has to be it." She placed her hand on the gleaming brass knob, turning quickly.

Just as she stepped inside, the very air around her shouted that Kaitlin had entered the wrong room. Everything was covered in plastic. Inside stood the man with the scar, holding a gun pointed at another man seated in the center of the room. The man was begging and pleading for his life.

The loud blast and the sudden burst of fire seemed to culminate simultaneously. When half of the man's head and brains splattered all over everywhere, Kaitlin couldn't handle the shock.

She fainted.

Coming out of a thick haze, Kaitlin groaned and placed her left hand on her temple. Her head was hurting something fierce and a large knot was forming. She slowly opened her eyes.

"Kaitlin?"

She turned her head. It was A.C., and she was wearing a shoulder holster. After what she'd witnessed, the fact that this woman was wearing a gun made Kaitlin fearful. "W-what are you doing in here?"

A.C. moved closer. "Kaitlin, we don't have much time." She was talking fast. "All I can say right now is that I'm not going to let anything happen to you. But you must do exactly as I say. You hit your head pretty hard. I also heard Marta mention that you were pretty shaken up by that plane crash in Phoenix. From this moment on, you can't remember a thing. Not even your own name."

"Why?"

Her eyes hardened. "Because Elian will kill you."

"Elian? The man with the scar?"

A.C. nodded.

Kaitlin gasped and tried to rise. She no longer cared about the throbbing ache in her head. All she could think about was finding a way to escape from this madness. She had witnessed a murder and now her own life was in danger.

A.C. gently pushed her back down. "Don't worry. I'm not going to let anything happen to you, but you will have to follow my instructions to the letter. Stay close to Marta at all times, and most important, you're going to have to fake amnesia. You have to be convincing.

Your life depends on it. Kaitlin, there is one more thing, you must never contact your family."

"But . . ."

"Not until I can get you safely away from here, and I give you my word that I will."

Kaitlin squeezed her eyes shut to hide her tears. Just when all of her dreams were about to come true, she'd stumbled into a nightmare. Fate couldn't have been more cruel.

ONE

Two and a half years later

"This was a great idea, Kaitlin. Taking a ride around the city has given me a new appreciation for Valle de Bravo."

She smiled politely. "You need to get out every now and then, Hector."

"It's not as chilly as it was last January," he observed.

"No, it isn't. It's real nice out. You should be glad to get away from that fortress you call home."

His cold hand covered hers. "It is your home, too."

Kaitlin didn't respond. She simply stared out the window at the neat, white stucco houses trimmed with red balconies and tile roofs, giving the town a colonial feel. As they neared Lake Avándaro, she heard Hector saying something. She had no idea what. Turning to face him, Kaitlin murmured, "I'm sorry. What did you say?"

"You are not happy here?" he asked in heavily accented English.

Kaitlin remained quiet because she didn't want to make Hector suspicious. No, she wasn't happy in the lakeside village that lay west of Mexico City. She was surrounded by lush pines, picturesque mountains and sparkling waterfalls, but Kaitlin had little adoration for the beautiful scenery. She wanted to go home because she didn't belong here, especially not in Hector's world.

"Have you remembered anything of your past?"

"No, nothing," she lied. "I guess that's what really bothers me. I just don't know where I belong." She was so tired of pretending. Kaitlin wanted nothing more than to be herself and return to her family. She couldn't help but wonder if they were still looking for her. Surely they wouldn't give up.

Hector looked perplexed. "You've seen all of the leading specialists. The doctor in Houston seemed promising, I thought. I don't understand why you didn't want to go back to him."

"I got scared, Hector." In truth, it was because the doctor sensed that her amnesia was nonexistent. She could see it in his eyes and the way he questioned her.

"If you like, we can begin the search for your family—"

"No," Kaitlin quickly interjected. She certainly didn't want to put her family in harm's way. "I'm afraid that I won't remember them." She fingered her pearl necklace absently.

"Maybe seeing them would have the opposite effect. It might help you regain your memory," he suggested softly. After a moment, he spoke again. "I have to admit that I do not think you are telling me the truth, Kaitlin. I have suspected for a long time now that you are faking this amnesia . . ."

Hector didn't finish the sentence because the car suddenly came to an abrupt stop and the chauffeur started shouting in Spanish.

Kaitlin's body reacted. A thread of anxiety traveled down her spine as she spied a huge black truck blocking their path on the empty road.

Their driver tried to back up, but now another vehicle, a black car with dark tinted windows, prevented their exit. Kaitlin looked over at the man sitting beside her. "What's going on?" she asked fearfully.

"Get down!" Hector ordered, jarring her into action.

Kaitlin heard the panic in his voice. "What's happening?" she screamed from the floor of the limo.

"Just do as I say. Stay down and don't move."

Seconds later, the windows exploded into millions of pieces. Hector grunted as if in pain and threw his body over hers.

The shooting seemed to go on forever.

Kaitlin had no idea how much time had passed, but as quickly as they started, there were no more gunshots. Only the sound of the horn blaring nonstop shattered the silence. Kaitlin tried to place her hands over her ears to shut out the annoying sound, but she couldn't. Hector's body held her prisoner in the cramped space.

The sirens off in the distance meant help was coming. She was too scared to fall apart. Too afraid to cry. Instinctively, Kaitlin knew the driver was dead. Although Hector wasn't moving, she could hear his ragged breathing.

From all around the limo, Kaitlin heard doors slamming. *The police. The police are here.*

As soon as they opened the door and pulled Hector out, Kaitlin crawled out screaming, "*¿Puede usted aycudarme?* Can you help me? Someone just tried to kill my husband."

Los Angeles, California

She'd had the dream again.

Sabrina Melbourne sat up in bed. Her palms were wet, her body wringing with perspiration and her heart pounding heavily. After she had met the Ransom family a year or so ago, this dream had continued to haunt her. It was a dream about Kaitlin.

She remembered Jillian telling her about seeing someone in the Houston airport that strongly resembled her sister. Then there were the dreams that Laine had been having, and now her own. Sabrina knew what it meant. Kaitlin Ransom was still very much alive.

It was time the family knew the truth. But how did you go about telling someone a thing like that? And without any real proof. Sabrina's thoughts traveled to Matthew St. Charles. The poor man was still in Arizona searching for his lost love. Although Sabrina didn't have any real idea where Kaitlin was, she had a strong notion that it wasn't Phoenix.

Feeling a bit chilled from the damp gown she wore, Sabrina climbed out of bed and slipped on a fresh one. Experiencing a sense of disorientation, she grasped hold of the footboard for support. Sabrina crawled back into bed. She lay in the middle of the bed just staring into darkness.

The next morning, Sabrina picked up the phone several times, only to put it right back down. This was not an easy task for her. Finally she decided to forge ahead. The Ransom family needed to know that Kaitlin was alive.

"Hello, Ray. This is Sabrina."

"Hey, Sabrina. What can I do for you?" He sounded in a good mood.

She felt encouraged. "I really need to talk to you. It's important. Can we meet somewhere for lunch?"

"Hold on for a minute. Let me check something."

Drumming the desk with her fingers, Sabrina rehearsed what she would say in her mind while she was on hold.

Ray came back on the line asking, "What time were you thinking about?"

"How about two o'clock?"

"That's fine." They discussed a location and hung up.

Hours later, Sabrina was already at the restaurant when Ray arrived. They were seated immediately.

"It's good to see you, Sabrina. How have you been?"

She smiled at him. "Okay. How about you and your family?"

"Everyone is fine. Carrie's pregnant again. She's due in October."

"I know," Sabrina responded. "Allura's pregnant, too."

Ray was surprised by her revelation. "How do you know?" Then he gave a short laugh. "I forgot. You're supposed to be psychic."

"Now you sound like Regis. My sister finally realized that I have the gift. I wonder how long it'll take you."

Ray laughed even harder.

After they gave the waiter their orders, Sabrina decided it was time to tell him why she wanted to meet. "Ray, I need to tell you something. I know you're going to find it a little hard to believe, but please keep in mind—"

"What is it?" Ray cut in. "Just spit it out."

"It's about Kaitlin. Ray, your sister is alive."

His expression pained, he shook his head in disbelief. "Don't . . ."

"Please believe me," Sabrina implored him. "I wouldn't tell you something like this to hurt you. Ray, you know me better than that."

He leaned forward, his voice low but exact. "Sabrina, I wish to the good Lord above that you were right. My family has had a hard enough time with this. We can't go through anymore. It hurts too much."

"Jillian saw her. She *saw* Kaitlin when she was in Houston. That was your sister. It was!"

"No, it wasn't," Ray stated flatly. "Kaitlin died when that plane went down. In July, it'll be three years. Jillian knows that."

"No. Jillian doesn't," Sabrina argued. "She won't tell you this, but that day still haunts her. What about Laine? He still has dreams of her—troubling dreams. Kaitlin's in some kind of trouble."

Their food arrived, but neither one could eat.

Finally Ray said, "Sabrina, do me a favor. Please don't discuss this with anyone else in the family. Don't ever mention this."

"But, Ray . . ."

He rose to his feet. "I've got to go." Dropping a twenty-dollar bill on the table, he added, "This should cover lunch."

"I'll pay—"

"No. I'll do this. You just remember what I said." His tone held the threat of a warning.

Ray was gone before Sabrina could respond. Things had not gone as well as she'd hoped. But she could understand why. Ray was too afraid to hope or believe. Glancing up toward the heavens, she whispered, "I'm going to need some help down here, Lord."

It was Sunday afternoon and everyone had gathered in Riverside at the home of the family matriarch, Amanda Ransom.

During dinner Allura announced, "Trevor and I are expecting again. The baby's due around the middle of September."

Her sisters were the first to respond.

"That's wonderful," Jillian stated. "Your baby and Carrie's will be a month apart."

"When did you find out?" Elle wanted to know.

"On Friday," Allura answered. "I didn't even have a clue. I thought I was just run down or something. That I could be pregnant never entered my mind."

"But didn't you tell Sabrina?" Ray asked. "She told me that you were pregnant two weeks ago."

Allura shook her head. "I didn't tell anyone anything. I didn't know. Hmm. I wonder how she knew?"

"My sister has visions," Regis responded. "Some things come to her in dreams as well."

Ray eyed her. "Do you truly believe that Sabrina's psychic?" Although he'd been present during one of her episodes, he had a hard time digesting any of it.

Regis nodded. "I do. I don't know what would have happened the night Jonathan was born."

"I believe she's psychic," Carrie stated. "I was there that night when she had the vision of Regis going into labor alone in that cabin at Big Bear. Besides that there are too many things she's predicted that have actually happened. I certainly wouldn't take anything she said lightly."

Excusing himself, Ray pushed away from the table and left the room abruptly.

"What's the matter with him?" Ivy inquired. "That brother of mine is sure acting weird today."

Carrie shrugged. "I don't know. He's been acting strange for a couple of weeks now. Being pregnant, I thought I was supposed to be the moody one."

Amanda cut off a piece of catfish. "Men are entitled to mood swings every now and then. Just leave him be."

"I don't know, Mama Ransom. I think something's bothering him. Only he won't open up to me." Carrie picked up a glass of iced tea. "This just isn't like him."

"He'll be fine," Jillian assured her. "Knowing Ray, he'll take care of whatever it is that's bothering him. That's just how he is."

After giving it some consideration, Carrie nodded in agreement. "I guess you're right."

Ray stood in the hallway, listening to the conversation. Was there a possibility that Sabrina was right? Could Kaitlin really actually be alive somewhere?

* * *

January 24. Today was Kaitlin's birthday. Had she lived, she would have been twenty-six years old, a year younger than him.

Before picking up his suitcase, Matthew St. Charles looked around the apartment where he'd spent the last two years. His eyes filled with tears. *Kaitlin is dead*. It was long past time he accepted that fact and moved on with his life. "Good-bye, Kaitlin," he whispered. "You will always own my heart."

A glance down at his watch indicated that his flight to Los Angeles would be leaving within the hour. This was the only gift he could give Kaitlin. Allowing her to finally rest in peace.

A news bulletin flashed on television, catching Matt's attention.

". . . there has been no confirmation from the Mexican authorities, but the reports are that Hector Rosales died a few minutes ago from the gunshot wounds he sustained. WPBN News reported the attempt on Hector Rosales's life two weeks ago. He was shot several times. . . . Reports also say that his young wife was with him at the time. . . ."

Matt was in no way sympathetic. How long had he prayed for Rosales's death? Live by the sword—die by the sword. . . .

Turning off the television, Matt picked up his luggage and left.

Matt told himself that the decision to leave Phoenix was a good one. His friend, Bob Steele, had been managing Matt's chain of restaurants and the photography studio in his absence, but it was high time he returned to the forefront.

The early-morning sun glared bright against the soft, clear blue backdrop of the heavens, but Matt was still too immersed in his grief to relish the splendor of his surroundings.

While he waited for his plane, Matt remembered happier days. No matter how much time passed, he knew the grieving for Kaitlin would never stop.

Throughout the hour-long plane ride to Los Angeles, Matt kept his eyes closed and pretended to sleep. He didn't want to talk to anyone, not even the beautiful flight attendant who kept trying to flirt with him. He only wanted one woman, and that woman was gone.

He would never forget Kaitlin's shapely five-foot-ten-inch frame, her big beautiful smile, her milk-chocolate complexion and dark brown eyes. He would also miss that incredibly sexy mole just above her top lip.

As soon as Matt entered the terminal at LAX, he spotted Bob and strolled toward him purposely.

Bob embraced him. "Matt, it's good to see you, man." Shaking his head regretfully, he added, "You don't look like you've been sleeping well."

Matt's face ached with inner pain as he tried to reassure him, "I'm managing. How's everything going?" He hoped Bob hadn't noticed his strained tone of voice.

"Everything's going just fine, but I'm glad you're home. You did the right thing in coming back."

Matt shrugged. "I guess I'm still too numb to feel anything right now. I know I've got to let Kaitlin go."

"There are some people here who are very excited about seeing you."

Glancing around, Matt asked, "Who?"

Bob gestured to his left. Matt followed with his eyes and found that Carrie, Ray, and Mikey were standing nearby. Permanent sorrow weighing him down, he straightened his slender frame and walked slowly toward them.

As he neared, Carrie held out her arms to him. "Matt, I'm so glad you decided to come home. We've really missed you." She looked him up and down. "My goodness, you've lost so much weight."

Matt didn't miss the fact that Carrie seemed heavier and she was practically glowing. "It looks like you're gaining. Is there another little one on the way?"

Grinning, she nodded. "The baby's due in October."

Although Carrie appeared genuinely happy over seeing him, Matt didn't miss the look of sadness that passed over her face.

Suddenly a little boy lunged forward. Sandy-haired, with light brown eyes, he looked like his mother. "I missed you, too, Uncle Matt," Mikey announced. "I thought you weren't never coming back."

Trying to appear as excited about his homecoming as they were, Matt smiled. "You don't have to worry about that anymore. I'm home now." Deep within, his heart constricted, and he reached for the little boy. Picking up his nephew, Matt held him close, holding back his tears. When he put Mikey down, Matt was once again in control of his composure. He turned to Ray.

"It's good to see you again," Ray said as he reached out to shake Matt's hand.

"Thank you for saying that." He and Ray had never been close friends, and Matt had to wonder if deep down, Ray blamed him for Kaitlin's death.

As if he knew what Matt was thinking, Ray insisted, "I mean it. I know you're not responsible for what happened to my sister. She died when that plane went down. You had nothing to do with that."

"I really thought she was alive . . ."

A strange look passed over Ray's face, causing Matt to wonder at the reason.

Carrie spoke up. "We know, and when Kaitlin's body was never recovered, we hoped against hope that you were right."

Ray cleared his throat loudly. "It's time to move on." He placed his arms around his wife. "Today is her birthday. Let Kaitlin rest in peace."

Matt knew Ray was right, but secretly he doubted he would ever find peace without the love of his life.

As they strolled along the corridor, Matt asked, "Where is that pretty little daughter of yours?"

"She's with Elle. They're having a girls' day out. Elle's taking Bridget and some of our other nieces to the movies."

Ray burst into laughter. "Elle's probably going to be bald by the time they get back."

Matt smiled. Elle was a shy, younger version of Kaitlin. "How is the rest of your family, Ray?"

"We're all doing the best we can. Some days are harder than others. . . ."

Carrie nodded in agreement.

They continued to walk along the busy corridor, each person immersed in his own private thoughts.

"Why don't you come over for dinner tonight, Matt? I know Mikey would love to spend some time with you," Ray suggested as they waited for Matt's luggage to appear.

He knew what Ray was doing. It would be hard returning to his home, but it was something that he could no longer avoid. "Thanks for the invite, Ray, but I've got to face that house sooner or later. Two and a half years ago, I vowed not to return there without your sister. . . ."

Ray nodded his understanding. "I would like to tell you that it gets easier, but I'm not sure I believe it myself. We just have to move forward. That's what Kaitlin would have us do."

"I love her so much. I don't know if I'll ever get over losing her." Matt's eyes grew bright, and he closed them. He blinked quickly when he felt Mikey tug on his hand.

"Would you like some ice cream, Uncle Matt? I saved my allowance so I could take you out for a treat. It might make you feel better."

Smiling, Matt nodded. "I'd like that." When he glanced over at Carrie, he saw that she, too, was trying to keep from crying.

TWO

Matt's first stop was La Maison, one of ten restaurants located from California to New Orleans left to him by his parents. The employees on hand seemed thrilled to see him. After a thorough but quick inspection, Matt was satisfied that everything was in order. He and Sasha, the manager, retreated to her office.

He stood over by the huge window. "It looks like you've kept everything under control, Sasha."

She smiled. "We've missed you, Matt. I was afraid you weren't going to come back." She advanced closer to him. "I'm so sorry about Kaitlin."

Turning away from Sasha to stare out of the window, Matt said, "Thank you."

"I can't help but notice, you've lost a lot of weight. You have to take care of yourself."

He turned around. "I'm okay."

After a few more minutes with Sasha discussing new dishes for the restaurant, Matt retreated to his own office. Bob was seated at the desk, going through a stack of reports. He pointed to the left at a stack of messages. "Those are for you."

Messages that needed to be dealt with urgently had been forwarded to Bob first, then on to Matt if necessary.

"I told them you were expected to return home shortly."

Picking them up, Matt mumbled, "Thanks." He peered over at Bob. "I really appreciate you taking care of the restaurants. Everything looks good." He went through the haphazard pile of yellow paper.

"It wasn't a problem. You took care of all the emergencies, although, I do have to tell you, your employees really missed you. We're all glad you're back. I hope you're ready to get back to work, too."

"I think work is what I really need right now. I'm going to be traveling for a while. I need to visit each of the restaurants, make sure everything's running smoothly." He thumbed through his messages once more.

There were several from Preacher Watson.

"I see Preacher's called a few times in the last couple of weeks. I haven't heard from this man in years. I wonder what's up with him."

"Isn't he the guy from your Night Ranger days?"

Matt nodded. "Yeah. Here's one from Gennai Li. I know why he's calling. He probably heard about Hector."

"He said it was good news."

Nodding again, Matt agreed. "Hector's death is good news. I guess I'll make Gennai my first call."

Bob stood. "I'll leave you to your calls then. I need to get back to my own office."

Matt walked Bob to the door. "I'll see you later. We're having dinner tomorrow night, right?"

"If you feel up to it. Give me a call." Bob paused. "How are you getting home tonight? Want me to come by?"

"No. I'll ask Sasha to drop me off. Thanks again, Bob. For everything." After Bob left, Matt returned to his office and picked up the phone. An answering machine picked up. "Hey, this is Matt. What's up, old buddy? Give me a call when you get home." He recited his home number before hanging up. Next he tried Preacher.

Another answering machine. He left a message.

An hour later, Matt had returned all of his calls. He was in the middle of checking the inventory when Sasha knocked on the door, carrying a plate in one hand.

"I thought you might be hungry, so I whipped this up for you myself."

Although he wasn't hungry, Matt gestured for her to bring in the food. "I don't know what I'd do without you."

Sasha placed the tray in front of him. "I'm hoping you never have to find out." Straightening, she added, "Matt, I care about you. I hate seeing you in all this pain." She placed a gentle hand on his shoulder.

Covering her hand with his, Matt nodded. "I know, Sasha. You're a good friend, and I'm grateful to have you in my life. But you don't have to worry. I'm going to be fine."

Removing her hand, Sasha backed away. "When I come back, I'd better find that plate of red beans and rice gone."

Matt laughed as he dove into the food. The savory smell of the spicy beans and sausage caused his stomach to grumble. His appetite was slowly returning.

When Sasha came back twenty minutes later, she found the plate empty. "Good, you ate it all."

After she left, Matt continued to work on the inventory until the restaurant closed. After helping Sasha with the closing, Matt had her drop him off at home.

"Are you coming to the restaurant tomorrow, or are you going to your studio?"

"I don't know right now. I'll call you in the morning, okay?"

Sasha smiled and nodded before driving away. She and Matt had been friends for several years now. Sasha was another woman who bore the scars of having known his now deceased brother, Martin.

Matt entered the house he'd bought in anticipation of the life he'd planned to spend with Kaitlin. He hadn't been there in more than a year, but the place was spotless. Bob had made sure that a maid came weekly.

Bob had already brought his luggage home and had neatly stacked it in the corner of his bedroom.

Matt stripped off his clothes and headed to the shower. His phone was ringing when he stepped out of the bathroom. Dressed only in pajama bottoms, he rushed to answer it. "Hello?"

"Matt! Where the hell have you been? I've been trying to reach you for days."

Sitting on the edge of his bed, he replied, "I've been in Phoenix, Preacher. Matter of fact, I tried to look you up recently. When did you move?"

There was a slight pause. "I moved more than two years ago. I live in Houston, Texas, now."

"How do you like it?"

"I love it. Hey, what were you doing in Phoenix all this time? Opening up another restaurant?"

Pain seared his chest and Matt closed his eyes. "It's a long story and not one I want to get into right now." He leaned against the solid pine headboard. "So what's going on?"

"Nothing. I just thought I'd better check in with old friends." He paused. "I heard about Rosales. Heard that it was someone in his own organization." Preacher's laughter was deep. "Poetic justice, don't you think? Heard something else, too. A.C.'s there."

Matt sat up straight. "What?"

"Yeah. She's still in Mexico. Still working the Rosales cartel. I thought she would've left the agency by now."

"It's been about six years, hasn't it?" Matt asked.

"Something like that."

"A.C. craves danger, I guess."

They talked for a few minutes more before hanging

up. Matt couldn't understand how a woman like A.C. could still want the life of a deep undercover agent. He had always thought she'd had way too much heart for that line of work. It was a dirty business and burnout was inevitable.

Until he'd met Kaitlin, Matt had once thought that Alison "A.C." Richardson would be the only woman he'd ever love. However, what he shared with Kaitlin far surpassed anything he'd ever experienced with A.C.

That night he prayed for A.C.'s safety. Whatever was happening within the Rosales organization, he hoped she could escape with her life. Matt didn't want anything to happen to his friend.

Ray replaced the phone in its cradle just as one of the other deputies dropped a stack of photos on his desk. "What's this?" he asked.

"Something I thought you'd be interested in. They're surveillance photos from Rosales's funeral."

Picking up one of the pictures, Ray studied it. "Who do you think is responsible, Armstrong?"

"Hmm. Hard to say. Rosales had lots of enemies. But I'd lay odds he was popped by one of his own. I've heard rumors about the cartel falling into disarray. Maybe they'll all kill each other over control of the organization."

Ray broke into laughter.

Armstrong picked up a photo. "Check this one out. Doesn't his wife look black?"

"What?" Ray looked up. "His wife was black?"

"She looks like it to me. Look for yourself." Armstrong handed the eight-by-ten photograph to Ray.

He stared at the picture. Ray's heart started to thump loudly. "T-This . . . this can't be . . ." He shook his head.

"What's up, Ransom? You look like you've seen a ghost."

It was hard for Ray to speak. He just sat there staring at the photograph.

"Ransom?"

Ray glanced up at Armstrong. "Do you have an identity for the woman?"

"We're checking into that. It seems that shortly after this was taken, the woman disappeared."

"What do you mean she disappeared?"

"Just what I said. No one seems to know what happened to her. She didn't return to the Rosales estate after the funeral. Rosales's daughter and her husband didn't either. They probably just went off somewhere for a little vacation. Do you know who she is?"

"No." Ray could swear that she looked like Kaitlin. But what in the world would his sister be doing in Mexico? And married to Hector Rosales, no less. There had to be some kind of mistake. His sister would never be married to a man like Rosales. But until he was sure of her identity, Ray decided he would say nothing.

For the rest of the day, Ray's mind stayed on the woman in the photograph. *Could it really be Kaitlin?* He thought about his conversation with Sabrina. She'd said that Kaitlin was alive, but in trouble. If the woman in the photograph was indeed his sister, then she was being held against her will. There was no way she'd ever marry a drug lord.

Ray picked up the telephone and dialed his friend who worked for the CIA. He could help him. His fingers tapped his desk impatiently. "Kevin Morrison, please."

"Morrison."

"It's me. I need a favor."

"Talk to me, Ransom."

The conversation was quick and to the point. Two hours

later, Ray received a list of people who had come in contact with the Rosales cartel. There was a deactivated unit called the Night Rangers. The members were rumored to be highly trained operatives who had been recruited from various areas of the military. Few people knew of the unit's existence. He quickly scanned the list, stopping at one name in particular. *Matthew St. Charles.* He was the elusive Jaguar. The legendary special forces agent had simply faded from view years ago. There had even been rumors of his death.

For the second time that day, shock filtered through Ray.

Secluded in a hotel off the coast of the Caribbean Sea, on the island of Isla Mujeres, Kaitlin paced back and forth in her room. *Where is A.C.?* she wondered.

Her eyes landed on the telephone. Kaitlin crossed the room in quick strides, reaching the table where it sat. She picked up the receiver and dialed.

Kaitlin's eyes filled with tears when she heard her mother's voice. It was a voice she'd only heard in her dreams for the last two and a half years.

"Hello, is anybody there?" Amanda questioned. There was a thread of impatience in her tone. "Look, if you're not going to say anything, then don't bother calling here."

As much as she wanted to say something, Kaitlin couldn't. A.C.'s warnings came back to haunt her. She hung up the phone and cried. She knew some of Hector's most trusted soldiers had small, plastic high-tech gadgets called scramblers. However, Hector recorded both incoming and outgoing calls. There had not been any way for her to contact her family without casting suspicion on herself. It was just much too risky.

She missed her family so much—and Matt. She missed the way he used to look at her. It was as if she were the only woman in the world. His smooth golden-honey complexion and those startling green eyes. *How she loved those eyes.* . . . Kaitlin cried harder.

"I want to go home. Oh, dear Lord, I just want to go home to my family and to Matt. Please make a way for me to leave this country."

Her thoughts centered on Hector. Although she was saddened over his death, she didn't grieve for him. The old man had been good to her, but had never won her love. She'd married Hector only for protection. One did what one had to do to stay alive.

Filled with nervous energy, Kaitlin wandered over to the balcony. She chanced a peek outside. *Isla Mujeres*, the Island of Women. The tiny fishing village was only five miles long and half a mile wide but she hadn't been able to experience the beauty of any of it. A.C. had advised her to remain inside the suite with the curtains drawn at all times.

It was late, but Kaitlin could still glimpse families gathered in the Caribbean-style homes. Seeing them laughing and enjoying one another made her all the more homesick.

Kaitlin checked her watch once more. A.C. should have arrived by now. "Where are you? I need you to keep your word to me, A.C. You promised you'd help me get back home. Please don't let me down. Please . . ." she prayed.

As the clock ticked on, Kaitlin grew more worried. Had something happened to A.C.? She was supposed to bring Kaitlin's passport and money. If she didn't show up by tomorrow, she would have to find another way home.

"You've been home a couple of weeks, and you're always here at the restaurant. Business must be pretty good."

Matt glanced up from his desk. "Ray, hello. I wasn't expecting to see you."

Ray dropped a manila folder down on Matt's desk. "Why didn't you ever tell me about this?"

Thumbing through the papers, he threw Ray a quick glimpse. "You must have friends in very high places."

Still standing, Ray replied, "You were part of Operation Foxfire—an eighteen-month multijurisdictional, multiagency investigation that tied drug trafficking activity within the U.S. to the highest levels of the international cocaine trade."

"Right before I left the agency, I was starting to feel like I'd lost myself somewhere. All the lies and the fabricated life I was supposed to have led started to mesh with my real life. It all seemed normal. I just couldn't learn to live with that. Or the danger." Closing the folder, Matt commented, "It's a part of my past. I didn't see where it was important." He eyed Ray. "What is this really about?"

"The one man everyone really wanted managed to disappear without a trace. Hector Rosales was considered one of the two most powerful international traffickers of cocaine in the world."

"He couldn't escape death, though," Matt retorted smugly.

Handing him a photo, Ray stated, "This was taken at Hector Rosales's funeral. Recognize anyone?"

Matt pointed to one of the men in the picture. "His name is Elian Cortez. He heads the security ring of the Rosales cartel. His father was Salvador Cortez. The Butcher."

"Salvador was killed ten years ago in Los Angeles by DEA."

Matt nodded. "Elian was shot but somehow he managed to escape. He and his father are suspected of murdering and torturing members of the Mexican police, prosecutors, and even a few reporters."

He stared blankly at Ray with confusion. "You want to tell me where this is going? Why all the interest in Rosales and Elian?"

Ray sank down in one of the chairs facing Matt's desk. Maybe it was best to go straight to the point of his visit.

"Well?" Matt prompted. Ray sure was acting strange, he thought to himself.

"There's something you should know." He took a deep breath and exhaled slowly. "Kaitlin's alive."

Shock flowed through him, and Matt found himself unable to breathe for a moment. He was afraid he'd heard wrong. Needing to hear it again, he asked, "What did you say?"

"You were right all along. Kaitlin didn't die in that plane crash. She wasn't even on the plane."

Matt could hardly contain his emotions. For so long he'd waited to hear those words. "Where is she then?"

"She's in Mexico."

Matt's mouth parted in surprise. *"Mexico?* What is she doing there?"

Ray seemed to be choosing his words carefully. He leaned back in his chair and eyed him.

"I'm not sure how it happened, but she ended up on Rosales's estate."

"Hector Rosales?"

"Yes."

Both eyebrows shot up. Matt wore a look of utter disbelief. "There must be some mistake—"

Shaking his head, Ray handed him the photo of Kaitlin at Hector's funeral. "This picture proves it."

"Kaitlin's alive," Matt murmured to himself. "She's alive. I knew it."

"We've got to get her out of Mexico. With Hector

dead, she could be in trouble. Especially with the leadership of the cartel in question."

"I still don't understand how she ended up in Mexico."

"I don't either. However, we can get all the answers we need after we bring her home."

"Ray, I'm going down there. I'll bring Kaitlin home. I've dealt with the Rosales cartel from the inside. I know how they operate."

"I'm going—" Ray began.

"No," Matt interrupted. *"No, you're not.* I know these people. You stay here with your family."

"Surely you're not thinking of going to Mexico alone?"

Matt shook his head. "No, I'm not going to be alone. I'm going to call a couple of friends from my agency days. As soon as I can get everything arranged, we're leaving for Mexico City."

"Are you sure your friends will help? This is all of a sudden. Can they just drop whatever they're doing just like that?"

"Yes. We're all used to packing and catching planes at the drop of a hat. I guess it's something you never forget. Like riding a bike. My friends seem to drift from place to place, from danger to a whole lot of danger. It's all in a day's work to them. Don't worry, Ray. I'm going to bring your sister home."

Ray headed toward the door. "Matt, I want you to know that I trust you. Do whatever it takes to bring Kaitlin home. Get her out of Mexico. *By any means necessary."*

Matt picked up the phone as soon as Ray left. He called Preacher first, then Gennai. An hour later, all arrangements had been made. He would be taking a flight in a few hours to Mexico. He jumped to his feet and grabbed his briefcase.

He was on his way out of his office when Sasha met him in the hall.

Pointing to his briefcase, she asked, "Where are you going in such a hurry?"

"I need to go home and pack. I'm leaving for Mexico City tonight."

Sasha walked beside him, pausing long enough to let one of the waiters pass. "Mexico City? But why?"

"I don't have time to explain right now, Sasha. But when I get back, I'll tell you everything."

"You just got home. I don't understand . . ." She eyed him. "Does this have something to do with the visit from Kaitlin's brother? This has something to do with her—with Kaitlin."

"I promise I'll explain when I get back." Matt hugged her. "If you need anything, call Bob."

Matt drove home and rushed upstairs. He packed lightly. In a few hours, he would be back in Mexico. Memories of a life he'd tried desperately to forget rushed to the forefront. He'd hoped that he would never have to pick up another gun in his life, but he would do anything to save the woman he loved.

After a quick shower, Matt dressed and drove to the airport. He was looking forward to seeing Kaitlin again. Once he had her within his reach, he would vow to never let her out of his sight again.

Whispering a prayer of thanksgiving, Matt rejoiced in the knowledge that Kaitlin was indeed alive.

Matt wanted to kick up his heels and shout his joy. There were no words to describe his feelings right now. Kaitlin had been spared, and he had been given a second chance. God owed him nothing, yet He had been generous with his miracles. For that, Matt was eternally grateful.

* * *

When Ray drove out of the La Maison parking lot, he headed straight to Riverside. He was going to see his mother and to tell her the news about Kaitlin. Carrie and the children were already out there, having ridden with Elle. By the time he arrived, everyone should be there. Ray had called an emergency family meeting. He wanted everybody there when he made the announcement.

While he drove, Ray prayed that Matt would be successful in rescuing Kaitlin. He wondered briefly if he'd done the right thing by not mentioning her marriage to Hector Rosales.

Ray didn't miss the hatred he heard in Matt's voice. He wasn't sure how he would react, and he needed his help. Matt was right. He knew the Rosales organization well and was the perfect choice to save Kaitlin.

The closer Ray came to the exit that led to his childhood home, the more nervous he felt. This was not an easy task. His family had struggled to deal with their loss for years. To enable them to move past their grief, they'd decided to hold a memorial service for Kaitlin a few weeks after the plane crash. Garrick had even ordered a gravestone.

Ray was filled with happiness. His beloved sister was alive and would soon be back home with him. He had every reason to believe that Matt would return Kaitlin safely back into the family fold.

He pulled alongside Garrick's Volvo and parked. His body trembling slightly, Ray climbed out. It was time to tell the family that Kaitlin was alive and would soon be home.

THREE

"I want you to find her!" Elian ordered in Spanish. "Check the airports. Check everywhere. And don't come back here until she's dead."

After everyone had gone, Elian strode over to the bar and picked up the crystal decanter. He poured himself a shot of tequila. Standing in front of the fireplace, he stared up at the portrait of Hector Rosales, his lips twisted into a frown.

Ever since Kaitlin had crawled into their lives, Rosales had gone weak. The old man had fallen in love. First he'd vowed to protect her at all costs. Then Hector had decided to turn his businesses into legitimate ones. Elian couldn't believe that he'd actually wanted to go legit because of a woman. Well, Elian wasn't about to let that happen.

His father had worked hard and had been very loyal to the Rosales family. He'd paid with his life for that loyalty. Now the family owed him.

The only people who stood in his way now were Marta Rosales-Guerra and Kaitlin. But not for long. As soon as he found Rosales's widow, she and Marta would die.

Everything was going according to plan. Wasn't it? Elian picked up his cellular phone and punched in a number.

"*Hola,*" the voice on the other end answered.

"Can you talk?"

"*Sí*. For a minute. Have you found our pigeon?"

"No, we are still searching." They were careful to avoid using names and spoke in code. The cellular phones were registered under fake identities but one could never be sure who might be listening.

The voice grew angry. "Find the bird."

"We are doing everything we can. What about you? Have you taken care of the baggage?"

"Do not worry. Everything is under control."

A wave of distrust washed over Elian. "How did the meeting go?"

"Fine. Things are moving. Everyone is pleased with the arrangement." Harsh laughter followed. "You worry too much."

They talked a few minutes more before hanging up.

So everything had gone the way they'd hoped. He was relieved to know that there would be no opposition from any of the other organizations.

Pouring himself another drink, Elian reminisced about his father. Salvador would be proud. This had been his dream for years. That the Cortez family would one day head the Rosales cartel. Only, Salvador hadn't lived to see it. Hector had paid for his mistake. Elian's spirits lifted a little at the thought.

Inside the Mexico City airport, Matt walked toward two men whom he trusted with his life. He greeted the tall, muscular dark-skinned one first. "Preacher, thanks, man. I appreciate your help in this situation." Thirty-seven years old, Preacher Watson was a pilot and a weapons expert.

"No problem," he mumbled.

Next, Matt greeted the other man. "Gennai, it's good to see you again." Thirty-two years old, and of Japanese descent, Gennai Li was an expert in ninjitsu and computers.

"You, too."

The three men headed toward the exit doors.

"I already have a car waiting," Preacher announced.

A few minutes later, they were inside the automobile. While Preacher drove, Matt told them everything.

"The woman we're rescuing is Kaitlin Ransom. Her brother is the guy who came to see me."

"There is more to this," Gennai stated. "You care for this woman."

"I love her more than my own life," Matt confessed. "Two and a half years ago, everyone thought she'd died in that crash in Phoenix. I didn't. I don't know why, but I refused to believe that she was dead. That's why I moved to Arizona."

"How did she end up here?" Preacher asked.

"I don't know. Right now I don't even care. I'm just glad she wasn't on that plane." Matt clenched his fists. "I'm not going to lose her again. Not this time."

Preacher broke into a wide grin. "Love's a powerful thing."

"Yes, it is," Matt agreed. "And I wouldn't have it any other way. Kaitlin is the other half of me. I love this woman like crazy."

Pulling his long, midnight-black hair back into a ponytail, Gennai said, "I am happy for you, Matt."

"Me, too," Preacher chimed in. "You're a lucky man. I don't think I'll ever meet a woman who'll make me feel that way."

"You will," Gennai assured him from the backseat. "No one is immune to love."

Preacher eyed him in the rearview mirror. "What makes you say that? Some honey got your nose stretched wide open?"

"There is a woman. I have loved her from the first time I ever laid eyes on her."

Matt turned around in his seat. "What happened?"

"She only had eyes for you."

"Who are you . . ." He paused, comprehension dawning. Surprised, Matt asked, "You mean A.C.?"

Stunned, Matt muttered, "You never said anything."

Gennai shrugged. "There was nothing to be said. The two of you were in love."

Wordlessly, Matt turned back around.

They rode in silence until Preacher announced, "Gennai got here late last night."

"Yes, and I decided to check out the Rosales estate. I was able to enter and leave the grounds undetected. This is what we're going to have to do. We're going to wait until it's dark to make our move. . . ." Gennai laid out his plan.

It was time to leave Mexico, A.C. thought to herself. She'd been getting some weird vibes from Elian lately and now even her room felt eerie to her. Earlier, when she was in the shower, A.C. swore she'd heard a noise. She'd developed an almost unconscious habit of looking over her shoulder from the years of being undercover.

A.C. had come out to investigate, but she found the room empty. Yet she couldn't escape the sensation that she was being watched. It was strange and unnerving.

Giving herself a mental shake, A.C. dressed quickly. Picking up her black leather backpack, she surveyed her room one final time. Inside the backpack were passports for herself and Kaitlin, as well as money and her gun, a nine-millimeter thirteen-shot Smith & Wesson. Just inside her pants leg was an ankle holster and a second gun. Satisfied that she had everything she needed, A.C. headed to the door.

She was sure Kaitlin had to be in a near panic by now, but A.C. needed to make sure she'd covered all of her bases before she disappeared. She felt pretty sure no one suspected anything, but her training had taught her that one couldn't be too careful.

It was dark outside, and the perfect time for her to make her departure. A.C. was glad to be getting out of this business. She'd called Tim Robbins, her case agent, two weeks ago to inform him of her decision. The agent-in-charge, Harold Jensen, approved her leaving because they were preparing to turn everything they had over to the DEA. It was time to close up Operation Unicorn. And time for A.C. to disappear.

She opened the door. Elian stood there leering at her. A.C. swallowed her disgust. "What do you want?" she questioned in flawless Spanish.

His gaze slithering up and down her body, he answered in English, "Where do ju think ju're going? Ju should be ow with the rest looking for Kaitlin."

"I work for Marta. So do you, by the way. She is now the head of the organization."

Still blocking her exit, Elian moved closer to A.C. "I bet ju know exactly where Kaitlin is, don't ju?" He lifted a finger and stroked the side of her face. "I wan ju to tell me the truth."

Keeping her expression blank, A.C. said, "I'm assuming she left with Marta and Armando."

"I don believe ju." He was standing a hairsbreadth away.

A.C. slapped his hand. "I really don't care what you believe. The fact remains that the three of them are not here. Marta was very distressed over her father's death. I imagine his wife was too. Now move out of my way, Elian."

"Ju should not cross me, A.C. I could prove to be a deadly enemy."

A.C. refused to cower, instead she chose another tactic. She attempted to wrangle the conversation in another direction. She believed that Elian was responsible for the hit on Hector. "I suppose Hector Rosales found that out, didn't he?"

Her question did as she intended. It surprised him. Elian struggled to maintain his composure.

"Wha ju talking about?"

"I know you had something to do with Hector's death, Elian. Marta knows it as well. Why do you think they left you behind?" A.C. laughed harshly. "You know, I used to think you had some intelligence, but you really screwed up this time."

"Shut up!"

"You were his right hand but Hector didn't tell you everything. Perhaps he knew you didn't have his best interests at heart."

"Wha ju talking about?" he asked a second time.

"Hector was dying, Elian. He was *dying*. All you had to do was wait."

Moving with amazing fluid quickness, Elian grabbed her roughly by the arm. "I gonna warn ju one more time. Keep jur mouth shut."

A.C. glanced down at her arm and then coolly lifted her eyes to his. "I think you'd better let go of me."

Elian laughed at her subtle warning, his glittering eyes studying her.

She slapped him as hard as she could.

Elian threw a right jab, then a left cross.

A.C. felt as if her head had been ripped from her body. Tasting blood, A.C. knew she was bleeding on the inside of her cheek. Moving as swiftly as she could, she swung her backpack at him, successfully knocking him down.

Elian dropped with a thud. Growling, he tried to

scramble to his feet, making it only to a sitting position. "Ju bit . . . ooow."

Every time he tried to stand up, A.C. struck him again and again.

Elian wrestled the backpack out of her hands.

A.C. balled up her fists and threw a punch his way. "I've been itching to do this for a long time." Her fist connected to his jaw. "Consider this payback."

Her hands felt like they were on fire but A.C. kept punching.

Elian fell down. From the floor, he kicked her legs from under her in a surprise attack.

A.C. tried to recover by kicking at Elian and scooting back out of his reach.

Elian reached for the gun strapped to her ankle and succeeded in getting to it before she could. Pointing the gun at her, he rose to his feet and motioned for her to stand up. "Enough of this. Now ju die."

A.C. muttered a curse.

Matt and Preacher waited just outside the Rosales estate, which included four hundred and fifty feet of shoreline and a private boat deck.

The magnificent estate sat majestically atop 8.2 acres, with a breathtaking view of Lake Avándaro and the Nevado de Touluca, a now-extinct volcano. Matt loved the area and had fond memories of Valle de Bravo. At least Hector couldn't poison that.

Matt, Gennai, and Preacher had changed into camouflage clothing. Only Preacher and Matt carried guns. Gennai preferred to work without one.

Before they neared the gate, Gennai jumped and disappeared into the trees.

Acutely aware of his surroundings, Matt climbed over the iron gate. A few feet away, Preacher did the same.

About fifty feet from the mansion, Matt stopped the advance. They encountered one of Rosales's soldiers, whom Preacher promptly knocked unconscious. One quick whack to the throat, and the man was out. The next one wasn't so easy. Matt ended up using the butt of his revolver. He didn't want to have to shoot anyone, but he would if it came to that.

Gennai was nowhere in sight but Matt wasn't worried. This was part of the plan.

Matt followed Preacher up and across the terrace. Cautiously, they entered through the French doors. He pointed at Preacher, then toward a hallway. Pressing himself close to the wall, Preacher moved alongside it.

While Preacher went in one direction, Matt searched the other way. His heart was beating wildly. The only thing that was on his mind was saving Kaitlin. Hearing the sound of glass breaking, Matt rushed down a long hallway. He put his ear to the door and listened. When he heard A.C.'s voice, Matt's hand touched his gun. He slowly and methodically turned the doorknob.

"Drop the gun!" Matt shouted. His own gun drawn, he walked cautiously into the room.

Elian was momentarily surprised, but he recovered quickly. "Jaguar. Good to see ju again."

"Drop the gun. Drop it now."

Elian wore a smirk. "Thees is so romantic. The hero sweeps into the room to capture his lady love."

Matt's eyes quickly searched the room. He caught sight of Preacher easing into the room through a window.

Elian glanced over his shoulder briefly. "Ah . . . re-inforcements." He fingered the jagged scar on his face. Gesturing toward Matt, he said, "I thought you were going to give me a chance to pay ju back for thees."

His eyes never leaving Elian's face, Matt replied, "Anytime, anyplace. Just let A.C. go. Leave her out of this."

"I see the rumors surrounding jur death are false. Where have ju been, Jaguar?"

"Missed me?" Matt questioned.

Elian laughed. "My only regret is tha I did not kill ju when I had the chance."

Matt inched closer. "You never had the chance," he sneered.

"Don't move any closer," Elian warned. "She means nothing to me."

"Let her go. This is the last time I'm going to ask."

"Are ju threatening me?"

Elian was visibly nervous. Matt spied movement from behind one of the curtains. He knew instinctively that it was Gennai.

Easing up behind Elian, Gennai quickly entrapped his arm, then proceeded to take the gun. A thin cord suddenly appeared from nowhere. In the blink of an eye, he had it wrapped around Elian's neck and had the man on his knees, struggling for air.

For a man Gennai's size, he had the strength of ten men.

"Don't kill him," Matt stated. "You don't want his blood on your hands."

"This murderer should die," Gennai snapped. "I should gut him like a fish for what he did to my sister and her unborn child."

"No," A.C. responded. "If you kill him now—it's the easy way out for Elian. Let him rot in prison."

When Gennai didn't look as if he was going to relinquish his hold, Matt strode over to him. "Come on, man. Not like this. I know he deserves it. Believe me."

A.C. placed a hand on his shoulder. "Gennai, let him go. He will pay for his crimes. I give you my word." She added, "Remember Grandmaster Toda's words: Choose the course of justice as the path for your life."

"Listen to A.C.," Matt suggested.

Gennai slowly released his hold on Elian. The man dropped to the floor like a rag doll, unconscious. "If I ever see him again, I will kill him," Gennai stated coldly.

FOUR

"I can't believe you guys are really here," A.C. announced. "Your timing is awesome." She pushed wayward strands of curling dark hair from her face.

Matt smiled. "It's good to see you, too."

She turned to Gennai. "I should have known you were behind that curtain. I could sense that someone had come into the room, but I assumed they'd gone. I must be slipping." Touching the area of her face that was now swelling, A.C. added, "In more ways than one." She turned away and spat out blood.

Gennai gently touched her bruised cheek. "You are still as beautiful as ever, A.C. You fought well."

There was a groan coming from one of the men sprawled on the floor. "Let's get out of here," A.C. said quickly. She bent to retrieve her gun.

"Wait," Matt stated. "A.C., I need to ask you something. Did you happen to see a young black woman somewhere here on the estate? We can't leave until I find her."

"You mean Kaitlin?" she asked without hesitation.

"Yes. Kaitlin. Where is she?"

The long lashes that shadowed her cheeks flew up. "You know her?"

"Yeah. Where is she?"

"I have her hidden away." Their eyes met and held.

"Is this why you're here, Matt? You came to get Kaitlin?"

Matt opened his mouth, but A.C. didn't wait for his answer, just walked away. He didn't miss her hurt expression. A.C. had assumed that he'd come for her.

He followed Gennai and Preacher out of the room. A.C. was surveying the hallways and rooms as she led them outside.

They left the house and hurried to the other side of the estate where the airfield was located. There were several small planes and a helicopter.

A.C. glanced over her shoulder. "We need to hurry and get out of here. Elian's going to have men everywhere looking for us."

"I don't think we're going to have to worry about Elian for a while, but you're right. We should get out of here." Matt turned around. "This house is heavily guarded, so I'm sure reinforcements have already been called."

"A lot of the men are out looking for Kaitlin." Leading them over to the helicopter, A.C. asked, "Preacher, do you remember how to fly one of these babies?"

"I sure do."

Matt heard a loud shot in the distance. "They're shooting at us. Let's get out of here."

As soon as they were safe inside, Preacher started up the helicopter. Amid gunfire, they were soon airborne. Using the throttle, Preacher moved the aircraft forward. During the climb, no one spoke until it was evident that they'd escaped.

"That was close," Gennai murmured.

A.C. agreed. "Too close for comfort. It would be my luck to get whacked just when I'd decided to get out."

"So where exactly are we going?" Matt questioned. "Where is Kaitlin?"

"First we're going to leave the helicopter in Cancun

and take the ferry to Isla Mujeres," A.C. replied. "She's staying at our special place."

Matt was surprised. "You hid her at the La Habra Club?"

A.C. nodded. "I was pretty sure nobody would find her there." She added, "I hadn't been back there since you left."

He didn't know what to say, so Matt remained silent. He felt a little awkward in this situation. Two women that he cared about greatly had suddenly resurfaced at the same time. One was his past and the other his future.

Kaitlin was suddenly wide awake. For most of the night she had tossed and turned, her thoughts spinning with fleeting images of her mother and her siblings. The other images, darker and more terrifying, jarred her awake. They were a kaleidoscope of ugly memories, some clearer than others. All of them, she wanted to forget.

Weary but unable to go back to sleep, she glanced over at the clock on the bedside table. It was well after midnight. Kaitlin turned on the lamp and sat up in bed, hugging her knees. A wave of apprehension swept through her. She was worried about A.C. Since Kaitlin hadn't heard from her, she could only assume that something must have happened. A volcano on the verge of erupting, she decided that maybe it was time to call Ray. He would know what to do.

Kaitlin maneuvered until she was sitting on the edge of the bed. She had just reached for the phone when she heard someone knocking.

Her mind a crazy mixture of hope and fear, Kaitlin rushed to answer it, but not before stealing a look through the peephole.

Her dark brown eyes widened in recognition and a

sound of pure delight burst from Kaitlin's mouth. She threw open the door.

For a moment both Kaitlin and Matt stood frozen in a stunned tableau. She managed to breathe one word: "Matt." Unwanted tears burned her eyes as she held on to Matt for dear life.

Kaitlin blinked rapidly. She could hardly believe that he had found her. "Oh, thank God! Thank God, you're here."

For two and a half years, she'd dreamed of this. The feel of Matt's arms around her. Those ice-green eyes staring hungrily at her. She'd missed him so much. "I can't believe you found me."

Without uttering a word, Matt leaned over and kissed her. His lips crashed into hers, as she pressed his tongue between her lips. The kiss was surprisingly gentle, but it left her blood fired with hot desire. Kaitlin could feel it sizzling through her veins, causing her knees to weaken.

When she thought she would just crumple to the floor, Matt held her tighter as he continued to shower her with kisses.

Kaitlin suddenly remembered that they were not alone. She reluctantly broke off the kiss. He was here with A.C. and two strange men she'd never laid eyes on before. How had Matt found her? She had so many questions, but this wasn't the time. For now, she just wanted to savor the moment.

"I'm sure you're wondering how I found you," Matt murmured.

"Yes, I am," she answered, her voice more breathless than it had been. "But right now, it really doesn't matter. I'm just so happy to see you. *All of you.*"

Although she hadn't been told, Kaitlin knew it was due in part to A.C. and the others that she and Matt were even having this reunion.

"Why don't we move this party inside the room," A.C. suggested. Her eyes quickly scanned the hallway.

After they were safe inside her room with the door closed, Matt pulled her back into his arms, reclaiming her lips. He crushed her to him. Neither one of them wanted the kiss to end. Each time one of them would try to break away, the other pulled back.

Preacher cleared his throat loudly. "Don't we even rate an introduction?"

Laughing, they reluctantly broke away from each other.

Matt made the introductions. "Honey, I want you to meet three of my closest friends. This is Preacher Watson, and this man over here is Gennai Li. You already know A.C. I wouldn't have found you without their help."

"It's very nice to meet you, Preacher. Gennai. I owe you both my life. There's no way I can ever repay you."

"We will happily accept a hug." Gennai's smile was bright.

With a laugh, Kaitlin gave them each a hug. Taking Matt by the hand, she said, "A.C. has been a good friend to me. I wouldn't have made it without her." Looking from Matt to her, Kaitlin commented, "I had no idea that you two knew each other. This is such a small world."

"It sure is. Matt and I go back a long way," A.C. muttered.

Kaitlin gestured toward the chairs. "Let's sit down."

A.C. and Gennai made themselves at home on the couch while she and Matt sat facing them on the love seat. Kaitlin quietly observed the couple. Matt had called them his closest friends, yet he had never mentioned them once during their time together. But he had not been very forthcoming about anything back then.

He had felt it necessary to keep his identity a secret. Or at least his relationship to Martin St. Charles, she amended silently. It was that very thing that broke up their relationship. Kaitlin felt that Matt had been using her to get next to Carrie and Mikey. Right now she desired nothing more than to put the past behind them while pushing her thoughts forward.

She noted how Preacher remained standing near the door. He seemed to be listening for something. *What?* she wondered. When his eyes met hers, Kaitlin awarded him a smile. She turned her attention to Gennai and A.C., silently watching as they talked and laughed with each other.

Everything about Gennai declared his feelings for A.C. The tender way he touched her face, his gentle smile, and the loving way his eyes locked with hers.

Kaitlin turned her attention to Matt. His handsome face was sculptured in a golden honey color, and those sexy green eyes still made her weak at the knees. His short-cropped hair lay in glossy waves. Matt's gentle nature contrasted with the sternness of his face.

Matt intruded upon her speculation. "What are you thinking about?"

Continuing her assessment of him, Kaitlin couldn't get over how much thinner he looked. "Matt, you've lost so much weight." She held back her comment on how tired he looked.

"When I thought I'd lost you for good, I couldn't eat or sleep. I was just waiting to die."

She wrapped her arms around him. "Ooh, Matt. I'm so glad this is over."

"Me, too. I love you so much."

"I love you, too. You were all I could think about."

Over by the door, Preacher shifted uncomfortably. "Eh . . . Maybe we should leave so that these two love-birds can be alone," he suggested.

"You all don't have to leave," Kaitlin announced. "I'm sorry if we made you feel uncomfortable. We're not really into public displays of affection. It's just that we haven't—"

Matt didn't agree. "They need to leave," he cut in. "I haven't seen you in a very long time, much less had a chance to be alone with you."

"Could you be any more obvious?"

Gennai and A.C. burst into laughter as they stood.

"We should check out the area anyway," Gennai announced. They joined Preacher over by the door. "We will be downstairs."

"Check in with us in about an hour," Matt told them. "No, make that two hours."

"Matt . . ." Kaitlin knew what they were thinking, and she tried to hide her embarrassment. When they were alone, she lit into Matt. "How could you treat them like that? They did help you find me."

"I wasn't being mean. I was being honest. Besides, they all know me well. They weren't offended."

"Are you sure?"

"Positive. Now that we have that straight." Matt pulled Kaitlin into his arms. "Where were we?" His mouth covered hers hungrily, devouring its softness.

Kaitlin matched his passion kiss for kiss. She still couldn't believe that Matt was really here. So many nights she'd dreamed of this day. The day when she and Matt would be back in each other's arms, and now he was really here.

Floating back to reality, Kaitlin awarded Matt one more kiss before he released her. Matt settled his arm on the back of the chair.

She raised her eyes to find him watching her. "What is it?"

"You are still so beautiful."

His compliment brought a smile to her lips.

Laying her head on Matt's chest, Kaitlin asked, "How's my family?" She looked up at him. "Are they still searching for me?" Matt swallowed hard. "Honey . . ." He paused as if trying to find the right words.

"Matt," Kaitlin prompted. She had a strong suspicion that there was something he was trying to protect her from. Had something happened to someone in her family? She sat up straight. "What is it? Tell me."

"Kaitlin, they thought you'd died in a plane crash."

Astonishment touched her face, and Kaitlin took a deep breath. "You mean all this time they've believed that I was on that plane to Phoenix? That I was dead?"

"No one knew you were in Mexico," Matt responded gently.

Disturbed by the news, Kaitlin raised her voice an octave higher. "You thought I was dead all this time, too?"

"Only until a few weeks ago," he responded honestly. "I'd given up hope."

"I see." Kaitlin was more than a little upset by his admission. In truth she probably would have done the same thing if the situation were reversed, but it didn't lessen the sting of hurt she felt.

"No, I don't think you do," Matt countered. "Kaitlin, I moved to Phoenix right after the plane crash. Your family and I went to Arizona as soon as we heard about it. You weren't among the survivors and your . . . well, your body was never found. But it didn't matter to me what they said. I wouldn't—no, couldn't—accept that you were dead. My heart wouldn't let me believe."

"But I don't understand." She hesitated, torn by conflicting emotions. "Sara never told my family what happened? I find that so hard to believe. That just doesn't sound like her at all."

His straight glance was filled with sympathy. Matt gently squeezed her hand. "Baby, Sara died a few hours before the crash. One of the employees found her dead in the store that morning."

Grief swept through Kaitlin. She put her hand to her

mouth and started to shake her head in disbelief. She and Sara were very close. "Oh nooo. I spoke to her that day. That morning, in fact. I knew she sounded strange on the phone. I remember telling Sara that she should see a doctor." Wiping away a tear, she asked, "What was the cause of death?"

His strong fingers continued to hold hers in his grasp. "She had a massive heart attack."

New tears sprang in her eyes. "I had no idea. All this time . . ."

"She was the only one who knew you'd gone to Mexico?"

Kaitlin nodded. "When I spoke to her, she mentioned that she was the only one in the store at the time."

"Why didn't you ever try to call home, Kaitlin? If we'd known, we would have come sooner," Matt whispered into her hair.

They parted a few inches.

"Well, for one thing, I had to pretend to have amnesia. It was the only way I could keep everyone safe. On top of that, A.C. told me that the phone calls were all recorded. She said Hector took all the necessary precautions to ensure loyalty."

"Yet someone from his own organization probably killed him."

Kaitlin shrugged. "I don't know. If so, I'm sure it was most likely Elian. He and Hector didn't exactly get along. I got the feeling that he didn't care too much for me either."

"He didn't hurt you, did he?" Matt practically ground out the words.

"No. I stayed as far away from him as much as possible. Matt, how did you know that I was still alive?" she asked, wanting to put all the pieces together.

He related how Ray had come across the surveillance photos and had come to him. Matt ran his fingers through her dark brown, shoulder-length hair. "I see you let your hair grow out."

Adjusting her body, Kaitlin assumed a comfortable posture on the love seat. "I didn't exactly have a hairstylist here in Mexico. I'm going to get it cut as soon as I get home." She glanced up at him. "Or would you rather I keep it this length?"

His eyes caressed her. "I'll like it no matter which way you wear it. I'm in love with you—not your hair." Matt pulled out his cellular phone. "Would you like to call your mother? It's late, but I'm sure everyone's wide awake and waiting to hear from you."

A cry of pleasure broke from her lips. "Yes. I really need to talk to her."

Amanda answered on the first ring. "Hello?"

"M-Mama . . ."

A soft gasp escaped from her mother. "Kaitlin? Baby, is that you?"

Tears running down her cheeks, she nodded. "It's me, Mama."

"Oh, my baby. When Ray told me that you were still alive . . ." Amanda broke into a loud sob. "A-All my d-dreams have come t-true. My little girl's alive and well. Thank you, Jesus."

"Mama, don't cry. Please don't cry." She wiped away her own tears.

"I'm so sorry, but I'm just so thankful. Oh, I just thank the dear Lord for giving me back my daughter."

Settling back against the cushions, Kaitlin and her mother talked. After that, she spoke with all of her brothers and sisters. Everyone insisted on hearing her voice for themselves.

Matt's eyes clung to hers, as if analyzing her reaction. She gave him a tiny smile.

Twenty minutes later, Kaitlin hung up the phone. "If it hadn't been for Ray seeing those pictures taken at

Hector's funeral, everyone would still think I'm dead." Her brows drew together in an agonized expression. "Oooh, when I think of what you all must have gone through. I feel so bad about this." She chewed on her bottom lip.

Matt took her face in his hand and held it gently. "Stop biting your lips like that, and don't start blaming yourself. You are as much a victim as the rest of your family. Besides, it wasn't as if you'd just taken off somewhere. You were held against your will. None of this is your fault."

In one forward motion, she was in his arms. "I keep pinching myself just to make sure this is real. All six feet of you is actually here in Mexico, after two and a half long, dreadful years of wondering if I'd ever see your handsome face again."

He kissed her tenderly, sending the pit of her stomach into a wild swirl. Kaitlin gave herself freely to the heady sensation of passion and desire. She wasn't shocked at all by her eager response to him.

A few minutes later, Kaitlin asked, "Your friend Preacher, he doesn't say much, does he?"

"No. Preacher likes to be left alone with his Bible."

They sat for a moment not saying anything.

Playing with her hands, Kaitlin glanced over at Matt. "You're nervous, too?"

"Actually, I'm just wondering if this is just some beautiful dream. However, I don't want to wake up and find out. I've wanted this for so long. Just to see you again."

Kaitlin stood. "If you don't mind, I'm going to take off these pajamas and change into something a little more presentable." Pulling on the bottom of the silk pajama top, she said, "I really wasn't expecting company tonight. Actually, I take that back. I was praying A.C. would show up. . . ."

Smiling, Matt nodded. "I'll be right here."

She paused, stopping at the bedroom. "This isn't a dream, is it? If it is, I'm never waking up."

Matt kept asking himself the very same question over and over. He was here in Mexico with the love of his life. Kaitlin was alive.

He exhaled a long sigh of contentment. They had been given a second chance. Matt couldn't resist a resounding "Yes." This time nothing would keep them apart.

There was a light rap on the door. Easing up off the sofa, Matt withdrew his gun from the holster. Stealthily he crossed the room and sidled up to the door. "Yeah?"

"It's me," a feminine voice replied from the other side.

Matt opened the door to let A.C. inside.

Scanning the immediate area, she asked, "Where's Kaitlin?"

"She's in the bedroom getting dressed." Matt regretted his choice of words the moment they were out of his mouth.

Her eyes lit up in amusement. "Mmm . . . I see."

"It's not what you're thinking. Kaitlin wanted to get out of her pajamas."

"Yeah, right. You practically threw us out of the room earlier." A look of sadness passed over her features.

The room was all at once filled with an uncomfortable silence.

Matt's eyes clouded with visions of the past. "A.C., I'm sorry."

She regarded him with a speculative gaze. "What are you sorry for?" A.C.'s tone sounded a little defensive. "You came after the woman you love. That's all there is to it. Might as well not try to explain it away. You can't."

"I know what this is doing to you, A.C. I'm not blind, you know. I see the look of hurt on your face." Matt stared at her with rounded eyes. "You were never good at hiding your feelings."

She dismissed his comments with the wave of her hand. "Don't worry about me, Matt. We had our time, and it just didn't work out. Why don't we just leave it at that?" A.C. strode briskly over to the veranda and stared out at the moon.

Matt knew she'd moved to keep him from seeing the shine of unshed tears in her eyes. He hadn't missed it, however. He waited a few minutes before joining her outside. "A.C., I still care for you. That will never change."

She turned around to face him. "I know that, Matt. I still care for you as well. I must admit there have been times when I am filled with some regret over losing you. I haven't had those feelings too often, though."

Matt bit back a grin.

"I've spent the last couple of years getting to know Kaitlin, and she's a wonderful person. I can see that she'll make you happy. She's the kind of woman you need."

"Kaitlin is a very special woman. She completes me. But I want you to know this: I will never forget our time together either," Matt confessed. "The memories of what we shared will always have a special place in my heart."

Tapping her fingers on the railing, A.C. screwed up her face. "Don't you dare get mushy on me." She turned to walk away, but not before adding, "I couldn't take it."

Matt laughed and shook his head. "You are still the tough girl, huh? The one who is always in control of her emotions."

She cast him a look over her shoulder. "I have to be. If I'm not . . . well, let's just leave it at that."

Matt followed her inside.

"A.C., it's okay to be scared at times. To need someone else."

Her eyes were full of remoteness. "Are you trying to

tell me that that was our problem? That I didn't share myself with you, or that I didn't need you enough?"

"I think we both know what happened between us. Besides, it's not important anymore." He didn't want to get into a debate with A.C. right now. Matt was trying to figure out when and if he should tell Kaitlin about his past with A.C. One thing for sure—he didn't want her finding out any other way.

"You're right, Matt. I do know what happened to us. And it doesn't matter anymore. The past is the past."

A.C. took a seat on the sofa. "Why don't you sit down and tell me what's been going on with you since you left Mexico."

Elian groaned when one of his men lifted him. "I'm going to get that . . ." His voice died when pain sliced through him. His voice was raspy due to his near strangulation. "Jaguar . . . Gennai . . . A.C. All of you will pay for this." He would find them and then he would take his time killing them.

In spite of his discomfort, Elian could feel the heat of his excitement as he fantasized about ways to torture the two men he hated most in this world. But that would have to wait. First, he needed to find Kaitlin.

Marta and Armando would be returning by the end of the week. There was much that still needed to be taken care of. Too many loose strings.

Once Kaitlin was found, he would make sure her body never surfaced again. A strand of nervousness crawled down his spine. She and Marta were close friends, and Elian realized that it would not be wise to make an enemy of Marta. There were murmurings that she would assume her father's role in the cartel.

Fury swept through Elian. He'd worked too hard to let that happen. Hector had crossed him and look what happened. Soon, he would deal with Marta. Many of Hector's soldiers had been loyal to his father and sought to avenge Salvador's death.

The ringing of the telephone reverberated throughout the room. The shrill ring caused Elian's head to hurt even worse. Groaning, he reached to answer it. *"Bueno."*

"I understand things got out of hand and our visitor escaped. I thought you said you could resolve our little situation. Perhaps I should have—"

"Everything is under control," Elian replied. "I just had a little problem. Nothing I can't fix."

"What happened?"

"I caught A.C. trying to leave—"

"She's got you sounding like this?" The man on the other end burst into laughter.

"She had help. Her lover returned," he responded with detached inevitability.

"The one who almost ripped out your eye?"

Elian swallowed hard, trying not to reveal his anger. "I thought you said he was dead."

"It's obvious the rumor was just that."

"What do you know of A.C.? Did it ever occur to you that she could be an undercover agent, no?"

Elian remained silent. The thought had occurred to him once, but everything she'd told them checked out. If what he suspected turned out to be true, then he would feel like a fool. Just the thought made him furious.

"Are you still there?"

"Sí. You have given me much to think about. I will talk to you later."

"Elian . . ."

"Yes."

"If you can't take care of the situation, I will."

Elian reacted angrily to the challenge in the caller's voice. "I said I'll take care of it." He slammed down the phone without waiting for a response.

The next day Elian met with an old associate of his late father's.

"I need a favor from you, Jose."

"What is it?"

"Find me a weak link in the DEA. I want to know everything about the person. Family, habits, everything."

FIVE

Seeing Matt and A.C. huddled together and laughing, Kaitlin could not stop herself from wondering if they had been lovers at one time. If Kaitlin had to take a guess—it would be yes. It was the way A.C. looked at Matt that made her believe so.

A.C. was the first to spot her. Shifting her body, she leaned back against the cushions of the couch. "Oh, Kaitlin. We didn't see you."

Moving into the room, Kaitlin asserted, "I hope I'm not interrupting anything."

"No," Matt responded a little too quickly. "We were just discussing the old days."

Kaitlin dropped down beside Matt on the love seat. "Since we've been up all night, I hope you guys are as hungry as I am. I was thinking that we could all have breakfast downstairs in about an hour."

Matt shook his head. "No. It would be better if we just ordered room service."

A chill raced down Kaitlin's spine. "You don't think it's safe?" she asked, her heart jumping in her chest. "You said no one would find me here."

"One can never be too careful," Matt remarked.

Kaitlin's mind fluttered away in anxiety. Chewing on her bottom lip, she clenched her hand until her short uneven nails entered her palm.

Rising to her feet, A.C. added, "I don't think we were followed, or that anyone knows where we are, but we can't afford to make any mistakes now."

Leaning against Matt, Kaitlin swallowed hard. "I can't wait to get out of this nightmare. I want my life back."

He kissed her forehead. "Soon, baby."

Retreating out of the room, A.C. cleared her throat and pointed toward the door. "Um . . . I think I'll join Gennai and Preacher down on the beach. They are both probably meditating somewhere."

Kaitlin sat up straight. "You don't have to leave, A.C. I really don't mean to keep running you all away."

"No, it's fine," she assured Kaitlin. "You and Matt need some time alone. The sun'll be rising in another hour or so. I think I'll take my morning run."

"Would you like for me to order you guys something to eat? I'm sure you all have to be hungry."

Smiling, A.C. nodded. "That's fine. Order fresh fruit for me and Gennai, and a three- or four-egg omelet for Preacher. In the meantime I'll take my run, round up the guys, and we'll be back shortly."

When they were alone, Kaitlin stated, "Your friends are really sweet. I like them a lot."

Matt smiled. "They're all good people. We've been through a lot together."

Kaitlin's gaze met his. "I have to wonder just how much or how little I really know about you."

"When we get home, I'll sit down and tell you everything. I promise."

"Even the part that concerns A.C.?" Kaitlin couldn't resist asking.

Matt didn't seem at all surprised by her comment.

"A.C. and I have a history together, Kaitlin, but it's all in the past," he replied.

"But you still care for her." It wasn't a question.

"I do. She's my friend. Nothing more. You don't have anything to worry about."

"I'll be the judge of that."

Matt broke into laughter. "Girl, since I've met you, I haven't been able to think about anybody else. You dominated my mind and my heart."

"That means so much to me because I feel the exact same way. I can't even put into words how much I missed you."

He was suddenly very serious. "Kaitlin, sitting here with you like this is just . . . wow."

She nodded in agreement. "While I was in the room changing, I had to stop for a minute. I got down on my knees and I prayed. I just had to give praises to God for delivering me into your hands."

She caught Matt staring at her hands. She folded them so that he couldn't see her nails. During her stay in Mexico, she'd started to bite them. It helped to calm her nerves. If he noticed, Matt was too polite to mention them.

Matt and Kaitlin talked nonstop for the next hour. Then they ordered breakfast for everyone, which arrived twenty minutes later. By that time Preacher, Gennai, and A.C. had returned.

Around the small dining room table in the suite, Preacher gave the blessing. Minutes later, everyone dug in. Conversation was kept to a minimum while they ate.

After they had eaten their fill, Preacher stood and announced, "Gennai and I will be staying in the room next to this one. A.C. is in the one right across the hall."

The next ten minutes were spent discussing an emergency escape plan, should the need arise. Kaitlin felt like she was part of a high-action movie. She could hardly believe this was her life.

Around seven A.M., the others retired to their rooms. They had all been up for hours and were exhausted.

Kaitlin yawned. "I can't believe we stayed up all night."

"My body can feel it."

Taking Matt by the hand, she led him to the bedroom. "Come on. Let's get some sleep."

When they entered the room, Kaitlin turned on the television. She watched for a moment before speaking. Her eyes still on the TV, she asked, "Matt, do you think there's a possibility that Elian and the others will find us here?" She was scared and couldn't hide it. "I know Elian wants me dead."

Shaking his head, Matt answered, "Don't worry about Elian. I will kill him before I let him harm you. But I don't think you have to worry about him anymore. He's probably out looking for me by now."

This surprised her. "Why? Why would he be looking for you?"

"Kaitlin, Elian doesn't have a clue that you and I even know each other—much less that we're together somewhere. I don't think he's smart enough to connect us." Matt didn't add that Elian knew he and A.C. were once lovers and had naturally assumed she had been the reason for his return.

"What does he know about you?"

"I was what you'd call a penetration agent. I was able to successfully infiltrate the Rosales cartel. During my undercover career I was known as Jaguar, one of the few men Hector trusted. He once told me that I was like a son to him. Whenever Elian would come to Hector about some big score, Hector would always ask my opinion. If I wasn't for it, neither was Hector."

Wrapped in memories, Matt continued, "That set Salvador and Elian off. To them I was nothing but an outsider. A kid from the United States who thought he knew everything. They resented me."

Kaitlin's reaction was a delicate shudder, but she continued to listen.

"I made several cases for the DEA and CID."

"CID? What agency is that?" she asked.

"It's a division of the FBI. Foreign Counter-Intelligence Division. We set up a sting operation called Foxfire. During the fallout, Salvador Cortez was killed. One night, I simply disappeared. There were rumors that I'd died, but I think that was around the time of Martin's death."

"So he thinks that you and Martin were one and the same."

"Could be. I don't know for sure."

This time her fear wasn't for herself. She was scared for Matt. "He's out to kill you, isn't he?"

"I'm not on his Christmas card list, that's for sure."

Kaitlin trembled involuntarily. She knew firsthand what Elian was capable of. She sent up a silent prayer for their safety.

Moving toward her, Matt removed his shirt. "I don't want to talk about Elian or anything else. I want to concentrate on us."

Her attention temporarily away from her fears, she broke into a sexy grin. "I thought you were tired."

"I'm not that tired."

Matt unzipped his pants and let them drop to the floor. Stepping out of them, he crossed the room and closed the bedroom door, while Kaitlin, now undressed, settled into the king-sized bed.

Matt slid under the covers and lay next to her. When his body touched hers, she shivered.

"Are you cold?" he asked.

She sat up, pulling the covers up to her chin. "No. Just nervous." Kaitlin broke into a flustered laugh. "It sounds silly, I know. Still, it's been a long time." Suddenly shy, she looked away. Her muscles were so tense. Kaitlin rubbed the back of her neck.

Matt propped up two pillows, sat up, and began kneading the back of her neck. "We'll take our time, sweetheart. There's no need to hurry."

"Could you just hold me?" she asked softly.

Matt pulled Kaitlin into his arms and placed a soft kiss on her temple. "Feel better?"

Her body slowly relaxed, the tension melting away like butter. "Much better. I feel so safe with you."

"That's a good thing. I never want you to feel anything less."

Kaitlin smiled. "With you, I don't think I will." Turning toward him, she pressed her lips to his.

Reveling in his nearness, she allowed herself to feel those sensations of loving and being loved. Kaitlin was soon caught up in a wave of passion. For the moment, the memories of her life in Mexico and the feeling of imminent danger were pushed to the back of her mind.

Cradling her close to him, Matt ran a hand up and down her body until Kaitlin thought she would go mad with want. Her body burned with her need for him.

Matt was just as impatient as she was. When they became one, he felt a soaring of spirit that was nothing less than joy. Together they pulsed in a steady rhythm that quickened. It grew so intense—sensations they never could have dreamed existed.

Kaitlin's world exploded. She held on to him as wild tremors took possession of them both.

His body slick with perspiration, Matt stared down into Kaitlin's eyes. What he saw there mirrored his own feelings. They had both been drawn into a world of primal pleasure where reason had no place.

Entangled in the bed sheets, Kaitlin snuggled against Matt. She felt protected and loved as she succumbed to a lover's sleep.

Around noon, Matt woke up. Feeling the warmth of another body next to him, he grinned. His hand slid down her arm.

"Wake up, sleepyhead."

Kaitlin mumbled something unintelligible. Her eyes remained closed.

Matt gently shook her. "It's time to get up. We've got a lot to do."

Kaitlin's eyes opened. Seeing him lying next to her brought a smile to her lips. "What time is it?"

"Twelve-ten."

She sat up, pulling the covers with her. "Are we leaving today?"

"I don't know. Preacher's working on that."

Kaitlin tried to hide her disappointment.

Matt didn't want to upset her. Instead, he sought to reassure her. "We're going to see that you get home, baby. We just want to keep you safe."

"I know."

He checked the clock a second time. "We should get up. Preacher should know something by now."

Kaitlin climbed out of bed and padded naked to the bathroom. Matt lagged behind just so he could enjoy the view of her well-toned body. Long legs, curved hips—her body was definitely made for loving.

Feeling his body's own response to hers, Matt eased up behind her. Gathering her into his arms, he held her tight. Whispering in her ear, Matt molded his body to the contours of hers.

Kaitlin turned around so that they were now facing each other. He stared into her incredible bedroom eyes. In one solid move, he picked her up and sat her on the vanity then wedged himself between her thighs. For one ecstasy-filled moment there were no other people in their world.

Kaitlin wrapped her arms around Matt's neck and held on for dear life. She felt hot, hungry, impatient and filled with wanting and excited—and a hundred other emotions all at once.

Mostly she felt safe. "Matt," she whispered against the curve of his shoulder, holding him tight.

He shifted closer, his body wedged firmly against hers. Matt's body melted into hers, needing release.

The peak of pleasure struck them both with tremendous force. Matt and Kaitlin held each other until the tremors passed.

By the time they had showered and dressed, Preacher arrived.

They sat down around the circular glass table located near a huge window. Matt had allowed Kaitlin to open the drapes a crack. Just enough to let the sun slip in, giving the room a golden tint.

"Any news?" Matt queried.

"Elian's got his people all over the airport and near the ferry. It's not going to be easy getting out of here. Chartering a boat is out of the question."

"That's what I was afraid of. What about chartering a plane?"

"I'm looking into that. I still have a couple of friends down here who owe me some pretty big favors. I should know something by tomorrow morning. In the meantime, I think we should just sit tight."

Kaitlin gave a frustrated sigh. "I'm going to go stir crazy if I don't get out of this room soon."

"I understand," Preacher acknowledged. "We're going to get out of here as soon as possible."

Feeling contrite for her outburst, she said, "I'm sorry. Please don't think I'm being impatient or ungrateful. It's just that it's been a very long time since I've seen my family, or felt safe for that matter."

Matt took her hand in his. "It's going to be over soon. Real soon. Just hang in there for a little while longer."

His voice had an infinitely compassionate tone. "Everything's going to be okay, sweetheart. I promise."

Nodding, Kaitlin pushed away from the table and rose. "I'm going to leave you two alone to talk. I guess I'll get back to my book. Thankfully, it's a good one."

When she was gone, Preacher shook his head sadly. "If we don't get her out of here soon, she's gonna lose it."

"Man, I know it. She's only hanging by a thread." Matt was worried. Kaitlin had developed a habit of chewing on her bottom lip and she was constantly biting her nails now.

"I'm going to make a few more calls. Hopefully I'll have better news later on."

"Thanks, Preacher."

"You just take care of your lady. She needs you."

"I need her too."

After Preacher left, Matt joined Kaitlin in the bedroom. Motioning toward the bed, he said, "You know, I'm feeling kind of tired. How about you?"

"Hmm . . . I'm feeling a bit fatigued myself. What do you suggest, Doctor?"

Grinning, he answered, "Bed rest. Lots and lots of bed rest." He quickly turned on his heel and headed out of the room. Matt went to the door and hung out the Do Not Disturb sign. When he returned, he unplugged the phone. "Now we should be able to rest without interruptions."

After spending the afternoon making love, Kaitlin and Matt finally emerged from the bedroom in time to join the others in A.C.'s room.

"We weren't sure you two were going to make it," A.C. commented.

"Leave them alone," Gennai uttered. "They have not seen each other in quite a while."

"If I'd had my way, we would still be holed up in that suite."

Kaitlin elbowed Matt. "I can't believe you said that."

"Why not?" he countered. "It's true. Besides, I know they would probably feel the same way."

"I know I would," Preacher confessed. "Y'all wouldn't see me for the next month."

Everyone broke into laughter.

"I ordered fruit and burritos," A.C. announced. While she continued to talk, she braided her hair. "I made a call to the agency and gave them a rundown of what happened."

"What did Jensen have to say about you getting out? I'm sure he was plenty mad. He was always saying how you were one of his best agents."

"It was Robbins who was upset in the beginning, Preacher. Jensen agreed with me. It was time for me to close up and get out. I was getting itchy because it seemed to be a dead end."

"How do you think you will feel a few months from now?" Gennai asked.

Kaitlin noticed he kept his expression blank. She had a strong feeling that Gennai wanted A.C. out of the business.

A.C. raised her eyes to his. "I meant what I said. It's time to get out—while I still can."

Gennai smiled. "I am very glad to hear that."

While everyone waited for the food to arrive, they sat around discussing tentative plans for leaving Isla Mujeres.

"I'm waiting on a call back from my friend, Foster. Once we get the plane, we can leave."

A.C. stretched her arms. "I for one can't wait to leave Mexico. I've been here way too long."

"I'm glad you're coming out the same way you went

in," Matt acknowledged. "You've been under for a long time."

"Six years is a long time," A.C. agreed. "We have enough information to bust up quite a few small-time drug deals, some burglaries, and even a hijacking, but I wasn't moving up in the organization. Jensen wanted me to be able to make the cases directly."

The food arrived.

Kaitlin dug into her chicken burrito with gusto.

Reaching for another burrito, Matt said, "I sure can't wait to get home. I'm looking forward to some of your mother's cooking."

She wiped her mouth with a napkin. "Me, too." Kaitlin glanced over at A.C. "I truly don't know how you did it. Staying here and being out of contact with your family for so long. These past few years nearly killed me. Not to mention how much it wore on my nerves."

"It was hard, I won't lie about that. I miss my family so much. They understand, though. All three of my sisters are in law enforcement. My father was with the FBI for almost thirty years."

"How did your mother feel about that?"

"My mother died when I was two. I don't have any clear memories of her. But had she lived, I don't think she would have been very pleased. I know I wouldn't."

Placing her hand in Matt's, Kaitlin said, "I never would have figured Matt as an undercover agent." She smiled at him. "You are a man of many talents."

He returned her smile.

"Matt was one of the best," Gennai stated matter-of-factly. "I trained under him."

"I always wanted to be a part of law enforcement," Matt revealed. "It's all my best friend Ted and I used to dream about when we were growing up. When he died, everything changed for me. Shortly after that, I left the agency."

Kaitlin's heart ached over the sadness she glimpsed in Matt's eyes. She had lost someone close to her, her father, so she could relate to his anguish.

Kaitlin ran as fast as she could. Elian was chasing her. Somehow, he had found her and the others at the hotel. Just as Elian raised his gun and was about to shoot her, Kaitlin awoke with a start, a scream poised on her lips.

Matt was instantly alert. He reached out to comfort her. "Honey, it's okay. You're safe. I won't let anything ever happen to you. I promise."

Kaitlin couldn't stop trembling. Her heart pounded, the terror gradually beginning to dissipate. It had only been a dream, though you couldn't tell by the way her heart was pounding. The dream had triggered something. It was a vague memory. But of what?

Matt kissed her softly, cutting into her thoughts. "It's okay, baby," he murmured in her ear.

Throwing her arms around him, Kaitlin pulled Matt close to her. "I'm so glad you're here." In his arms she found a feeling of security. "I'd go crazy if you weren't."

"Want to tell me about it?"

She looked up at him, feeling very vulnerable and a bit afraid. "I would rather forget everything." She rubbed her arms as she fought off a chill.

Running his hand up and down her back, Matt whispered, "If Hector wasn't already dead, I'd kill him myself. The—"

Kaitlin stiffened at the cold hatred in his voice. She'd never heard him sound that way before. Still, she contended, "Hector was nothing but kind to me, Matt. He treated me well."

Matt looked at her as if she'd lost her mind. "You call holding someone against their will good treatment?"

"It wasn't quite like that," Kaitlin countered. "There were other circumstances. Hector actually saved my life."

His green eyes never left her face. "How?"

She hesitated for a heartbeat. "He married me."

Matt felt like he'd been punched in the gut. Bile roiled in his stomach and beneath his skin, his muscles quivered in his rage. Surely he'd heard her wrong. "What did you say?"

"Hector and I were married." Kaitlin was confused. Surely Matt had known about her marriage. "Matt . . ."

"I don't believe you," was all he could manage to sputter. Matt put his hands to his face. "I don't believe this," he repeated over and over. "How could you marry a cold-hearted murderer?" Matt demanded through tightly clenched teeth.

"Matt, I thought you knew this already." She stretched out her hand to touch him but he moved out of her reach.

Climbing out of bed, Matt reached for his clothes. He dressed quickly. "No, I didn't know anything about your marriage. If I had, I don't know that I would have rushed down here. . . ."

Kaitlin reacted as if she'd been struck, but she managed to keep her face bland. "I see," she stated coldly.

Matt headed to the door, his stride long and brisk. "I need to get out of here."

Kaitlin didn't try to stop him. They both needed time to gather their thoughts. She was stunned by his reaction. She'd known Matt wouldn't be happy about her marriage, but Kaitlin just assumed he had found a way to deal with it. But now that she was thinking of it, the fact that he hadn't kind of surprised her. Perhaps she should have mentioned it earlier. Then another thought occurred to her. Why hadn't A.C. said something to him?

SIX

Matt took a stroll around the hotel, muttering a long string of curses as he went. Kaitlin and Hector? How could she have married a man like that? He shook his head in confusion. The woman he loved more than his own life had married the man he hated with his entire being.

The more he thought about it, the more incensed Matt became. His anger had become a scalding fury. As hard as he tried, he simply couldn't understand. Kaitlin had been Hector's wife. A rock-solid knot formed in his stomach. For a moment he thought he might be sick. All this time he had grieved for her. . . . Matt's hands clenched into tight fists. He was so angry. He wanted to hit something or someone. Jealousy and fury consumed him.

By the time Matt reached the beach, his eyes were filled with tears. Reaching the water's edge, he sank down and cried.

There was a knock on her door, and Kaitlin rushed across the room to answer it, hoping all the while that it was Matt. She was more than a little surprised to find A.C. standing there.

Following Kaitlin over to the sofa, she said, "I saw Matt leaving, and he looked irate. Is everything okay?"

Kaitlin shook her head sadly. "No, it's not. He didn't know that Hector and I were married."

"I kind of figured he didn't," A.C. admitted.

"Then why didn't you tell him?" Her tone was accusing, but Kaitlin didn't care. Matt should have been told from the beginning. She didn't speculate on whether or not she would have told him herself.

"Because I knew he'd react the way he did. I wanted you two to spend some time together. I thought after that everything would be fine."

Gazing into A.C.'s eyes, Kaitlin saw that she was sincere.

"A.C., tell me something. Why does Matt hate Hector so much?"

"Remember when Matt mentioned his friend, Ted Chambers?"

Kaitlin nodded.

"Well, they were as close as brothers. Ted was a DEA agent. During a raid on one of Rosales's operations, he killed Salvador Cortez, Hector's right hand. I'm sure you know that Hector and Salvador were very close, as well. Salvador was Elian's father."

"I take it Hector went after Ted."

A.C. nodded. "But not only did he kill Ted. Ted's wife and unborn child died in the explosion, too."

Kaitlin was horrified. "Oh, dear Lord!" It was hard for her to imagine the fragile, soft-spoken old man that had been her husband in this way. A stone-cold murderer.

"Ted's wife, Kyoko, was Gennai's sister."

"How awful . . ."

A.C. nodded a second time. "It was a bad time for all of us. Ted and Kyoko were nice people. They shouldn't have died that way."

"I'm so sorry. After hearing this, I'm actually kind of surprised that Elian is still alive."

"Just barely. It was a struggle to stop Gennai from killing him. Gennai and his sister were extremely close," A.C. went on to explain. "Ted and Matt were like brothers. It hit both of them really hard. Gennai swore revenge."

Sighing loudly, Kaitlin said, "I guess I can understand why Matt's so angry then. He feels like I've betrayed him."

"Did you tell him what happened? All of it?"

"I can't, A.C. I just can't do it. Not right now. Matt's been through a lot. I can't hurt him any more than I already have."

"I will help you any way that I can, Kaitlin."

"I know, A.C. You've kept your promises so far." Kaitlin paused for a moment. "There's something else I need to know. Are you still in love with Matt?" Her stomach clenched, and the muscles at the base of her neck tightened, but she had to know.

"I'm sure I'll always love Matt, but not in the way you mean. I realized that when I saw him again. We will always be friends. We went through a lot together."

Kaitlin wasn't sure she believed her, and told her so.

"I'll admit that I used to have dreams of Matt coming back for me, but that was such a long time ago. And the truth of the matter is that he didn't. He came for you. And I'm very happy for you both. I'm a very proud woman, Kaitlin. I don't want a man who is in love with another woman. I believe there's someone else out there for me." A.C. gave a wry smile. "I'm just going to have to hunt him down."

A more relaxed Kaitlin grinned. "I appreciate your honesty."

"I will always care for Matt, but only as a good friend. The same as I feel for you, Kaitlin."

She stared down at her hands. "Do you think Matt and I will be able to get past this?"

A.C. nodded. "Oh yeah. The man loves you. Just give him some time. And be completely honest with him. Tell Matt everything. He will understand."

Nodding, Kaitlin agreed. "I just wish I knew where he went. He shouldn't be out there all alone. Especially with Elian and his goons running around looking for us."

"He's probably at the lighthouse. That's where he used to go when he wanted to think about things. Don't worry about Matt. He's probably safer than we are right now."

Yawning, Kaitlin covered her mouth. "This was not supposed to happen."

"You two will kiss and make up. Just watch and see." Rising to her feet, A.C. added, "Go get some sleep. And don't worry about Matt. He'll come back when he's ready."

"Maybe I should wait up for him."

A.C. burst into laughter. "Girl, you can hardly keep your eyes open. Go to bed. Matt will think things over and come home. Tomorrow, everything will look much better. You'll see."

The two women embraced.

"Good night, A.C., and thanks."

"Night, Kaitlin." A.C. opened the door. "Remember that Matt loves you. He came all the way to Mexico to rescue you. He's your black knight."

"I'll try to remember that. Thanks again." Kaitlin closed the door, being careful not to use the dead bolt. She navigated over to the sofa and sat down to wait for Matt.

Kaitlin had fallen asleep out of pure exhaustion by the time Matt returned. He studied her for a long moment, wondering how she could have hurt him this way. Finally he nudged her gently.

She woke up with a start. "Matt. You scared me." Sitting up, she said, "I'm so glad you're back. I was getting worried."

"There wasn't any need," he replied dryly. "As you can see, I'm fine."

For a second there was silence. Deafening and condemning. "It's been a long day. Why don't we go to bed and sleep on everything that's happened, okay? We can talk in the morning." Kaitlin stood and headed toward the bedroom, pausing long enough to see if he would follow. "Aren't you coming?" she asked, her expression imploring.

Shaking his head, Matt replied, "No. I'm going to sleep out here."

Her throat closed for a second. "Why?"

"Under the circumstances, I think it's best." Distaste colored his voice.

She was tired and her irritation built. "Don't act this way, Matt."

"Kaitlin, it's late. Let's just go to sleep."

"I don't believe this is happening. After all that we've been through . . ." Her voice died. Kaitlin sighed heavily. Waving her hand in resignation, she muttered, "Whatever!"

Matt stretched out on the sofa. It wasn't a comfortable fit, but it was a better option than the floor. He closed his eyes even though Matt knew sleep wouldn't settle over him for hours to come.

No matter what he did, Matt couldn't get the image of Kaitlin and Hector making love out of his mind. It was almost enough to drive him insane. In a jealous rage, he'd wanted to have it out with Kaitlin. But in the end it really wouldn't help anything. They couldn't change the past.

How could Kaitlin expect him to understand? For the last couple of years, he'd remained celibate because he couldn't get her memory out of his mind. She had spoiled him for other women. Hot fury washed over him. While he had been grieving, Kaitlin had been playing house with a drug lord and murderer.

"Matt, this isn't right," Kaitlin announced from the doorway. "You should come to bed. You can't be comfortable on that sofa."

"Go to sleep, Kaitlin," he snapped.

She slammed the bedroom door shut.

Matt stared at the closed door for a long time that night. Barely twenty-four hours earlier, he'd found the love of his life, and now . . .

Life just wasn't fair at times. Placing his hands on his face, Matt tried to relax. He wanted nothing more than to be able to go into the bedroom and join Kaitlin. That's where he should be, but he couldn't do it.

The fact that she'd married and bedded Hector really bothered him, to a point where Matt wasn't sure they would ever get past it.

Tears slipping from her eyes, Kaitlin climbed into bed. Why couldn't Matt understand? Her marriage to Hector had been nothing but a matter of survival.

She lay in the middle of the bed, hoping that Matt would eventually ease into the room. An hour later, Kaitlin was asleep.

Morning came, and when Kaitlin opened her eyes, she found that she was still alone. Matt had stubbornly stayed on the couch. She hoped and prayed that he was in a better frame of mind. If not, then she hoped he'd had a miserable time of it on the sofa.

She was sitting on the side of the bed when there

was a soft knock on the door. "Come in," Kaitlin called out.

Matt slipped inside. "I need to take a shower."

Kaitlin didn't utter a word. The man could have graced her with at least a good morning. But she couldn't stand the distance between them. She had to get Matt to talk to her. When he came out of the bathroom, she decided to close the gap a little. "Morning, Matt."

He seemed puzzled at first. "Kaitlin, I apologize for my rudeness."

Feeling encouraged, she forged ahead. "How long have you been up?"

"I woke up around four."

"What time did you finally fall asleep?"

His voice was resigned. "Around three."

Kaitlin sat on the edge of the bed watching him.

When nothing more was said, Matt turned to leave the bedroom.

Moving quickly, Kaitlin blocked his path, practically knocking over a lamp on the nightstand. "We need to talk. We have been apart much too long to let something like this stay between us."

Matt's eyes traveled from her face and slid down her body.

She knew the transparent lacy negligee she wore held his attention. "Please talk to me."

His eyes darkened with emotion. Fingering the fragile material, he asked, "Did you wear this for Hector?"

Kaitlin's shoulders stiffened a fraction. She couldn't believe she'd heard right. "What did you say?"

His expression unforgiving, Matt repeated his question. "I asked if you wore this for Hector."

"I can't believe you just asked me that question. And you had the nerve to repeat it."

"I'm sure you didn't buy it with me in mind. If Hector hadn't died . . . well, it goes without saying."

Kaitlin glared at him with burning, reproachful eyes. "You're—"

A knock on the door interrupted her.

Irritated, Kaitlin muttered a curse.

Matt tossed her a look that spoke volumes.

There was a second knock.

Walking away from her, Matt headed toward the door. "I'd better get that."

Kaitlin gave a frustrated sigh. Tears of outrage stung the back of her eyelids, but she wasn't about to fall apart. After closing the bedroom door behind Matt, she headed for the shower. However, the hot water did nothing to soothe her tension. She got out, dried herself, and dressed, putting on a long floral-print skirt and matching lavender knit top. When Kaitlin left the bedroom, she found Preacher and Matt in a huddle, discussing something.

"Am I interrupting?"

Matt shook his head. "No."

"Any news?" Kaitlin inquired. "Will I get to go home soon?"

"Preacher was just telling me that Elian's got men posted everywhere," Matt explained. "But he's found a way for us to get off the island undetected."

Kaitlin was thrilled. "When do we leave?"

"We can leave as soon as everybody's ready," Preacher answered. "The sooner the better. There are pictures of Kaitlin everywhere, and people in Cancun asking questions. I've heard talk of a reward. Twenty-five thousand for the whereabouts of Mrs. Hector Rosales."

He glanced over at Matt. "The bounty on your head is much higher. One hundred thousand for the elusive Jaguar. It doubles when you are dead."

Kaitlin spoke up. "I can be ready in fifteen minutes."

Approximately fifteen minutes later, Kaitlin and the others left the hotel by taxi and headed to a tiny airfield. There, Preacher had secured them a helicopter that would take them to Texas. Once there, they would fly via commercial aircraft to California.

"Can the driver be trusted?" Gennai asked Preacher.

"Yeah," he answered. "I saved his brother's life once. One of Hector's goons had taken him out for a swim. I happened to be there fishing."

"What happened to him after that?" Kaitlin asked.

"As far as the Rosales cartel knows, the man is dead. In reality, I helped him leave the country. Shortly after that, his family joined him."

Kaitlin drew up the slim length of her skirt and climbed into the plane with Matt's assistance. Brilliant sunlight pierced through the windows of the helicopter. She felt a slight breeze, but it was too warm to be refreshing.

As soon as they were safely inside the aircraft, Kaitlin was fervent in her prayer of thanksgiving. She was finally going home! If Matt weren't acting so distant, this would be perfect. But not even Matt's behavior could destroy her happiness. She was finally going to see her family again. Kaitlin settled back into the helicopter.

Stealing a peek at Matt, she took note of his grim expression. A feeling of dread slid down her spine. Kaitlin had never seen him so angry. It was in the firm set of his jaw and in the way he sat. His back was ramrod-stiff and his muscled arms were folded across his chest.

If Matt decided that he didn't love her anymore, then at least she still had her family, Kaitlin decided. They would always love her. No matter what.

She stole another look at Matt, and Kaitlin grew a little sad. She loved him dearly, and the mere thought that she could lose him again tore at her. "I hope we can get past this," she whispered.

He glanced over at her. "Did you say something?"

Kaitlin shook her head, then turned away to stare out of the window. She didn't want him to glimpse her

tears. For just the briefest of moments, she thoug
about the plane crash in Phoenix. Her body shudder
involuntarily, and she felt like she couldn't breath
Kaitlin felt dizzy, causing her to reach out for Matt.

He seemed to read the fear in her eyes and unde
stood, because he immediately wrapped his arms arou
her. "It's okay, baby. Preacher knows what he's doing
He pointed outside. "Look how clear it is. It's a go
day for flying."

She nodded, unable to speak.

"Just lay your head on my shoulder."

Kaitlin did as she was told.

"Now close your eyes. Relax, baby. It's going to
okay." Matt squeezed her right hand. "I'm right he
with you."

Her last thought before she fell asleep in the secur
of his arms was that he still loved her. In spite of e
erything, Matt still loved her. She was filled with ho
that they would find a way to get past all that had ha
pened.

SEVEN

Elian enjoyed his breakfast on the terrace, surrounded by a breathtaking view of Lake Avándaro. As he cut his meat with enthusiasm, his companion watched him fearfully.

"Do ju have the information I requested?"

He nodded and tossed a large manila folder on the table. "Please let my family go. You have what you need."

"Not so fast, my freen. How do I know that thees is not some kind of trick?"

"I-I wouldn't do that," the man sputtered with indignation. "You have my family."

Laying down his knife and fork, Elian picked up the folder. His eyes never left the man's face. He loved seeing the fear in another person's eyes. It made him feel powerful. "Let's see what we have. . . ." He quickly scanned through the contents.

Satisfied with what he'd found out, Elian grinned. "I was pretty sure that Jaguar was undercover, and A.C." He placed a finger to his mustache. "Interesting." He gestured at the man's plate. "Ju not hungry?"

"M-My f-family. Please release my family. I've given you what you wanted."

Elian gestured to one of the men standing nearby. "See that Manny here joins his family." He grinned to himself, knowing the fate that awaited the poor man.

He would join his family all right. All the way to the depths of hell.

Hearing the clink of feminine heels on the tile floor, Elian looked up. He retained his affability, but there was a distinct hardening of his eyes. "Marta, I didn't know you were back."

"Who was that man?" she demanded in Spanish.

Waving his fork, Elian answered, "No one."

Tapping her fingers on the table impatiently, she stated, "I asked you a question."

"And I answered you." His lips puckered with annoyance as he reached for his glass and downed the last of the juice. "Where is your husband?"

"That was a question, Elian. I'm the only one around here asking questions. You're doing the answering." Marta's lips thinned with irritation. "Make no mistake, I am now the head of the cartel. If you are not with me then you are against me. You do not want me as an enemy." Her full skirt swirling around her, Marta turned and walked briskly back into the house.

Furious, Elian hurled the glass across the terrace, and watched it shatter into a million pieces when it hit the floor.

Kaitlin released a squeal of pure joy when they pulled up alongside a black Ford Explorer parked in front of her mother's house. Judging by the number of cars parked in the driveway and in the front, she could tell that all of her siblings were home.

"Looks like everyone is here," Matt observed. To his companions, he explained, "Kaitlin comes from a big family."

"I'll say," Preacher commented. "Looks like a small car lot over here."

"I can't wait to see everybody." Kaitlin jumped out

of the car and dashed up the steps. She ran her hand alongside the white railing that spanned the complete length of the two-story house. The two large Boston ferns that adorned the front door looked as full and healthy as they did the last time she was here. Tenderly, she ran her fingers through the leaves.

Matt came up behind her. "Ready?"

Tears filling her eyes, she nodded.

Matt rang the doorbell.

The door was thrown open, and Amanda Ransom stood there.

As soon as Kaitlin spotted her mother, she rushed into her open arms, causing Amanda to abandon her quad cane. "Mama, I'm so glad to see your face. I missed you so much."

"Oh, baby. My miracle . . . Thank God!"

Kaitlin ached inside as she saw how much her mother had aged. There were now tiny age lines where previously there had been none. Amanda's hair had more gray, and she was thinner. Kaitlin swallowed the urge to just break down altogether.

One by one, Kaitlin greeted the other members of her family with hugs and kisses. Even two of her uncles from North Carolina and Maryland had flown out for this occasion. A host of her other relatives were present as well.

She navigated around the room saying hello to family and close friends. It gave her a warm feeling to know that she was loved by so many and had been missed.

Kaitlin looked over at Mikey. He was standing in the corner, just watching her. She smiled and gestured for him to come to her, but he wouldn't move.

Putting aside her hurt feelings, she coaxed, "Mikey, honey, don't tell me that you've forgotten me?"

"No."

"What's wrong?"

His eyes filled with tears. "I thought you were dead. We had a church service and everything for you. You're not dead, are you?"

"Mikey, I'm alive and well." Kaitlin moved at a snail's pace toward him. She didn't want to frighten him. "Really, I am. I didn't die in that plane crash. I never even set foot on the plane. Honey, I went to Mexico."

"I know," he whispered. "Daddy told me that you went there on business."

She held out her hand. "Touch me. You'll see that I'm alive. Just like you."

Cautiously, Mikey reached out. He touched her gently, then gripped her hand.

"I missed you," Kaitlin whispered.

"I missed you, too." Crying, he fell into her arms. "Aunt Kaitlin . . ."

"Aunt Kaitlin, did you forget our phone number or something?" one of her older nieces asked. "Why didn't you call us? We were so sad because we thought we'd never see you again."

Wiping his tears with his hand, Mikey stepped away from Kaitlin. "Yeah. Why didn't you call us? Daddy could've helped you."

Carrie laid a gentle hand on Mikey's shoulder. "Honey, Daddy and I will explain everything to you later."

"Actually, I'd like to talk to him," Kaitlin interjected. "To all of the children myself. But not right now. I'll do it later, though. I think all explanations should come from me."

Carrie murmured her agreement. Reaching out, she and Kaitlin embraced. "Girl, I'm so glad to see you."

"Same here," she quietly acknowledged.

She pulled Kaitlin off to the side. "It's so good seeing you together with Matt again."

A blank expression settled over Kaitlin's face, causing Carrie to give her a questioning look.

"Is everything okay between you and Matt?"

Before Kaitlin could respond, she was called away. With a promise that they'd talk later, she ran off to join her mother.

She was polite while Amanda introduced her to several of her friends. Kaitlin was grateful that no one bombarded her with questions, because she wasn't ready for that.

While Amanda was deep in conversation about the many blessings that had been bestowed on the Ransom family, Kaitlin slipped off.

She wandered along the hallway that was decorated with huge sprays of flowers from Amanda's garden. There were countless family portraits greeting her along the way.

Kaitlin wiped away a tear as she strolled from room to room. A faint smile touched her mouth when she entered her old bedroom. Everything in the room smelled new. How in the world had they managed to redo an entire room from top to bottom so quickly?

She was revisiting a place she knew and had dwelled in most of her life. She was home.

Matt stood back with Preacher and the rest, watching the tearful reunion. Kaitlin was beaming with happiness and so were the rest of the Ransoms. Matt was thrilled over being able to return her to the safety of the family fold, especially since he'd felt responsible for Kaitlin leaving in the first place.

Ray strolled over toward him. "I can't thank you enough."

"No problem, Ray."

"I really mean it. My family and I are eternally

grateful." He lowered his voice. "Let's step outside for a minute. I don't want the others to hear what I have to say."

Matt followed Ray outside to the patio. The warning hairs on the back of his neck prickled. "What's up?"

"Yesterday, they found a DEA agent dead in Mexico. He and his family had been shot execution-style. He's suspected of printing out a list of agents who are involved in deep-cover operations. Especially those that were involved in Operation Foxfire."

Leaning against a post on the patio, Matt asked, "You think he sold them to Elian Cortez?"

"I think he may have been forced into stealing the information. His coworkers said that he'd been acting strange for about a week. He'd cited marital problems and told a few people that his wife had taken the kids and gone to Mexico. The last day he was seen alive, he left work early. He made it known that he intended to go to Mexico to get his family and bring them home."

"Sounds like he was trying to leave clues."

"Same impression I got."

Every muscle in Matt's body tensed. Through lips that barely moved, he asked, "The children were murdered, too?"

Ray nodded.

He felt sick inside. "I should have just let Gennai kill him."

"There are rumors that Elian's left Mexico. No one seems to know where he went. I believe he's going to come after Kaitlin sooner or later."

"He's after me," Matt stated. "And if he really does have the printout, then he knows exactly where to find me."

"If he finds you, then he finds Kaitlin."

"Do you think he perceives her as a threat to the cartel?"

Ray nodded. "Don't you? You've had dealings with the man firsthand."

Matt rubbed his chin thoughtfully. "With Elian, it's hard to tell. However, I don't think he's acting alone. Although he's a brutal murderer, he doesn't have the guts to go against the organization. Not without some power behind him."

"You think Hector's daughter is behind this? What do we know about her husband? What's his name? Armando Guerra."

"I don't know anything about him," Matt answered honestly. "But until we know something for sure, what do you have in mind, Ray?"

"I want to put my sister in protective custody. What she knows could probably destroy the whole Rosales operation."

Matt was a little stunned. "You're going to use her to put the others behind bars? I would think you'd want to keep her as far away from this mess as possible."

"I don't want Kaitlin involved, but I'm going to find out what she knows. I'll do whatever I have to, because I want her safe."

"Ray, I need to know something. Why didn't you tell me about Kaitlin's marriage?"

He responded with, "Have your feelings changed for my sister?"

Before Matt could reply, Kaitlin announced, "I'd like to know the answer to that myself." She joined them outside.

"I'll leave you two alone. Matt, we'll talk later." Ray left them alone.

Matt turned ice-green eyes toward her. Her steady gaze was riveted on his face, boring into him in silent expectation.

"Well?" she prompted.

"I could never stop loving you. Not even when

everyone else thought you'd died in that plane crash. My heart just wouldn't let me move on."

"I never stopped loving you either. Matt, I want to tell you why I married Hector. It was only because I feared for my life. I figured if I married Hector, I would be safe. He was also dying of prostate cancer."

Kaitlin shook her head sadly. "Hector was a very sick man and in constant pain. There were days he could barely get out of bed. He rarely ventured outside the estate. It had taken a lot of nagging on my part to get him to take a drive the day he . . . the day he was shot. He died saving me, Matt."

He was quiet.

She laid a hand on his arm. "Don't you see, honey? Hector took your best friend away, but in the end, he saved me. I know it doesn't make up for what he did to Ted . . ."

"I know what you're saying. Really I do."

Kaitlin removed her hand and retreated a step. "But it doesn't change how you feel about him?"

He didn't want to hurt her, but he had to be honest with her. "No, it doesn't."

"Matt, Hector suffered greatly. The pain was horrible, and it was hard watching him deteriorate. After the shooting, well, Hector wanted to die. He couldn't take the pain anymore. And he was tired of hiding his dying from his men." Her voice faded, and she cleared her throat.

Shrugging, Matt said, "I'm sorry, but I have no pity for the man. No compassion for a murderer. He deserved to suffer."

"So, where does that leave us?"

Matt backed up a couple of steps and rested his butt on the edge of the whitewashed rail. "I don't know the answer to that right now."

Kaitlin was persistent. "Can we get past this? I have to know."

His silence was Kaitlin's answer. Without another word, she walked to the edge of the patio and eyed the mountains.

Matt followed.

He reached out and tried to get her to look at him. Matt figured Kaitlin didn't want him to see how much he'd hurt her.

With her back still turned to him, Kaitlin stated coldly, "Leave me alone."

Crossing the patio, Matt held open the door, causing it to scream in protest. "You coming inside?"

"Not right now," Kaitlin said through tight lips. "I'll be in later."

He paused. "You okay?"

She gave him a look that clearly asked, *What on earth do you think?* Her gaze found his and held. Finally she spoke. "Tell me something. Are you okay, Matt?" she asked. "After everything that's happened, this is how we end up."

His heart slammed against his rib cage in response to her question. "Do you want me to lie to you, Kaitlin?"

"It's not like it hasn't been done before," she snapped in anger.

Cold dignity created a stony mask of his face. "I'll be inside."

Kaitlin turned back around to stare out at the mountains. He watched her for a moment before joining the other men in the family room.

Matt didn't know what the topic of conversation was, because he couldn't get his mind off Kaitlin.

Kaitlin dodged several family members to get to her old room. She needed a few minutes to gather herself after Matt's rejection.

Hot tears slipped down her cheek. Angry, she wiped at them. How could Matt do this to her? Although she didn't want to think about it, Kaitlin had to consider that just maybe they weren't meant to have a future together.

The door to her room opened. Kaitlin glanced over her shoulder. Her brother stuck his head inside.

"You okay, sis?" Laine asked.

Using both hands, she hastily wiped her face. "I'm fine. Just needed a minute to myself. I'll be out there in a few."

Stepping all the way inside of the room, Laine surveyed her for a minute. "You sure you're okay?"

Smiling, she nodded.

Kaitlin stayed inside her room until she felt she was able to deal with seeing Matt. She decided it was best to keep her distance from him right now.

Twenty minutes later, she left the safety of her bedroom.

"I was looking for you."

"Mikey." She bent down to tickle him. "You have no idea how much I missed you, cutie."

He stared into her eyes. "What's wrong with you? Are you sad?"

"I'm just a little tired, that's all." Taking him by the hand, she said, "I want to talk to you and your cousins about what happened. Help me gather up everybody and meet me in the family room, okay?"

"Okay."

Kaitlin could feel the heat of Matt's gaze on her. Her eyes met his briefly. She rifled him with an unreadable stare before finally turning away.

She spent the next thirty minutes fielding questions from her nieces and nephews. Kaitlin looked up to find A.C. standing in the doorway watching her. She smiled and gestured for her to enter. "I'm going to talk to my friend for a while, okay? You guys run along and play."

Before Mikey left, he hugged her again. "I love you so much. Please don't leave again."

"Honey, I'm okay," she assured him. "Really I am. And I love you, too."

When Mikey left, A.C. said, "You're very good with the children."

"I love my babies." Kaitlin stopped short. She put her hands to her face.

"You will be a wonderful mother."

A.C. placed a reassuring hand on her shoulder.

"I can't say thank you enough for the way you protected me. I don't know what I would've done without you."

"You were the innocent. Caught up in something that was not your doing. I'm thrilled with the way things have turned out. I really am."

"Thank you for being my friend. I want you to know that I'm going to miss you when you leave tomorrow."

"I won't be gone long. I'm flying to Washington, D.C., for my debriefing. We've got lots of information that will lead to a few indictments."

"You're going to have to testify?" Kaitlin asked.

A.C. nodded. "It's a part of my job."

"Is Gennai going with you?"

"No. We thought it best that he stay here with Matt and Preacher. I'll be back in a day or so. Gennai and I have to discuss where we're going to settle down."

Kaitlin was surprised. "Settle down? Really?"

A.C. grinned. "Yeah. Gennai and I have been talking."

"That's wonderful."

"We'll take this as far as it can go, I guess."

"He loves you, A.C. He really does."

"I know. I've known for a long time."

"But Matt was in the way," Kaitlin stated.

A.C. nodded.

"Are you truly over Matt?"

"Yes, Kaitlin. My season with Matt was just that. A season. Gennai is not a rebound. He and I have been friends for a very long time. I know him well, and this just feels right. I don't know how else to explain it."

"I think I know what you mean, A.C. That's how I felt when I met Matt." Kaitlin sighed. She hated this tension between them, but there were so many people around, so now was not the time to try to have a conversation.

A.C.'s voice cut through her thoughts. "I'm going to see what the guys are up to. Are you staying in here for a while?"

"I'll be here for a few minutes." Kaitlin twisted her fingers in her lap. Feeling anxious, she took slow, deep breaths and forced herself to relax. She was home, and she was safe. Soon she would start to heal.

As soon as Sabrina entered the house, she was met by Ray. Smiling, he said, "I guess I owe you an apology, Sabrina."

She waved her hand in dismissal. "It's no problem. I understand, Ray. No apologies are necessary."

"I just wish I'd listened to you. Maybe we could've found her earlier."

"I didn't know where she was. But—" Sabrina swayed.

Ray reached for her. "Sabrina, what's wrong?" he asked. "Did you just get another one of your visions or whatever you call them?"

In a low whisper she answered, "Ray, Kaitlin's still in danger."

He looked worried. "Are you sure?"

Sabrina nodded.

Kaitlin came into the living room. Looking from one person to the other, she asked, "What's going on?"

Ray ignored her question. Instead, he said, "Sis, I want you to meet someone. She's the other person who never believed you were dead. This is Sabrina Melbourne."

Smiling, Kaitlin held out her hand. "You're Regis's sister, right?"

Sabrina took the offered hand. "Yes, I am. I'm so glad to finally meet you."

"Me, too," she said slowly. Kaitlin surveyed Sabrina. She'd reacted almost as if she'd been burned when her hand touched hers. "Is there something wrong?"

Sabrina's eyes filled with sympathy.

Ray interrupted them. "Kaitlin, I want you to stay in a safe house for a while. And I don't want you to argue with me on this."

Kaitlin cast Ray a sidelong glance. "But why?"

"I think your brother's worried that you might still be in danger," A.C. announced from behind. "I just got off the phone with my superior. Honey, I hate to tell you this, but Elian's left Mexico. He could be anywhere."

Ray and Sabrina exchanged a glance.

"You both already knew this, didn't you?" Kaitlin asked. "Sabrina had a vision. That's why you two looked so solemn when I came into the room."

Matt and Preacher joined them just as Ray announced, "You're going to be all right, sis. We're going to take you to the safe house as soon as possible."

"I'm going to stay with her," Matt decided.

Preacher nodded in agreement. "We're all going to hang around until Elian and his men are taken down."

"Do you think he'll come after the rest of the family?" Kaitlin asked fearfully.

"What does he know about you?"

A.C. answered for her. "Not much of anything. Marta

and I created a fictional background for her. She didn't want Elian going after anyone in Kaitlin's family. On top of that, I've already asked Jensen to erase all traces of her life. School records, credit cards, and stuff like that."

"Did Marta know about Kaitlin's amnesia?"

Shaking her head no, she replied, "Only Kaitlin and I knew she was faking. I wasn't sure just how much Marta could be trusted, so I thought it best to not take any chances."

"I'm not going to a safe house. I'm staying with Mama."

"Kaitlin—"

"Ray, I mean it. I'm going to stay with Mama. I'm not leaving her."

"Then at least come stay with me. You and Mama both," he suggested.

"You know Mama. She's probably not going to do that. Can't A.C. stay with me? Gennai and Preacher are welcome as well." Kaitlin looked over at A.C. "Do you mind? I know you're going to be out of town for a few days, but you said you were coming back."

"I'll stay with you. I don't have a problem with that. I don't think the guys will either."

Preacher nodded his agreement. "Looks like we're going to be hanging around for a while."

EIGHT

Kaitlin found Regis in one of the bedrooms on the floor playing with her son, Jonathan. They had been introduced earlier by Laine. She was thrilled that her brother had managed to find someone who would love him the way he deserved. Silently she watched them from the doorway.

Regis looked up. She smiled when she saw Kaitlin standing there. "Hi."

"He's such a good little baby, and he looks just like Laine."

"Yes, he does."

She dropped down on the floor beside Regis. "Laine adores him."

"We went through a lot for this little guy. But I wouldn't change a minute of it."

"I've never seen Laine so happy. I'm glad he found you." Kaitlin remembered Thelma and had never liked her. She found out earlier that Laine had married Thelma shortly after . . . Kaitlin didn't want to finish the thought. It was still a little unsettling knowing that everyone had thought her dead until a few days ago.

Smiling, Regis said, "I'm glad you are back with your family. They were so lost without you."

Kaitlin reached for the thirteen-month-old little boy. "May I hold him?"

"Of course." Kissing her son, Regis cooed, "Say hello to your Auntie Kaitlin. This is your daddy's sister."

Holding the child close to her, Kaitlin reveled in his baby scent. "He's sooo precious." She tried to ignore the persistent ache in her heart as she cuddled her nephew. It had been a while since she'd held a baby. Not since . . . Kaitlin pushed the thought away.

"I think so."

"I just love babies." Kaitlin kissed Jonathan's cheek, enabling him to grab a handful of hair. "Ouch, little man."

This only served to make him burst into giggles and secure his hold.

She worked her hair out of his hands. "I see I'm going to have to get this cut, huh." Kaitlin rubbed her nose against his.

Jonathan attempted another grasp for hair.

"Oh, you like pulling hair, do you?"

Regis laughed. "I've learned to keep mine pulled back and out of his reach. He loves to grab."

"I see." Looking over at Regis, she said, "I just met your sister. You two look a lot alike."

"She's a sweetie. Sabrina kept getting vibes whenever she was around the family. She had dreams of you and felt that you were alive, but in trouble."

"You know this has been such a strange and terrifying experience. I mean, my family thought I was dead all this time."

"But Matt never believed for one minute that you'd died."

Jonathan was beginning to get restless, so Kaitlin handed him back to his mother. "He'd started to believe it. That's why he moved back to California. He was moving on with his life."

"It may not look like it right now, but things will

work out for the best, Kaitlin. You two were meant to be together." Regis planted a kiss on her son's forehead.

"I don't know about that, Regis. I used to believe it. Matt's regretting that he found me at all."

Regis's mouth dropped open. "I don't believe that for one minute. When I met him, I could see how much he grieved for you. It was like he was just going through the motions of living. If you don't mind my asking, what in the world happened?"

"How much do you know about my being in Mexico?"

"Just that you were held against your will by some drug lord."

"It was more than that, Regis. I married Hector Rosales."

"I see." If Regis was surprised, she didn't show it.

"I'm sure you're wondering why."

"Kind of."

"It was to stay alive, pure and simple. It wasn't a love match."

"Oh, I understand. We have to do what we must to survive sometimes."

Kaitlin sighed. "I wish I could get Matt to see it that way."

"I take it he's upset over the news."

"Huh! Upset doesn't come close."

Regis tried to reassure her. "You and Matt will work this out, I'm sure."

"I don't know about that. Right now he's barely speaking to me."

"Maybe he just needs some time."

"Maybe," Kaitlin agreed.

Regis placed a squirming Jonathan on the full-sized bed, then rose, before picking him back up. "Do you know where I can find Sabrina?"

"She was out back somewhere talking to Ray. At least that's where I last saw her."

"Are you looking for me?" Sabrina asked from the doorway.

Kaitlin and Regis looked toward the door.

Regis smiled. "Yes, I was. I wanted to make sure you're not getting into trouble."

Sabrina pretended to be offended. "Why on earth would you even think something like that? I was just describing to Elle the man that she's gonna marry."

"See what I mean? Girl, you need to quit that mess. Look into your own future."

Kaitlin watched in amusement as the two sisters bantered back and forth. She decided to take her leave at this point and went in search of Jillian. She wanted to get her hands on John Jr.

It was still a surprise that Jillian and John had gotten married. She'd known for a while that they'd had feelings for each other, but she never really imagined they would end up together. Jillian couldn't have found a better mate, in Kaitlin's opinion.

Kaitlin caught a glimpse of an intimate moment between Ray and Carrie. It was good to see that they were still very much in love. All of her married siblings had chosen well.

Her heart ached as she recalled how happy she and Matt used to be. Now, after such a long separation, they were acting like polite strangers. "It just isn't fair," she moaned softly.

Sabrina played with her nephew. "You are growing up so fast, little man."

Jonathan gave her a big lopsided grin.

She tickled him, and he burst into laughter.

"You two look like you're having a good time together."

Sabrina glanced over her shoulder. "Hey, Matt."

He strolled into the room and embraced her. "It's good to see you again." Matt stroked one of Jonathan's chubby cheeks. "Hey, fella."

"Same here. It's good seeing you smile for a change." She shifted Jonathan to the other hip. "This little boy is getting so heavy. I need to find his parents."

"I'll walk with you." Matt took the baby from her. "There are some other people I'd like for you to meet."

After Jonathan was placed in Laine's arms, Sabrina followed Matt outside to the patio.

"Sabrina, this is my friend, Preacher Watson."

Sabrina shook his hand. "Nice to meet you."

"And this is Gennai Li and A.C. Richardson."

"Nice meeting you both."

Preacher kept staring at her. Sabrina stared boldly until he finally had the manners to look away. She couldn't resist an impish grin.

"What are you up to?" Matt whispered.

"Nothing," she whispered back.

Garrick joined them for a minute, announcing, "There are some juicy steaks out back waiting for you all. Come on out and eat." To Gennai, he said, "Mama has a couple of vegetarian dishes out there for you. Matt told her that you didn't eat meat."

Preacher and Gennai excused themselves and followed Garrick to the patio.

"Matt, I sense that there is something going on between you and Kaitlin," Sabrina said, now that they were alone.

"She's married. She married Hector Rosales."

"He's dead." Sabrina wondered just how much Matt knew of Kaitlin's life in Mexico.

"That makes her the widow of Rosales. That's the problem. It doesn't make me feel any better."

"You're angry, and it's somewhat understandable, but a dead man shouldn't come between you two."

"He has."

"Only because you've let him," Sabrina pointed out. "This isn't easy for Kaitlin. Surely you know that."

"She didn't have to marry Rosales."

"How do you know that?" she questioned. "How do you know Kaitlin wasn't forced into this marriage? There could be a number of reasons why she married him."

"Maybe she fell in love with him."

"I know you can't believe that."

"I don't know what to believe."

"Have you asked Kaitlin about it, or given her a chance to explain how all this happened?"

"We've talked about it," was all Matt would say.

Sabrina gave a slight shrug. "If I were in your shoes, I wouldn't let love get away a second time."

She left him standing there. Sabrina prayed he would have the good sense to move forward with Kaitlin.

After giving Sabrina's words careful thought, Matt sought out Kaitlin. He found her in the kitchen. She and Elle were finishing up the dishes. She glanced his way when he walked in, but said nothing, just continued to dry the plate in her hand.

He cleared his throat. "I wanted to say good night."

"You've said it," she stated coldly. Kaitlin wouldn't even grace him with a look.

"Kaitlin . . ." Matt began.

She cut him off quickly. "Bye, Matt."

She wasn't going to make this easy for him. Matt hadn't expected she would. Right now Kaitlin was extremely upset with him.

"See you later, Elle."

She gave him a sympathetic look. "Bye, Matt."

He looked at Kaitlin. She was still ignoring him. Matt decided he'd give her some time with her family and time to readjust to being back home. It would also give him time to deal with his hatred of Hector Rosales.

Kaitlin felt like crying as she watched Matt walk out of the door, and out of her life. Fate had dealt her another blow.

"You were kind of rude to Matt back there, don't you think?"

She turned around, facing Elle. "No, I don't."

Elle looked at her with questions in her eyes. "What's going on with you two?"

"Nothing."

Taking the towel out of Kaitlin's hand, Elle inquired, "Why are you acting like this? You love Matt, and he loves you, so why are you two acting so distant with each other?"

"Matt has issues."

"We all do," Elle shot back. "Why should that keep the two of you apart?" She studied Kaitlin for the answer. "What on earth could be so bad that it would break you two up?"

"He can't handle the fact that Hector Rosales and I were married."

Elle dropped the towel she was holding. "Married!" she shrieked with surprise.

"Yes. I thought you knew," Kaitlin replied calmly.

Elle shook her head. "No, somehow I missed that piece of information. I don't think anyone else in the family knew either."

"Ray knew about it."

"Well, he didn't share it with the rest of us. Maybe he thought Mama would have a heart attack or something."

Kaitlin folded her arms across her chest and leaned against the kitchen counter. "I don't know, but I'm going to have a talk with him. He should have prepared y'all. I guess I should call a family meeting and tell everybody."

They could hear voices. It sounded as if they were coming from the living room.

Tiptoeing to the door, Elle peered out into the dining room. "Matt's leaving."

Kaitlin shrugged nonchalantly.

"Why don't you go to him? Get him to understand what happened. Don't just let him get away like that."

"He doesn't want me, Elle. He thinks I'm tainted or something. Nothing I say will ever change the way he feels."

"You don't know that for sure."

Kaitlin glanced sidelong at her sister. "Let's talk about you. Is there a man in your life?"

Elle smiled. "There's someone I'm crazy about, only he doesn't have a clue."

"Why don't you tell him?"

"Because I can't just walk up to Brennan Cunningham and announce that I'm in love with him—"

Kaitlin stopped her. "Who did you say?"

"Brennan Cunningham. He's—"

"I know who he is. Baby sister, I have to tell you. When you set your sights on someone . . . you really aim high. That man is practically a billionaire."

"I don't care a fig about his money. It's just something about him." Elle shrugged. "He's handsome and fine. Fine, fine, and did I say fine?"

Kaitlin laughed. "I take it the man is fine."

"And he's real nice, although he comes off as being unapproachable. He's shy in a way."

"You don't even know him."

"Yes, I do. I've been around him quite a few times. He and my boss are best friends. He's always coming through the office, and he's even gone on a few business trips with us."

"How does he act around you?"

"He's real nice to me. He watches me an awful lot."

"Really?"

"Yeah. Do you think it means anything?"

"He might be attracted to you."

"I hope so."

"Elle, if he doesn't go after you, then it's his loss. You're a wonderful person and will make some man a phenomenal wife."

"Kaitlin, I really missed you while you were gone. I'm so glad you're back."

"Me, too."

The two sisters embraced.

For just the briefest of moments, Kaitlin wished it were Matt whose arms were around her.

Sabrina muttered a curse. She had a flat tire. She was a few miles from Amanda Ransom's house, but not close enough to chance walking back.

Reaching into her purse, she searched for her cell phone. Although she could easily call for one of the Ransoms, Sabrina decided to call for roadside assistance. After all, this is what she was paying for.

Bright headlights almost blinded her as a car slowed to a halt.

"What's wrong, Sabrina?"

She looked up. Her initial fear was replaced by relief. It was Matt and his friends. "I have a flat."

Preacher climbed out of the car. "Would you like me to take care of that for you?"

"If you don't mind. I know nothing about changing tires."

Sabrina stood off to the side while Preacher removed the spare from the trunk of her automobile. Matt got out to see if he could be of assistance.

Preacher's response was, "No, we got it. Thanks."

While Matt and Sabrina watched, Preacher and Gennai worked diligently.

"Did you get a chance to talk to Kaitlin before you left?" Sabrina asked Matt.

He shook his head. "No, she wasn't in a real talkative mood. It's my fault though. I've hurt her by my reaction. I think I may have messed up big time."

"You two are the golden couple."

Matt grinned. "I thought so, too."

"Well, I'm not sure you're going to believe me, but I'm going to tell you anyway. You and Kaitlin *will* grow old together."

"I believe that. But I think we need some time apart. I need to work through this issue."

Sabrina made a face and gave him a playful punch. "You've had nothing but time! Either you love Kaitlin and you want to be with her or you don't. Stop trying to make this into something hard."

Preacher put the jack and the flat tire into the trunk. "Be careful on that donut. Remember, it's not made for the same wear and tear as the regular tires."

"Oh, I know. First thing in the morning, I'm going to take it to the dealership. Thank you so much, Preacher. I owe you."

"It was all my pleasure." Preacher's eyes slid over her face and down her body.

It was clear to her that he liked what he saw. Sabrina was flattered by his interest. Extremely conscious of h virile appeal, she found herself attracted to him as well. The thought sent her spirits soaring. Maybe her drought was finally over.

NINE

Ivy stormed briskly into the kitchen early the next morning. Kaitlin glanced up from the newspaper she'd been reading. "You're here awful early. Do you have an appointment in Riverside this morning?"

"No. I had to come out here to see you." Ivy slapped her palm down on the breakfast table. "Girl, have you lost your ever-loving mind?"

Her brown eyes widened with false innocence. Kaitlin calmly put aside the newspaper. "What are you rambling about, Ivy?" She pushed away from the table and strolled across the floor toward the oven.

Her sister followed her. "What is this I hear? Elle says you were married to Hector Rosales. Please tell me that she's wrong."

Without looking up from her task of taking hot raspberry muffins out of the oven, Kaitlin declared, "What Elle said is true."

A loud gasp escaped Ivy. "Why did you marry that man? From everything I've read, he was a horrible person, Kaitlin."

After carefully placing the hot muffin pan on the counter, Kaitlin turned around to face her sister. Ivy was now wearing her judgmental furrow. The muscles at the base of Kaitlin's neck tightened—the way they always did whenever she was faced with a confrontation.

Kaitlin sighed heavily. "Ivy, I was never in love. It was never about that. I married Hector because he cared for me, and I thought it would help me stay alive."

Ivy's lips parted in shock at the news. "But . . . how could you?" She shook her head in despair. "It's almost like prostitution."

Kaitlin felt a surge of anger. She glowered at Ivy. "I beg your pardon!"

"Good morning," Amanda announced when she entered the kitchen. She glanced from one daughter to the other. "What is going on in here?"

Still glaring at Ivy, Kaitlin replied, "Morning, Mama. If you all will excuse me, I'm going upstairs." She tossed the towel on the kitchen counter and rushed out.

Just as she climbed the stairs, Kaitlin heard her mother ask, "What in the world did you say to your sister?"

Ivy's response was simply, "I told her exactly what I thought of her marriage to Hector Rosales. I guess the truth hurts."

As she climbed the stairs, Kaitlin could hear Ivy and her mother arguing.

In her room, Kaitlin lay across her bed, fighting a tension headache. She was furious, and tired of having to explain herself. Why couldn't anybody understand that her fear motivated her heart and her mind to operate for one purpose—survival.

What did it matter now? The man was dead. No one knew what she was going through. Memories of what happened haunted her still. Nobody could possibly understand unless they'd had to endure it firsthand.

Regis ran her fingers gently through Sabrina's hair. "It's time for a trim."

Sabrina frowned. "Already? I thought you did that a few weeks ago."

Putting away her hair dryer, Regis replied, "It's been eight weeks. I trimmed your hair the last time I did your retouch."

"Oh." Flipping through the latest issue of *Essence,* Sabrina asked, "How's my little nephew doing?"

"He's busy. Girl, Jonathan wears me out. You know, Laine's been talking about us having another baby. He's ready. His doctor gave him the good news two weeks ago."

Sabrina glanced up into the mirror. "What about you?"

Regis smiled. "To tell you the truth, I'd like to wait another year. You know I'm so busy right now, I barely have time for myself."

"Did you tell Laine?"

"I did, and he says he understands. However, he's worried that if we wait, we won't be able to conceive. Laine's even promised to cut back on his work schedule to help me more. He really wants to have another baby, and he's a wonderful father."

"Girl, you're going to be pregnant before this year is out."

Regis picked up a curling iron. "I ought to burn you for that. I'm too exhausted nowadays to keep up with a toddler, a husband, and a new baby."

Sabrina shook with laughter. Suddenly her expression changed. Her body trembled slightly, and she put a hand up to her face.

"Sabrina, are you okay? What's happening?"

"Nothing. I just got this weird feeling and all of a sudden I got a vision of Preacher. I remember when I touched his hand the other day, I experienced this exact same feeling. His touch seemed so familiar. Why in the world would he be so prominent in my mind like this? What connection could we possibly have?"

"I don't have a clue. The two of you are as different

as day and night. You're a talkaholic and he—well, h
doesn't seem to have much to say. He just sits off b
himself somewhere and reads that Bible he carries wit
him."

"Hmm . . . silent, Bible-toting, and deadly. Nov
that's a combination."

Regis's eyes lit up in amusement. "Girl, I knov
you're not interested in that man." She held up a portio
of Sabrina's long hair and clipped the ends.

"Why not? He's good-looking."

"And he has a dangerous job. Sabrina, you won
know if or when the man is coming home half th
time."

"It's a job."

"It's life or death," her sister argued.

"Regis, don't worry about me. You're always tellir
me that I need to find a man. Well, I have. Now mal
me look good."

After Sabrina left the hair salon, she stopped off
La Maison. She was craving some of the spicy Caju
seafood dip that was the house specialty.

Just as she strolled into the restaurant, Sabrina felt
tap on her shoulder. She turned around.

"We meet again," Preacher declared.

Her breath caught in her throat. Subconscious
Sabrina placed a hand to her throat. "Hello, Preache
How are you?"

"I'm blessed. How 'bout yourself? Take care of th
tire?"

Sabrina nodded. "I'm doing fine, and the car is a
taken care of. I didn't know you were still in town."

"We're going to hang around for a while. We're sta
ing with Mrs. Ransom. Make sure things are safe."

"I understand. I'm sure that takes a load off her mir
having you all there."

He gestured toward the dining room. "Are you having lunch here?"

"Yes, actually I am." Sabrina paused. "Are you here to see Matt?"

"He asked me to drop off some stuff for him."

The dark depths of his eyes enchanted her. "Would you like to join me? I'd like to pay you back for helping me the other night."

"You don't have to do that."

"I want to, and besides that, I really hate to eat alone."

Sasha approached them. "Will you two be having lunch?"

Sabrina glanced up at Preacher, who responded, "Yes. A table for two, please."

She released a subtle sigh of relief. Sabrina really wanted to get to know this man better.

A few minutes later, they were seated.

"This is the second time you've rescued me."

He smiled. "The pleasure is all mine." Preacher's eyes scanned her face. "You don't strike me as a woman who needs rescuing."

"You'd be surprised," Sabrina shot back.

Picking up his menu, Preacher scanned the contents. He laid it down a few minutes later. "Matt tells me you're psychic."

Shrugging, Sabrina stated, "I have a gift. I'm glad I've been able to help people."

"Praise God," he murmured.

The waiter arrived.

Sabrina said, "I already know what I want. Do you need a few more minutes?"

"No, I'll have whatever you're getting."

"Are you sure?"

He nodded. To the waiter he said, "For starters we'll

have the Cajun seafood dip followed by two garlic shrimp platters and two tall glasses of iced tea."

Sabrina's mouth dropped open in her surprise. Preacher wasn't psychic. Was he?

The waiter left with their orders.

"How did you know?"

"I have a confession to make. Sasha told me that you always order the Cajun seafood dip and that you love the garlic shrimp."

Sabrina burst into laughter. "You and Sasha had some discussion about me."

"Yeah, we did. I wanted to know as much about you as I could find out."

Her full lips smiled in delight. "Why?"

"I find you a very attractive woman. You intrigue me."

Sabrina murmured, "I see." She was a little taken aback by his straightforwardness.

"I don't apologize for my bluntness. I find it cuts out a lot of misunderstandings in the long run."

"You sound like my cousin, Marc. That's something he would say."

"It's a true saying."

Preacher's physical appearance and serious demeanor sent off a warning that he was not a man to be crossed, but his smile was soft and gentle. Nervous, Sabrina played with her water glass. She had never met a man quite like him.

"I was also told that you're not seeing anyone."

She raised her eyes to meet his. He was staring intently at her. Beneath her fine linen suit, Sabrina felt the stirring embers of a smoldering fire.

"I also know that you lost your husband a few years back. I can only imagine how you must feel, and I don't want to intrude upon your mourning. However, I would like to know if you're interested in dating again?"

Sabrina could only nod.

He was visibly relieved. "I'm glad to hear that, because I would like to take you out sometime."

Preacher seemed to be waiting for an answer, so she responded, "I'd love to go out with you."

"Is tomorrow night too soon?"

"No, tomorrow night is fine. What time should I be ready?"

"Eight o'clock."

Sabrina scribbled her phone number and her address on a napkin, which she handed to him.

Preacher stuck it into his shirt pocket.

"If I'm going to have dinner with you, I'd better know more about you—like your birth name. I'm sure your parents didn't name you Preacher."

"My parents were the first ones to call me Preacher, because I used to give sermons when I was a child. I loved Bible stories, and I loved the Lord. However, my legal name is Thaddeus Jacob Watson. My friends call me Preacher and my enemies make sure to never call me anything within earshot."

Sabrina burst into laughter.

The waiter returned with their food.

Over lunch, Preacher and Sabrina discussed the pros and cons of being single and dating in today's world. He proved to be quite an interesting man. He was well versed in the arts, literature, and politics; they conversed on a number of topics.

Three hours later, Sabrina left Preacher with Matt and she headed home. She was filled with excitement and looking forward to seeing him tomorrow night.

She had just turned on her laptop and was preparing to do a lesson plan for her next computer class when she started to feel dizzy. Sabrina was surrounded by a thick haze. Turning up her nose, she frowned over the rancid smell of death in the air. Sabrina fought the over whelming urge to scream. Someone was going to die

Elian tossed the papers in the trash. Who was Kaitlin All of his leads had turned up nothing. It was as if th woman simply didn't exist. He picked up the phone an called another one of his contacts.

Marta had burned up Kaitlin's information shortly a ter the shooting. He knew that she and Kaitlin had onc attended school together. Even there, his contacts ha turned up nothing.

The thought occurred to him that Kaitlin was an ur dercover agent, but he didn't think she had the stomac for such a job. She was quite an actress though. Elia had never believed that she suffered from amnesia—nc for a minute.

He wouldn't soon forget the day when Hector ha come to him stark-raving mad over the hit that had bee done while Marta and Kaitlin were in the house. Elia had tried to explain how the man had been stealing fror Hector. How he had been skimming 10 percent off th top. He further explained how he'd taken it as a person: affront since he'd been the one to introduce the man t Hector.

In truth, it had been Elian who'd been stealing fror Hector and had been called on it. In order to keep hi secret safe and his plans in motion, he'd had to silenc the threat.

Hector had turned a deaf ear to him. He was so angry Elian had feared that Hector would have him whacke

A few days later, he summoned Elian to his offic and extracted a vow that Kaitlin would not be harmec He explained that she suffered from amnesia and there fore was not a threat to the organization. When Elia suggested that her memory could one day return, Hecto dismissed the idea with a wave of his hand, and stated that he would deal with Kaitlin personally. Elian hadn't wanted to incur the old man's wrath, so he gave his word and decided to bide his time.

Elian's face now was a glowering mask of rage. Kaitlin was supposed to have died with Hector.

For the time being, he would have to push Kaitlin from his thoughts and attend to the matter at hand. He knew the identity of Jaguar. And he knew where to find him.

Marta was oblivious to his plans, and he planned to keep it that way. In a couple of weeks, he would travel to Los Angeles. For now, he needed to lie low. When Marta questioned him, Elian lied about meeting a young lady and wanting to spend some time with her.

Whether Marta believed him, Elian couldn't be sure. It didn't matter to him because she would soon join her father. Yet he'd seen something in her eyes. It was the same deadly look Hector would have when he wanted someone dead.

Although Elian found it hard to believe that Marta was as dangerous as her father, he decided to play it carefully. Marta and her father had become very close in the last few months of Hector's life. They had spent many hours in closed-doors meetings. He could only surmise they had been making plans for her to take over after his death.

When he felt a hand clasp his shoulder, Elian jerked around. "Stunts like that can get you killed," he uttered.

"I heard you were leaving?"

Elian regarded his visitor over steepled fingers. "Is she suspicious?"

The man shrugged. "She says that you are planning to break someone's heart. I don't think you have anything to worry about."

"I have everything to worry about. I have gone to

great lengths for you, but I am not so sure you will not
betray me."

The man laughed. "Now why would I do that? We
are *familia*. You and I." He headed for the door and
peeked out. Before leaving, he said, "Make sure you
finish the job this time."

As quietly as he'd come, the man disappeared, leaving
Elian to his thoughts. He and the man might be blood
relations, but when it came to a multimillion-dollar em-
pire . . .

Elian continued to reflect. His cousin was clever
enough to play both sides without him knowing, but
then again his cousin was in a much more dangerous
position. Elian had the advantage because of what he
knew. Only time would tell if they were truly partners.

It was Valentine's Day and Matt had never felt more
alone. He couldn't get Kaitlin out of his mind. Yeah
Hector was dead all right. But he had managed to take
away another person Matt loved. *Only if you allow him
to do so,* a tiny voice echoed inside.

Eyeing a couple who had just entered the restaurant,
Matt made a decision. He wasn't going to let Hector
ruin this for him. Kaitlin was the only woman he wanted
to share his life with. He headed straight to his office
and picked up the phone, calling a florist. He ordered
two dozen red roses. Next, he ordered candy.

A.C. rapped on the door to his office. "Hey, Matt.
You busy?"

He put down the phone. "No, come on in." When
she was seated he asked, "How did it go?"

A.C. leaned back in her chair. "Everything went okay.
I'll be going back and forth for the next couple of years
or so."

"I don't miss it at all."

3 QUICK STEPS TO RECEIVE YOUR "THANK YOU" GIFT FROM THE EDITOR

Send this card back and you'll receive 4 FREE Arabesque novels! The introductory shipment of 4 Arabesque novels – a $23.96 value – is yours absolutely FREE!

There's no catch. You're under no obligation to buy anything. You'll receive your introductory shipment of 4 Arabesque novels absolutely FREE (plus $1.50 to offset the costs of shipping & handling). And you don't have to make any minimum number of purchases—not even one!

We hope that after receiving your books you'll want to remain an Arabesque subscriber. But the choice is yours to continue or cancel, anytime at all! So why not take us up on our invitation to receive 4 Arabesque Romance Novels, with no risk of any kind. You'll be glad you did!

Call us
TOLL-FREE
at 1-888-345-BOOK

THE EDITOR'S "THANK YOU" GIFT INCLUDES:

- 4 books absolutely FREE (plus $1.50 for shipping and handling)
- A FREE newsletter, *Arabesque Romance News*, filled with author interviews, book previews, special offers, and more!
- No risks or obligations. You're free to cancel whenever you wish... with no questions asked.

BOOK CERTIFICATE

Yes! Please send me 4 FREE Arabesque novels (plus $1.50 for shipping & handling). I am under no obligation to purchase any books, as explained on the back of this card.

Name _____

Address _____ Apt. _____

City _____ State _____ Zip _____

Telephone ( ) _____

Signature _____

Offer limited to one per household and not valid to current subscribers. All orders subject to approval. Terms, offer, & price subject to change. Offer valid only in the U.S.

Thank you!

AN061A

Accepting the four introductory books for FREE (plus $1.50 to offset the cost of shipping & handling) places you under no obligation to buy anything. You may kee the books and return the shipping statement marked "cancelled". If you do not cancel, about a month later we will send 4 additional Arabesque novels, and you will be billed the preferred subscriber's price of just $4.00 per title. That's $16.00 for all 4 books for a savings of 33% off the cover price (Plus $1.50 for shipping and handling). You may cancel at any time, but if you choose to continue, every month we'll send you 4 more books, which you may either purchase at the preferred discount price. . . or return to us and cancel your subscription.

ARABESQUE ROMANCE BOOK CLUB
P.O. Box 5214
Clifton NJ 07015-5214

PLACE
STAMP
HERE

"Well, this is the end of it. Outside of testifying at the trials, I'll be able to go back to being plain ol' Allison again. I'm looking forward to that." She tossed a card across Matt's desk. "Do you think Gennai will like it?"

He read the message inside and grinned. "This is nice." Matt handed the card back to her. "You never got me anything like this. I'm a little hurt."

A.C. broke into laughter. "Don't even go there, Matt."

"You love him a lot."

"I'm getting there. I can't even imagine my life without him. Sometimes I think about running away. This is so intense, these feelings I have for Gennai."

"I'm glad to see you so happy."

"I am," A.C. confessed. "I can't wait for him to meet my family."

"Have you been able to contact any of your sisters?"

"I spoke to Sherry. Felicia's on assignment somewhere in Washington State. Perri is in Canada right now."

"What about your dad?"

"I spoke to him. He wants me to come home as soon as I can."

Matt scanned her face. "You miss him, don't you?"

A.C. nodded. "I do." Playing with her braid, she asked, "Are things any better between you and Kaitlin?"

"I ordered her a huge bouquet of flowers just before you came in. I'm hoping we can have dinner tonight."

"I'm glad you're coming to your senses."

"Don't pull out your pom-poms yet. She may not want to see me."

"Oh, I don't think you have anything to worry about. Kaitlin loves you, and she's not going to let you go that easily."

Silently, Matt prayed she was right. The one thing that was abundantly clear was that, like A.C. felt about Gennai, he couldn't see life without Kaitlin.

* * *

"Honey chile, I'm telling you that you and Matt will get past this." Carrie leaned forward. "You didn't see him, but I did. When he heard about the crash, Matt rushed straight to my house. I could tell he'd been crying, Kaitlin. When he looked me straight in my face and told me that he knew you weren't dead, I thought he was crazy. Matt placed his hand over his heart and said that you were the other half of him."

Kaitlin's eyes were bright with unshed tears. She glanced down at her hands.

Carrie continued. "He went with us to Phoenix, and he ended up staying there. He vowed that he would not return without you. Now tell me, Kaitlin. Do you really think Matt will give up so easily?"

Kaitlin wiped away a tear. "You don't have any idea how much he hated Hector. He sees this as some sort of betrayal." She told Carrie about Ted and his family.

Pressing a hand to her chest, Carrie gasped. "How horrible!"

"I'm so sorry that happened to them. I really am. Nobody deserves to die that way." She chewed on her bottom lip.

"Kaitlin, how does this make you feel? Knowing that you were married to someone like that?"

"I feel sick to my stomach. Carrie, I never loved Hector. But he wasn't like that with me. The man I knew had changed. He was sick and dying. He wanted to go to heaven, so he begged for forgiveness and set out to make things right."

"He couldn't give those people back their lives."

"I know that. What he did was horrific. I realize all that. I just find it hard to hate a dying man. I saw the way he suffered. Girl, there were days the pain reduced him to crying like a baby. All I could do was stand there and just watch him suffer."

"I guess no one can really imagine just how hard this was on you."

"They can't. Especially Ivy. She looks at me with such disgust."

"Don't let Ivy get to you. That's just her way. She'll come around."

Kaitlin glanced down at her watch. "I'd better get out of here. I want to get back to Riverside before the rush-hour traffic kicks in." She stood up and yawned. "I'm so tired."

"Tell me about it," Carrie agreed. "I'm not that far along, but this pregnancy is really wearing on me. I'll be glad when this child is born."

"So what are you guys hoping for? You already have a boy and a girl."

"Ray wants another girl."

"Really?"

Carrie nodded. "He doesn't want to risk Mikey thinking that he'll love his own flesh-and-blood son more than him."

"He's a sweetie."

"Yes, he is. I love him like crazy."

"Has he given you your Valentine's gift?"

"No. Ray's been so busy, he's probably forgotten. I'm not going to be upset. He gives me gifts all year round. He's a very loving and generous husband. Not to mention romantic."

"Uh-huh. That's how you got this little one."

Carrie put a hand to her mouth to hide her giggles.

"I hope I'll find a man who'll love me like that."

"You have, silly. Girl, I'm telling you, Matt is the only man for you. Don't let him get away."

Kaitlin checked her watch a second time. "I'd better get out of here."

The two women stood and headed over to the front door. She and Carrie embraced.

"I'll talk to you later in the week. Take care of yourself, and if you need me to take the children this weekend, just let me know."

"Okay. Drive safe," Carrie advised.

In the car, Kaitlin's fingers tightened over the wheel. Memories flooded her mind as she drove along the 405 freeway south. Traffic was heavy, and up ahead there was yet another accident. As she slowly inched along, memories of her and Matt skipped through her mind. Recollections of a love that was no more. She swallowed hard. *Not today,* she screamed in silence. *I am not going to take that stroll down memory lane.* It was a painful path.

She turned on the radio, scanned the channels, then turned it off again. Kaitlin didn't want to hear anything romantic, especially not today. Searching through her mother's tiny CD collection, she found a gospel album. Kaitlin popped it into the disc player.

The usual hour-long trip home had turned into an hour and forty-five minutes today. Kaitlin didn't mind too much. There wasn't really anything to rush home for. She knew that Preacher and Gennai were going to be down at March Air Force Base today, and she wasn't sure when A.C. would be back.

As she drove through Riverside, Kaitlin noticed that nothing much had changed in the area near her mother's house. The grocery store looked the same. So did the video store and local merchants in the midsized strip mall. Nothing had changed but yet everything seemed different.

"These just came for you." Amanda carried a beautiful bouquet of flowers. "You also got a big box o candy. I bet I know who these are from."

Kaitlin wasn't so sure. "I don't know, Mama. You might lose that bet. They're probably from one of your sons."

"Well there's only one way to find out. Read the card."

Kaitlin gave a small laugh. "Might as well." She pulled the tiny envelope from its plastic holder. Opening it, she read the card.

"Well?"

"They're from Matt. He wants me to meet him for dinner tonight. He wants to spend Valentine's Day with me."

"You just got back home. I know you're not going all the way back to Los Angeles tonight."

"No, I'm not. Matt can come out here if he wants. We can have dinner at Gregory's."

"That's a real nice restaurant."

"What do you think I should do, Mama? I'm still a little hurt over his attitude."

"I think you should have dinner with him. The two of you should sit down and really talk about everything. I know how much you two love each other. It's a love that only comes around once. And that's if you're lucky."

Matt arrived promptly at eight to pick up Kaitlin. In honor of Valentine's Day, she was wearing a red dress that accentuated her curves. Her hair was a mass of spiral curls and the style suited her. She looked so stunning, he couldn't take his eyes off her.

As he continued to appraise her, he murmured huskily, "You look so beautiful."

Kaitlin saw the heartrending tenderness of Matt's gaze and smiled warmly. "Thank you."

As an afterthought, she added, "Happy Valentine's Day." She handed him a large envelope containing a card she'd chosen for him when she went looking for

an anniversary card for John and Jillian the previous
night. Kaitlin had originally planned to mail it, but after
finding the flowers and candy, she decided to wait and
give it to him in person.

They stood staring at each other. Kaitlin's body ached
for his touch. From the way Matt's eyes traveled over
her face and her body, she knew he felt the same way.

"Are you two just going to stand there gawking at
each other?" Amanda asked from behind them. "You're
going to miss your reservations."

Matt chuckled. "We're leaving now."

Kaitlin blew her mother a kiss and picked up her
purse. "I'll see you later."

"Have fun."

Kaitlin didn't see her mother giving Matt a thumbs-up.

Outside, Matt held the car door open for Kaitlin. She
slid onto the passenger seat. When Matt got in on the
other side, Kaitlin said, "I'm glad you asked me out. I
missed you."

"I'm sorry about the way I've been acting. I can't
help the way I feel about Hector, but I shouldn't hold
it against you. You did what you had to do. I understand
that."

"Are you sure that you understand? I don't want you
saying that just to make up."

"I'm being honest, Kaitlin. I do understand. I still
don't like it, but I do understand."

"Matt, I didn't love Hector."

"I know that."

"Can we please move forward? I really want to go
on with my life, and I'm so tired of being apart from
you. I love you, and I know that you love me too."

"We can. I want that too."

Throughout dinner, Matt and Kaitlin continued to discuss their relationship. It was important to her that they
clear the air.

After dinner, Matt suggested that they go to a comedy club in Riverside.

"That's fine. It's something I've missed while I was in Mexico."

They arrived in time for the second show. Although they enjoyed the comedian, Matt and Kaitlin only had eyes for each other.

Afterward, he drove her back to her mother's house. Matt walked her to the door. "Thank you for having dinner with me."

"I'm glad we did this. We really needed to talk."

He agreed. "There's something else I really need to do."

"What's that?"

"I need to kiss you."

She awarded him a sexy grin. "Then what's stopping you?"

Matt's hand settled over her shoulder, his fingers on her back. He pressed warm lips to the crook of her neck, causing Kaitlin to moan.

Embers of a long-awaited fire smoldered. Backing her against the wall, Matt lowered his head. His lips touched hers, and Kaitlin quivered. His muscled arms held her fast, and her knees threatened to give way altogether.

When Matt kissed her, it felt as if he did so with his whole body. The touch of his lips was a delicious sensation, arousing her passion.

She broke the kiss after a while. "I'd better go inside."

He nodded. "Yeah. You're right." Using his thumb, Matt wiped away a smudge of lipstick from Kaitlin's chin.

They said a final good night, and Kaitlin went inside. She found her mother in the den watching television.

"Where's everybody?"

"Preacher had to meet someone in L.A. A.C. and Gennai are on the patio."

Kaitlin sat down beside her mother. "And what are

you doing up so late? Don't tell me this movie is that good." She stuck her hand in the bowl of popcorn in Amanda's lap. She tossed the popcorn in her mouth.

"I wanted to find out how things went between you and Matt. Good, I hope."

Grinning, Kaitlin nodded. "We had a nice time, Mama, I think we're on the right track now."

"I never doubted it for a minute."

Laying her head on her mother's shoulder, Kaitlin watched television until her eyelids grew heavy. Sitting up, she yawned. "I'm tired."

Covering her mouth, Amanda agreed. "Me too. I was trying to make it to the end of the movie, but I don't think I can."

Kaitlin assisted her mother in getting up. "I'll see you in the morning, Mama."

"Okay, baby. You get a good night's sleep." Amanda kissed Kaitlin's cheek. "I'm glad to see you and Matt together again. He's a good man."

Kaitlin couldn't agree more. Matt was her soul mate, her best friend. In Matt, she saw her future.

TEN

Their first two attempts to have dinner had been a failure, so when Preacher hadn't called to cancel by five o'clock, Sabrina went ahead and started dinner.

Thirty minutes before Preacher was due to arrive, she stood in the middle of her huge walk-in closet, trying to decide between a jade-green dress and a purple pants set. After a few minutes of trying to decide, she pulled a blue wrap skirt and matching knit top off their hangers.

Next, Sabrina searched through a mountain of shoe boxes, looking for the shoes that matched the outfit. Before getting dressed, she pulled her hair up into a ponytail and applied just a touch of makeup.

Ready for her date, Sabrina strode into the kitchen to check on dinner. When the doorbell sounded ten minutes later, she smiled. Preacher was prompt, she noted.

Sabrina welcomed him into her home. Preacher walked inside carrying a dozen pink roses. Handing them to her, he said, "I hope these will make up for having to cancel our other dates."

"They're beautiful. Thank you." Stealing a peek at him, Sabrina admired Preacher. He was dressed in a well-fitting, single-breasted suit that looked as if it had been made just for him. He wore an ivory shirt beneath the black jacket and a stunning black-and-ivory-patterned tie.

Sabrina was tempted to ask if he were coming fro
church.

She noted that his observant eyes missed nothin
Turning around to face her, he said, "Nice place."

"Thank you. Why don't you have a seat." Sabri
gestured to the plush navy blue leather sofa. She f
lowed him over to the chair and sat down. Sabrina w
careful not to sit too close to him because she did
want to send out the wrong message. "Dinner will
ready in about five minutes."

He smiled and nodded. Preacher's eyes scanned t
room a second time. His eyes landed on the pictures
her late husband, Marcus.

Playing with her fingers, Sabrina broke into a sm
laugh. "This is awkward. You would think we'd outgr
stuff like this."

Laughing, Preacher nodded again.

Sabrina gestured toward the kitchen. "We're havi
steak and lobster for dinner. It should be ready in a f
minutes."

"My favorites."

"I'm relieved to hear that. I wasn't sure what y
liked but I remember you talking about steak and lo
ster when we had lunch together."

She checked her watch and stood up. "I'll set ever
thing out on the table."

"Would you like some help?"

"No, I have it. Just make yourself comfortable."

"Sabrina . . ."

She turned. "Yes?"

"You look real nice."

"Thank you. You look nice yourself. I have to adn
I would not have ever pictured you in a suit. Don't g
me wrong, you look wonderful. I just figured you f
a military uniform or something like that."

"My military days are long over."

"I'll be right back."

Sabrina had everything ready in a few minutes. She went back into the living room and took Preacher by the hand, leading him to the huge dining room table.

"You must host quite a few dinner parties," Preacher observed.

"Not too many. But you have to remember now. My sister is married to one of the Ransoms, and there are quite a few of them."

He broke into a grin. "Yeah, you're right about that. They seem like good people, too." He pulled out a chair for Sabrina.

"They are. I really like all of them."

"It's obvious that they've adopted you into the family. Not just your sister."

"It's true. I do feel like I'm part of their family."

Preacher volunteered to say a prayer of thanks. When it was over, Sabrina picked up her knife and fork. She was pleased when he dove right in to the salad. He seemed right at home.

She served the main course after they finished their salads.

"Dinner was great!" Preacher announced. "I can't remember when I've eaten this good. Mrs. Ransom is a good cook, but you worked a miracle with this lobster."

"I'm glad you enjoyed it because I have a confession to make. This is the first time I've ever made a lobster. Regis and Laine had to come help me. You should have seen us trying to put the thing in the pot."

"Was it still alive?"

"Yeah. Of course Regis's conscience got the better of her, and she wanted me to keep it. Like I'd want a lobster for a pet. Anyway, Laine put it in the pot for us."

"You didn't have the heart to do it."

"I didn't," she replied truthfully. "But I didn't want it as a pet either. I wanted to eat it."

For dessert, Sabrina served a chocolate cheesecake which she'd made from scratch. To her delight Preacher had a second slice. Afterward, he finally pushed away from the table. Sabrina had done some investigating of her own and found out that he loved cheesecake, especially chocolate cheesecake.

She couldn't talk Preacher out of helping her with the dishes. While washing dishes, they discussed the homeless project she was involved with.

"How did you get involved with the project? What it called again?"

"The First Step Program. I have a friend named Khalil Sanford. Well, his family founded this project about four years ago. They buy old vacant and run-down buildings, then they renovate them into apartments for the homeless. In each building there are three training rooms on the first floor, where they teach you skill that will enable you to go out into the workforce."

"So they give you a place to live and teach you skill? The first steps into getting your life back."

"Yes, that's it exactly. I volunteer there three times week. I teach a computer class and an English class.

"That's admirable of you."

"I really enjoy it. A lot of people turn their head when they see a person begging on the street, but even though they may not realize it, many of them are on one paycheck from being homeless themselves."

"I have to admit that I never thought about it th way."

"We usually don't." Sabrina's eyes met his. "No on really knows this, but Regis and I were homeless once Our father died, leaving my mother with a lot of hospital bills. She had always been a stay-at-home mom and really had no skills. Mom tried to find a job, but it was hard for her. She was sick herself. Anyway, w ended up losing our home, and Mom couldn't keep a job."

"Did you have any family to help you?"

"We had family. You remember my cousin Marc? You met him the day you all brought Kaitlin home."

Preacher nodded. "His wife is the scientist?"

"Yes. They own Chandler Pharmaceuticals. But my mother was too proud to ask for help."

"What happened?"

"I called my aunt Lillian. She's Marc's mother. Anyway, she flew to Florida and got us. Aunt Lillian took care of Mom and sent us to school. Mom died about six months later.

"I miss my parents a lot. For a long time I was angry with them for dying, but my aunt and uncle loved us. They treated us like we were theirs. Regis and I wanted for nothing. In fact, they paid for the wedding when Marcus and I got married. When they died, it broke my heart all over again. So much death . . ." Sabrina grew quiet.

Gently, Preacher grasped her hand, his fingers fondling its smoothness.

Sabrina felt the heat from their closeness. Her attraction to him was much more than that. She felt a kinship with him. Boldly, she wrapped her arms around his neck.

Preacher lowered his head and kissed her, opening her mouth with his.

Sabrina gave in to the unleashed desires of his mouth against hers. They clung to each other in a fervent embrace.

"It's getting late," he whispered to her, moving his lips against hers. "I think I should go."

"You don't have to leave. I mean, I don't have to be anywhere until tomorrow evening. There's no need to rush off."

"Are you sure?"

Sabrina nodded. "I really enjoy your company."

"Same here."

Her eyes glued to his, Sabrina met Preacher's lip
with her own. Shivers of desire raced through her an
sent the pit of her stomach into a wild swirl. His lip
left hers to nibble at her earlobe.

Sabrina was wild with wanting him, but she was n
going to give in to her passion. It was against the grai
of her beliefs.

They parted slowly. "I really should go," Preache
announced.

"You're not driving back to Riverside tonight, ar
you?" She could have kicked herself for saying tha
Sabrina didn't want Preacher to get the impression tha
she was inviting him to stay with her.

He didn't appear to have taken it that way. "No, I'r
staying at Matt's."

Relieved, Sabrina walked him to the door. Sex wa
something she was ready for, but not on the first date

"Dinner was wonderful, and the company was eve
better. I really enjoyed myself, Sabrina."

"We're going to have to do it again."

Preacher agreed. "Soon."

After locking up, Sabrina retired to her bedroon
Humming to herself as she changed into her nightgowr
Sabrina was ecstatic.

It felt good being held again. Although she'd denie
it repeatedly, Sabrina was lonely. She loved being mai
ried and hoped to remarry one day. Preacher gave he
renewed hope for the future.

Matt found Sasha in her office working on the montl
end reports. "Hey, you're back. How was your vaca
tion?"

She glanced up from the computer monitor. "Hey, Matt. I had a good time. Went down to Baton Rouge."

"Went to see the family?"

She nodded. "It was good to go back and visit, but I have to confess, I'm glad to be home. Family can get on your nerves after a while. How were things here?"

"Fine."

"Are you going to be around for a while? I'm tired of you abandoning me like you did."

Matt chuckled. "It's a show of how much I trust you and how efficient you are. I know I can leave everything in your very capable hands."

Leaning back with her hands folded across her chest, Sasha grinned. "I'll remember that when it comes time for a raise. Better yet, I'm thinking bonus."

"You've earned it. Tell you what, we'll sit down next week and talk about it."

"Great." Sasha turned off her computer. "Now are you going to tell me what in the world was going on before I left for vacation? You took off like a crazy person."

"I found Kaitlin."

"You what?" Her face was frozen with shock.

"Kaitlin's been in Mexico all this time."

"Really?"

Matt gave Sasha a quick rundown of what had transpired over the past two and a half years.

When he was done, all she could utter was, "Wow."

"That's how I felt when I first found out."

Pushing away from the desk, Sasha moved to where he was standing. She gave him a sisterly hug. "I'm so happy for you, Matt. This is incredible news."

Something in Matt's expression caused her to retreat and ask, "Is there something more you're not telling me?"

"Kaitlin got married while she was away." Just sayir the words bothered Matt.

"Noooo." Sasha rolled her eyeballs in irritation.

"She married the man that killed Ted and his family Sasha was floored. "How do you feel about that?"

"I don't know that I can get over this rage that I fee While she was gone, I thought my life was over, Sash Even when I moved back here, I really thought that would have to pretend I was among the living. I ju couldn't get over her."

"You were in so much pain. It broke my heart ju seeing you that way. It really did."

"Then Ray comes to me and tells me that Kaitlin's st alive. All I could think was *thank God it's over.* I was : grateful to have another chance for a life with Kaitlin.

Hugging him again, Sasha said, "And you still ha that chance. Matt, don't let that monster take anoth person from you. Don't let him have that kind of pow over you from the grave. You and Kaitlin can still ha that life together that you both want so much."

"I do want that. But I have to be honest. I just dor know if I'll ever get past the fact that she shared a be with Hector Rosales."

"I don't know why Kaitlin married him, Matt. But do know this: She loves you, and you love her. Tha got to mean something."

"It does. Kaitlin and I are trying to work throug this, but it's not easy."

"Take it one day at a time."

"You have been such a good friend to me, Sasha."

"As you have to me. You saved my life."

"My brother—"

Placing a finger to his lips, she whispered, "Let's n speak of Martin. He was a very sick man. We'll lea it at that."

"He almost killed you."

"But he didn't. By the grace of the good Lord, he didn't."

"On a brighter note, Kaitlin's coming here tonight for dinner."

"Well, I'm going to have the chef fix you both something special."

"You are a sweetheart, Sasha. And you take good care of me."

"Well, now you have Kaitlin, so you don't need me anymore."

"It's time for you to find yourself a good man to pamper you. You deserve it, Sasha."

She waved her hand in dismissal. "I don't know about that . . ."

"Practice what you preach, Sasha. Don't give Martin this much power over you. It's time to let someone into that great big heart of yours, sweetheart."

"Maybe. . . ." Giving him a push, Sasha said, "Let me get back to work, and don't worry about this evening. I'll have everything ready."

Throughout the day, Matt's thoughts centered on Kaitlin. Just seeing her smile. She gave his life new meaning each day. He was looking forward to their date tonight.

Kaitlin arrived that evening wearing a beautiful dress in royal blue and sporting a new haircut.

Matt greeted her with a kiss.

Doing a slow spin, she asked, "You like?"

"You look beautiful, baby."

"How are A.C. and the others?" she asked as soon as they were seated in the private dining room.

"Gennai and A.C. have been doing some sight-seeing." Matt laughed. "At least that's what they're calling it. As for Preacher, I haven't seen him much. I wonder what's going on with him."

Kaitlin laughed. "From what I understand, he's been spending lots of time with Sabrina."

"Really? I knew he was interested in her but I didn't know they had actually started seeing each other."

She nodded. "I think they make a cute couple."

Matt agreed. "He needs to settle down."

"I don't know anyone more settled than Sabrina. Preacher may actually find that kind of lifestyle boring."

"I don't think so. I think it's what he's been looking for. He was married before, but his wife couldn't handle his being gone all of the time. One day he came home and found an empty house. She didn't even leave a note behind."

"How heartbreaking that must have been."

"It sure devastated him."

"Well, he won't have to worry about Sabrina doing that to him. She'd at least leave a note."

Both Kaitlin and Matt burst into laughter.

A waiter arrived with a cart of assorted appetizers.

Kaitlin glanced over at Matt. "You went all out, didn't you?"

"I can't take the credit for any of this. Sasha arranged everything. Including the champagne."

Matt couldn't take his eyes off her. Kaitlin looked exactly the way he'd remembered her. He liked her better with short hair, he decided.

Kaitlin picked up a shrimp and stuck it into her mouth. Catching him watching her, she gave a tiny smile and continued to chew. Matt had never seen a woman sexier than she was, while eating, he decided as he stared into the eyes he loved so fiercely.

Seeing her like this fired his blood, and Matt was filled with longing. Since he had been given a second chance with her, Matt wanted this time to be perfect. He was eternally grateful to God for this blessing.

He glanced over once again at the woman who owned his heart, and smiled. Yes, he had been truly blessed.

Matt couldn't seem to stop staring at her, and Kaitlin had to admit she loved the attention. Being with him like this caused memories to flood her mind; memories that were trapped in another time. A time when her life wasn't filled with shadows. A time when they were free to live and love without bodyguards and guns.

Matt touched her cheek. "What are you thinking so hard about?" he asked.

Kaitlin raised her eyes to Matt. "About us."

Matt bit into the last shrimp as their entrees arrived. As soon as the waiter left, he asked, "What about us?"

"I was just remembering the old days. It's funny what we tend to take for granted—like feeling safe."

Matt reached for her hand. "Listen to me, Kaitlin. I'm not going to let anything happen to you."

"I believe you. I really do, but I'm still scared. I'm just real jumpy these days. Maybe it's going to take some time to adjust."

"Maybe . . ." Matt agreed.

Kaitlin's hands shook so much she had to hide them in her lap. Her nerves were so bad these days.

He gestured toward her plate. "Aren't you going to eat?"

"I am." She reached a trembling hand toward her water glass, but thought better of it. Kaitlin picked up her fork and began to eat.

When Matt and Kaitlin had finished their meals, they found they still had room for dessert. Sasha surprised them with a six-layer lemon cake.

After dessert, Matt took Kaitlin dancing at a nearby club called The Wanderer. Inside they ran into Kaitlin's brother Nyle and his girlfriend, Chandra Davis.

Nyle greeted them. "What are y'all doing here?"

Kaitlin and Chandra embraced. To her brother, she replied, "Same as you. Matt and I came to do some dancing."

Nyle laughed. "Like you know how. Matt, I hope you keep your feet out of the way. My sister can't dance a lick."

"Real funny. Boy, I taught you how to dance."

They continued their light bantering as they walked over to the table where Nyle and Chandra had been sitting. Nyle found two more chairs for her and Matt.

When a song by Dru Hill came on, Chandra jumped up, grabbing Nyle by the hand and leading him to the dance floor.

Kaitlin watched the couple on the floor. "Mama says that Nyle's been seeing a lot of Chandra. She says they've been together about a year and a half."

"I know it's been a good little while."

Kaitlin gave Matt a knowing smile. "He's in love. Pretty soon we're going to have another wedding in the family."

The thought of another wedding thrilled her on one hand, but depressed her on the other. It was her dream that one day she and Matt would marry. But he had yet to say anything about marriage, and she was a little uneasy about bringing up the subject herself. She couldn't help wondering if Matt was still bothered by the fact that she was Hector's widow.

"What's wrong, baby?"

"Nothing," Kaitlin lied.

Standing, Matt walked around the table and pulled Kaitlin out of her seat, enveloping her in his arms. "Don't go getting quiet on me. Let's dance."

After dancing, Matt drove her over to Jillian's. Kaitlin tried to hide her disappointment. She'd hoped to spend the night with him. *Maybe he's just trying to take things slow,* she reassured herself.

"I'll stop by here in the morning before you leave," he was saying.

Kaitlin needed to know why he hadn't tried to make love to her since their return. "Matt . . ."

"Yes?"

She chickened out. "I'll see you tomorrow. Drive carefully."

"Go on inside. I want to make sure you're safe."

Kaitlin did as she was told. From the huge picture window in Jillian's living room, she watched Matt drive off. "What's really going on?" she whispered.

The following Saturday, Matt left the restaurant around noon and drove out to Riverside.

Amanda greeted him at the door. "Hey, honey. Kaitlin's upstairs. She should be down shortly."

Amanda had been gone no more than a few minutes when Preacher entered the den through the patio doors. His eyes bounced around the room. "Where's Kaitlin?"

"She hasn't come down yet. Why?"

"I tried to reach you all last night. Did you get my message?"

"Kaitlin and I went to dinner, and afterward, we went dancing. You're the one who's been MIA. I had to hear it through Kaitlin that you're spending a lot of time wi—"

"I found out something," Preacher interjected quickly. "Elian's in California. Word on the street is that he's somewhere in Los Angeles. Could be he's looking for you."

"Do me a favor. Don't say a word to Kaitlin. I don't want to scare her."

"Don't worry, Matt. I've talked to A.C. and Gennai.

We're going to hang around long enough to take care of Elian—once and for all."

"I appreciate what you're doing. But I have to tell you, Preacher. This is not going to end until somebody ends up dying. I don't want it to be Kaitlin, or any of us for that matter, but I've got a bad feeling about this one."

They talked for a few minutes more. Preacher exited through the sliding glass doors and went back onto the patio, leaving Matt to ponder his predicament. How was he going to get Kaitlin to leave town without scaring her half to death?

Kaitlin strode into the den. "I thought I heard Preacher's voice in here."

"He was here, but he had to leave," Matt replied.

"Don't tell me I'm still running everybody away." She picked up the remote and surfed through television channels.

Matt laughed and shook his head. "I guess he had somewhere to go. Maybe he and Sabrina have a date or something."

"Oh." Kaitlin returned her attention to the television.

"Baby, I've got an idea. Why don't we take off and go to Catalina Island or Big Bear?"

Kaitlin glanced over at Matt. She searched his face but could detect nothing out of the ordinary, yet her instincts told her there was more to his sudden need to go away. "When?"

"How about right now?"

Kaitlin was suspicious. "Why so soon?" She didn't get the feeling that this was some sort of romantic getaway. Could this have something to do with Elian? Kaitlin swallowed her fear and refused to panic.

Matt moved closer to her. Lowering his voice to

whisper, he said, "I would like to be alone with you, that's why."

His voice caressed her, warming her all over, but Kaitlin was not quite convinced. "I see. Are you sure here's no other reason you want to get me out of town?"

Giving her an innocent smile, Matt implored, "You trust me, don't you?"

She nodded with a laugh. "I do. So, are we telling my family anything? I really don't think I should do another disappearing act."

"No, don't do that. Just tell them that we want to get to know each other all over again. In private."

"I'm not so sure my mama's going to be okay with this."

"I'm not asking your mama," he pointed out. "Honey, I want you all to myself. At least for a few days or so."

Kaitlin carefully considered his suggestion before responding. "I don't know, Matt. Mama's been feeling bad lately. Let me see how she's doing over the next couple of days and then I'll let you know. Okay?"

He nodded. "That's fine."

Kaitlin stole a peek at him. Matt kept his face void of expression but she still couldn't shake the underlying feeling that something was amiss.

Watching television, she nervously chewed on the nails of her left hand.

Matt pulled her hand away. "Stop that."

Kaitlin turned off the TV. Turning in her seat, Kaitlin asked, "If there was something wrong, you'd tell me, wouldn't you?"

"Honey, everything is fine. And I'm going to do everything I can to keep it that way."

Trusting him, Kaitlin let the matter drop. She wanted desperately to believe that everything was fine, and that there was absolutely nothing to fear. It was either that or suffer a nervous breakdown.

ELEVEN

Elian parked his rental car in a space across from La Maison. He had not been there long before he caught a glimpse of Matthew St. Charles, aka Jaguar. He had arrived at the restaurant just as Jaguar was leaving.

He smiled. Very soon he would have his revenge. Whistling, Elian climbed out of his car, and put on a pair of sunglasses. He carefully surveyed the buildings in the area.

Elian walked along the sidewalk, trying to blend in with the other pedestrians. Looking up and down the street, he took in every inch of his surroundings. This time he could not afford to fail, because there would not be a second chance. Mistakes were costly, and Elian wasn't ready to die.

Tuesday night, Preacher followed Sabrina into the computer room at Phase I Apartments. They were met by Khalil Sanford. She and Khalil embraced. When Sabrina made the introductions, he offered his hand to Preacher. "It's nice to meet you, Thaddeus."

"Just call me Preacher."

"All right. Preacher, it is."

Khalil gave Preacher a tour of the apartment building while Sabrina taught her class.

"Where does the money come from for the program?" Preacher wanted to know.

"We receive grants from the government in addition to donations from NBA wives, celebrities, and private citizens."

"I'm impressed by all you've done. If there is anything I can do to help, just let me know." Preacher pulled out his wallet. "In fact, I'm gonna put my money where my mouth is." He wrote a check and handed it to Khalil.

"Wow," was all he said.

Preacher chuckled. "It's good. I've made some wise investments. God's been good to me."

"Thanks, man We really appreciate this." Khahil spent the next hour talking to Preacher about the plight of the homeless.

Sabrina's class let out a little early, so they stopped off at a restaurant for dinner. It was Preacher's intent to just drop her off at home, but Sabrina invited him in.

It was getting increasingly hard for him to just stop at kissing her. It had been a while since Preacher had been with a woman. Just thinking about Sabrina could cause his body to respond.

Tonight Sabrina had surprised him by saying, "You don't have to leave." The only evidence that she was nervous was the spinning of a white-gold bangle. "You're welcome to stay here for the night."

Sabrina seemed perfectly serious, so now he was sitting on her bed and waiting for her to come out of the bathroom.

Sabrina walked into the bedroom slowly. She was dressed in a modest nightgown that reached to her ankles. She eased into bed and pulled the covers up to her waist.

A smile tugged at her lips when her gaze met his. Her shyness made him even more attracted to her. "Sabrina,

I'm crazy 'bout you. Real crazy, but I don't want to force you into something you're not ready to do. Making love is special. I think you're special too. I don't want to mess this up."

Sabrina looked a little stunned. "You don't want to make love?"

"No, I'm not saying that. I'd be lying if I did. I want you something bad . . ." Preacher cleared his throat noisily. "I want you bad."

"Well, what are you going to do about it?"

Preacher kissed her gently. "Nothing. We're going to sleep." He reached over and turned off the light.

Sabrina's eyes opened wide in her surprise. Stunned into silence, she lay flat on her back and stared into the darkness.

Preacher had rejected her. Well, it wasn't quite a rejection, she amended.

She had never met a man quite like him. Preacher was an original. He'd all but said that he wanted to wait until marriage. Sabrina respected his beliefs, but it had been a long time for her. According to Preacher, it had been a while for him as well.

Crossing her legs, Sabrina tried to smother her hunger for sex. But it was to no avail. Her body was wound so tight that she feared she would suddenly go into a spin. She needed release. And she needed it tonight.

Sabrina stole a peek at the man lying beside her. Preacher was hugging the edge of the king-sized bed. It was apparent that nothing was going to go on tonight, so she settled in and closed her eyes. Sleep would not come for the next hour.

She could tell that Preacher wasn't sleeping either. Her body starving for sexual gratification, Sabrina decided it was now or never. Summoning up her courage, she tossed the covers back and turned on the light.

Surprised, Preacher tried to sit up. Sabrina gently pushed him back down and straddled him. Pulling her gown over her head, Sabrina tossed it over to the floor. Grinning at Preacher's sharp intake of breath, she stated brazenly, "Consider yourself under attack."

After protecting themselves with a condom, they made love in a frenzy, both needing release from long pent-up tension. The second time was calmer, and they took their time, enjoying each other and their pleasure.

Sated, Sabrina fell asleep in Preacher's arms. But a couple of hours later, she awoke with a start. Wet with perspiration, she sat up.

Preacher mumbled something in his sleep, then turned on his side.

Sabrina put shaky hands to her face. The familiar smell of death invaded her nostrils, threatening to make her gag.

Easing out of bed so as not to disturb Preacher, Sabrina rushed to the bathroom. She felt sick.

Hanging her head over the toilet, Sabrina emptied the contents of her stomach. When she felt stronger and calmer, she rose to a stand. She brushed her teeth and took a shower.

Preacher was still sleeping when she crawled back into bed. Or so she thought.

His bass voice penetrating the dark, he asked, "You okay?"

"I'm fine. I think I ate something that didn't agree with me."

She put her head back on a pillow and closed her eyes. She was beginning to get a headache because she was concentrating so hard. Someone was in danger, but she had no idea who. How could she help anyone?

"Help me, Lord. I really need your help. . . ."

* * *

The following Saturday, Matt and Kaitlin attended a wedding. She handed Matt another roll of film. "She's a beautiful bride. And I love that gown she's wearing."

"She does look nice," he agreed. Matt loaded the film into the camera. "They are good kids."

"How long have you known her family?"

"She's Bob's second cousin."

Kaitlin took a seat while Matt resumed his work. He still owned a photography studio and had employed a full-time photographer, but he was doing this himself as a favor to Bob.

Matt was very good at what he did, and Kaitlin loved watching him work. He studied his subjects carefully before taking the pictures. The bride was extremely shy, so Matt gently instructed her, using humor to help her relax.

The photo session was nearing the end, and the newlyweds would soon be en route to the reception. Kaitlin gathered all of Matt's equipment while he took the last of the pictures.

They managed to leave before the bridal party and headed to the hotel where the reception was held. Matt wanted to be there to take pictures of the couple as they exited the limousine.

In the car, Kaitlin said, "I need to know something, Matt. Why haven't we made love? You haven't touched me since we came back to California."

"I know, but it's only because I wanted to give you time to settle. You've been through a lot and I'm trying to be sensitive to that fact."

"I thought maybe it was because I was married to Hector. Honey, he never touched me. It's still hard for me to think of that marriage as being real. Hector couldn't . . . he was impotent."

Matt glanced over at her. "You and Hector never once made love?"

Kaitlin shook her head no. "Do you still want n
Matt?"

"I do. Baby, I want you so much . . ."

He pulled up in front of the hotel. "After we get do
here, we'll finish this up at my house, okay?"

"You're meeting Laine afterward, remember?"

"That's right. Think it's too late to cancel?"

"I do." Kaitlin smiled. "After that we'll have the re
of the evening."

Bob was in the lobby when they stepped inside.

"Here you guys are."

"I was still taking pictures," Matt announced. "Mi
Helen wanted lots of pictures of Cindy and Emmanuel

Shaking his head, Bob said, "You'd think this w
Helen's day from the way she's running things. M
cousin needs to sit down and leave those two kids alor
They only wanted a small ceremony, and Helen veto
that. Most of the people here are her friends."

Matt and Kaitlin both burst into laughter.

"I used to see that all the time. Mothers want the
daughters to have the weddings they have alwa
dreamed about. In a way, it's a cycle." Kaitlin ran
hand through her short curls.

"Do you miss the bridal stores?"

Kaitlin bent and slapped dust from her shoes, the
gave her dress a little flounce. "I do. I called Sar
daughter, Barbara, a couple of days ago and asked abc
my old job. She said that sales have really been dov
since her mother's death. The stores are barely stayin
afloat. She's had to close three of them already. Ba
bara's even thinking about selling the other stores."

"That's too bad."

"I've got an interview set up on Wednesday wi
David's Bridal. We'll see what happens."

Matt turned to her. "Honey, you don't have to wor

about rushing out to find a job. I'll give you whatever you need."

Slipping her arm through his, Kaitlin replied, "I know you will, but I prefer to have my own. My dad used to always say: God bless the child who has got his own."

"I understand, but just remember that the offer holds."

"You're such a sweetheart."

Bob escorted Kaitlin inside and to their table. Matt joined them fifteen minutes later.

After all the photographs had been taken, Matt and Kaitlin said their good-byes to Bob and the newlyweds. They left the reception and drove back to Matt's studio.

Laine and Regis arrived shortly after them. Matt had agreed to take family photographs. Kaitlin watched in the background while Matt worked. Jonathan was in a cooperative mood, so the time passed quickly. They were done in a matter of minutes.

"Do you want us to pay you now?" Laine asked.

Matt shook his head. "Just wait until the pictures are ready."

Kaitlin reached for Jonathan. "Come here, sweetie."

He practically jumped into her arms. The first thing he went her for was her earrings.

"Oh, no, you don't. You're going to make Auntie Kaitlin pop your little hands."

Jonathan looked her straight in the face and burst into laughter.

Kaitlin's mouth dropped open. Glancing over at Regis, she asked, "Did you all see that? Your son is laughing at me."

"He gets that from your brother," Regis replied. "Laine does that to me all the time."

"Just give him a spanking," Kaitlin advised. "Then send him upstairs for a nap."

Matt and Laine cracked up.

Before Laine left, he said, "Mama called and wanted to know if you'd be staying with us or with Ray."

Matt chuckled. "Mrs. Ransom's not very subtle, is she?"

"No, she's not," Kaitlin agreed. "Tell Mama that I'm planning to stay with Matt tonight. Better yet . . ." Kaitlin strode over to the phone on the counter. "I'll call her myself."

After Laine and his family left, she asked, "Can we pick up where we left off?"

Matt's eyes filled with amusement.

"Come on and let's go. I'm ready to get out of here."

"I've never known you to be so aggressive," Matt interjected. "I like this side of you."

"You know that's not quite how I meant that statement."

"You don't have to be shy around me, baby." Matt continued to tease her.

He embraced her. "Baby, it took me a while to realize this is what I wanted." Bending his head, Matt covered her mouth with his. "I love you so much. I just want everything to be perfect."

"It feels perfect," she murmured against his chest. "I don't think we're going to have any more problems from now on. Feeling more secure than ever, Kaitlin released a soft sigh of relief.

The week passed quickly. On Friday evening, Kaitlin had driven into Los Angeles. She was spending the weekend at Ray's. He and Carrie had gone down to San Diego for a conference.

Kaitlin and Matt were taking Mikey and Bridget to see *Mickey's Birthday Party*. Matt still enjoyed cartoons himself, and so did Kaitlin. In fact, he suspected Kaitlin was using the kids as an excuse to see the movie.

At approximately one o'clock, they were all strapped inside his car and on their way to the theater.

"Auntie Kaitlin, I got a happy face on the story I did about you. My teacher said she thinks I'm gonna be a writer one day."

She turned around to face him. "That's wonderful, sweetie. I'm going to have to do something special for you. Especially since you're making me so famous."

"It's because you're special."

"You are such a precious little boy, Mikey. I just love you to death."

"Wuv me too?" Bridget asked shyly. "I good girl. I go potty by myself."

Kaitlin and Matt exchanged smiles.

Giving Bridget a playful pinch, she replied, "Of course I love you, too. I love you both to pieces."

"You're going to be a wonderful mother, Kaitlin. You're good with children."

A wave of guilt flooded through her body. How could she not tell Matt? Kaitlin was afraid. Afraid that he would not forgive her. But could they have the same foundation they both wanted when she hadn't told Matt everything? He deserved to know the truth.

Elian parked in the parking lot across from La Maison. Dressed as a janitor, he strode past security. He took the elevator to the tenth floor and got out. Elian took the stairs the rest of the way to the roof. The previous night he'd already brought up a high-powered rifle. Out of view of any security cameras, Elian rid himself of the clothing and prepared to take his revenge.

Setting her shopping bags next to her chair, Sabrina put away her change from her mocha latte purchase.

"I'm so glad we did this, Kaitlin. I really had a goo[ ]time. Regis hates to go shopping with me."

"No problem. I needed to pick up a few things an[y]way." Laughing, she pointed to Sabrina's five larg[ ]shopping bags. "You really had a good time. Your cred[ ]card is probably crying by now."

"It's not too bad. I usually do this only once a year[.]

Kaitlin looked down at her one shopping bag. "I ten[ ]to just get one or two items only when I absolutel[ ]have to have them."

"That's how Regis is—" Sabrina screwed up her fac[e]All around her was a red haze, and the smell of deat[ ]was in the air. "Oh, Lord, *noo*," she moaned. In h[er]mind, she had a clear view of Gennai. He was covere[ ]in blood. She caught glimpses of Matt and Preacher b[ut]the visions were not as vivid as the ones of Genna[i]Sabrina concentrated harder. That's when she saw th[ ]blood. It was everywhere. Feeling sick, she placed [ ]hand over her mouth.

Kaitlin set her glass back on the table. "Sabrina, something wrong?"

She could only moan in response.

"What is it?"

"We've got to warn them." Sabrina turned on her ce[l]lular phone and started punching numbers.

"Sabrina, what's going on? Please tell me."

She saw the frightened look on Kaitlin's face. "It[']Gennai and the others. They could be in danger."

Kaitlin grabbed her keys and her purse. "Come o[n]We've got to find them."

"Preacher's not answering his phone." She mutter[ed]a curse under her breath. "What is Matt's cell phon[e]number?"

Kaitlin quickly rattled it off to her. She stood. "The[y]are having dinner over at La Maison. We've got to g[o]over there."

Sabrina rose. "Why in the world do they have these things if they don't ever answer them?"

Kaitlin reached her car first. "I'll drive. You keep trying to reach them."

TWELVE

Gennai and Preacher sat in the private dining room of La Maison, playing dominoes. A.C. joined them half an hour later, wearing a sexy black dress with spaghetti straps.

Gennai recovered from his shock enough to whistle.

Her hair was curled, and she even wore a hint of makeup. Matt could not get over the change in her. A.C. was gorgeous. He couldn't ever recall seeing her in a dress before.

Even Preacher was impressed. "Girl, you clean up real nice. You should dress up more often."

Self-consciously, A.C. pulled down her dress. "You think it looks okay? Kaitlin picked it out for me."

Gennai rushed to his feet and pulled out a chair for her. "You look beautiful, A.C."

"Thank you," she murmured softly as she eased down onto the seat. Catching Matt's look of amusement, she warned, "Don't you dare say a word."

Matt grinned. "I was just going to give you a compliment. You do look good."

"Thank you," she replied.

Matt wasn't about to let her off that easy. "Wish I had my camera with me. I'd love to have a picture of this rare moment."

A.C. rolled her eyes at Matt. "You just couldn't leave it alone, could you?"

After the third game ended, Preacher asked, "Do they still have that little jazz club on Wilshire Boulevard?" When Matt nodded, he suggested, "Why don't we go there? It'll be like old times."

"Okay with me." Matt looked over at A.C. and Gennai. "What do you guys want to do?"

"The jazz club is fine with us," they both said in unison.

As they were walking out, Sasha waved to them and called out for Matt. He stopped and turned around to see what she needed. The others waited by the front door for him.

Matt joined them a few minutes later. "Sorry about that. Had to take care of something real quick. I'm ready." He led the way to his car. "I'll drive."

Matt turned around to say something to Gennai. "I thought—"

He never finished the sentence because he was quickly shoved to the ground by the small man. Matt caught sight of a tiny red dot. . . . He heard sounds, muted and sharp at the same time.

His astonishment turned to horror when the right side of Gennai's head exploded. The man crumpled to the ground, moving slightly when another set of bullets ripped through his back. Matt rolled behind a cluster of bushes, knocking down A.C. in the process.

"What the—" she yelled.

"Sniper," Matt managed to get out.

A.C. yanked a gun from her purse. Tossing it to Matt, she retrieved a second gun that had been strapped to her thigh.

Preacher had dropped behind a car and had his gun drawn. He made eye contact with A.C. and pointed toward the roof of a nearby building.

A.C. followed his gaze. "The sniper's somewhere on the roof of that building. I'd bet it's Elian." She looked around. "Where's Gennai?"

"He shoved me out of the way—" Matt pointed to her right. "He's over there."

A couple was about to walk out of the restaurant, but A.C. shouted for them to stay inside.

The woman screamed.

Matt tried to put his confused emotions in order. Someone was shooting at them. Pulling out his cell phone, he discovered the battery was dead. He muttered a string of curses.

Sasha appeared at the door. "Matt, I've called the police."

He could hear the fear in her voice. "Keep everybody inside," he yelled. "And tell them to stay down." He silently applauded her for having the forethought to lock the doors.

A.C. kept peeking over to where Gennai lay. "What is he doing? Playing dead?"

Matt stared at her, baffled.

Preacher was inching toward the street. He was going to try to cross to the other side.

"Gennai," A.C. called out. "Get your butt over here." A faint thread of hysteria was in her voice.

Matt realized that in the sudden scramble to protect themselves, A.C. didn't know Gennai had been shot. He searched for the right words. "Gennai saved my life, A.C."

She was looking at him now, momentarily disconcerted. "Matt?"

Another shot shattered the glass of the car, giving him a short reprieve.

"Are you telling me he was shot?" she asked.

His words hadn't registered in the midst of all the confusion, Matt reasoned. "Yes, Gennai was shot."

"And you just left him out there?"

Matt was unwilling to face A.C. and unable to turn away. She had to know the truth. Gennai had already departed this world.

A.C. moved to stand, but Matt pulled her back down. "It's not safe. The shooter is still out there."

"I don't care. I've got to help Gennai."

"Do you think I would have left him out there in the open just like that if he were alive?"

She sat there, her face void of expression. "What are you saying, Matt?"

"Honey, he's dead."

Before Matt knew what was happening, A.C. slapped him. Dropping her gun, she scrambled to her feet, only to be yanked down again by Matt. Still crouched low to the ground, Preacher made his way to where they were hiding. Thankfully, there had been no more shots. Sirens screamed in the distance, so maybe the sniper had fled.

Matt tried to hold A.C. He sought to stop her from running over to Gennai. She hit, punched, pounded, and pummeled hard enough to make him want to release her, but Matt held on.

Finally she broke his grip and pushed past him and Preacher. A.C. knelt down beside Gennai and pulled him into her arms. She kissed his lips.

Matt took a moment to catch his breath. He ventured out cautiously. Half of Gennai's skull had been shattered. There was blood everywhere. So much blood, and more coming.

Preacher followed him, his eyes scanning the area and searching. He critically covered every inch of the immediate area, while Matt did the same.

It wasn't long before they were converged on by the Los Angeles Police Department. Police cars were everywhere. Matt glimpsed several men across the street on the roof. They were searching for the sniper. Even in the distance he could tell they were not wearing LAPD uniforms. He fleetingly wondered who they were.

Sasha was standing beside him now. Following his line of vision, she said, "I called Sam. He's head of security in the building across the street. I told him that there was a man on the roof shooting," she explained. "That's his security team you see up there now."

Spectators were coming from all directions. Matt scrutinized the crowd. He was looking for one man in particular: Elian Cortez. He was also cognizant of the fact that the sniper could be someone hired to do the hit.

Matt brought his attention to Gennai. The paramedics had arrived and were tending to him. He didn't have to be told that his friend was dead. Matt could feel it in his heart. He was so filled with anger and sorrow that he was numb.

He searched for A.C. She was being questioned by a detective. Hearing his name being called, Matt turned around. Kaitlin was there. She and Sabrina were running toward them.

Kaitlin ran straight into his arms, saying, "Oh Lord, are you okay?"

"Where is Preacher? Is everybody okay?" Sabrina asked.

"He's across the street. They're checking out the building."

Kaitlin's eyes strayed to where the paramedics stood. A moan escaped her, and she swayed. Matt tightened his hold on her.

"Gennai . . ." She looked up at him. "He's going to be okay, right?"

Matt shut his eyes to hide his grief. "Honey, he's gone."

Sabrina gasped. "Oh, nooo. No! I didn't want this to happen. I tried to call . . ." She put her hand to her mouth, stifling her sob.

Kaitlin looked around. "Where is A.C.?"

Matt pointed a few feet away. "She's talking to th
detectives."

"How is she doing? She and Gennai had made s
many plans."

Shrugging, Matt responded, "On the outside sh
seems okay, but I'm worried about her. I'm afraid she
going to go after Elian."

"Do you think she'll try to kill him?"

"She won't try, Kaitlin. A.C. *will* kill Elian withou
blinking an eye."

Hours later, Matt drove Kaitlin and A.C. to Riversid
He took extra precautions to make sure they weren
being followed. Preacher had gone with Sabrina.

Matt intended to stay at Amanda's. He wanted t
make sure Kaitlin and her mother were safe.

A.C. sat stoically in a chair in the corner of Amanda
living room. Her head was tilted back, eyes blinkin
rapidly to fight the tears. Matt knew that for now, th
was the extent of her visible grief.

Kaitlin's heart ached over the news of Gennai's deat
Not only because he was Matt's friend, but because h
had become a part of her life as well. Her tears ove
flowed and rolled freely down her face. She wiped a
them with the back of her hand.

Matt was a few feet away talking to some very offici
looking men in dark suits. They had just appeared on h
mother's porch that morning. From Matt's reaction t
them, she could only assume that these were the me
he once worked for.

Giving them some privacy, Kaitlin decided to check c
A.C. She looked in the kitchen and out on the patio f

her. Worried, Kaitlin ran up the stairs. Easing open the door, she found A.C. alone in her bedroom. She was standing with her back to Kaitlin, just staring out of the window. Every now and then she would raise her hands to her face. Not daring to intrude on A.C.'s mourning, Kaitlin closed the door and went to her own room.

She was joined by Matt half an hour later.

"Your friends are gone?" she asked.

"They are not my friends. They are still here. Right now they're talking to A.C. Then they plan to leave."

"You used to work for them, didn't you? They are Night Rangers or something, right?"

He nodded, giving her a clearer view of his face. Matt's eyes were wet with unshed tears. Kaitlin wrapped an arm around him. "How are *you* doing?" she asked. "You've been trying to take care of everybody else."

"I don't know. I honestly don't know, Kaitlin. All I know is that I feel that same anger I felt when I thought I'd lost you. I'm tired of losing everyone I love."

She remained silent, not knowing what else to do or say.

Matt put both hands to his face.

Kaitlin held on to him while he cried over the tragic passing of a dear friend. Fighting tears, she closed her eyes, but her tears escaped anyway.

In the huge family room at Sabrina's house, she and Preacher sat side by side in silence. She could feel his pain burning her, but Sabrina continued to hold on to his hand. Preacher needed her strength.

Finally she spoke. "Gennai is at peace. I know how close you all were, and I know you miss him."

"He is in a much better place. He has earned his eternal rest," Preacher murmured in her hair. "The Bible says we're supposed to rejoice at a time like this, but

I have to tell you, I sure don't feel much like rejoicing. I still have a hard time believing last night really happened. We were on our way to a jazz club. Just like old times. . . ."

"Preacher, I saw it. At first, I didn't know who it was in my vision. I could see and smell the blood though. It was only last night that I was able to see Gennai's face. I saw only snatches of your face and Matt's." She sighed heavily. "If only I could have reached you. Maybe he would still be alive."

"Sugar, you can't blame yourself. My phone is usually on. I don't know why it was off last night. I must have turned it off at some point, but I don't remember."

"I do blame myself. Maybe I should have said something sooner."

"What good would it have done? You said yourself that you didn't know who it was. There was nothing you could have done. Gennai's journey had come to an end. But before he left, he gave Matt a tremendous gift."

"What?"

"His life. Matt was the intended victim."

Sabrina was stunned into silence.

THIRTEEN

On a rainy Tuesday afternoon right after Easter, a graveside ceremony was held for Gennai. Matt arranged for him to be buried beside Kyoko. Brother and sister were finally reunited.

Kaitlin held Matt's hand and rested her other on A.C.'s tensed shoulders. It was an uneasy situation for them all with so many agents present from all phases of law enforcement. The entire area was heavily guarded, calling back to mind her way of life in Mexico—only these were supposed to be the good guys.

After the funeral, everyone gathered at Matt's house. When they arrived, the bomb squad was leaving. After giving the house a thorough sweep, Matt was informed that it was safe to enter the premises.

La Maison had been closed since the incident. Matt decided to keep it closed because he feared Elian might decide to seek his revenge through his employees.

Sasha had the La Maison chef prepare the food. Kaitlin tried to get Matt to eat something.

He would only push the plate away. "I'm not hungry, sweetheart."

"Matt, you've got to eat something. You haven't eaten much since that night."

"Have you seen A.C.?" Matt asked her.

"I think she's in one of the bedrooms. She said sh|
wanted to lie down."

Kaitlin found she didn't have much of an appeti|
herself. She headed to the kitchen, carrying her pla|
of untouched food. She decided to just wrap it up ai|
take it home with her.

She and Matt searched for A.C. When they found he|
she had changed from the black pantsuit into a pair |
jeans and a T-shirt. Her hair was in a French braid ai|
all traces of makeup were gone. Her leather backpa|
was slung across one shoulder. A.C. looked like she w|
getting ready to leave town.

Matt blocked her exit. "Where are you going, A.C.?|

"I'm going to find Elian, and when I do, I'm goii|
to kill him. Gennai's death will not go unavenged."

"Sweetheart, you can't do that."

"Oh, yes, I can. I have a Smith & Wesson that sa|
I can do whatever I want."

"Why don't you stay here with me. You need to spei|
some time grieving."

"I can grieve later. I have the rest of my life to grie|
for Gennai. I spoke to Jensen and got myself assigne|
to the task force. If it's the last thing I do, I'm goii|
to get Elian Cortez."

"I'm not going to let you leave like this, A.C. You'|
in a lot of pain right now."

"Matt, I don't want to have to knock you out, but|
will. I'm leaving."

He held his ground. "You will have to go through me|

"Don't do this, Matt. We've been friends much t|
long."

"That's why I'm doing it. I can't let you go out li|
this. Gennai deserves better."

"Don't you dare say something like that to me|
A.C.'s eyes filled with tears. "I loved him, Matt. V|
never had a chance." Gesturing toward Kaitlin, she sa|

"If it weren't for me, you wouldn't have her. The way I see it, you owe me big time."

Kaitlin spoke up. "Honey, let her go."

Matt turned to her. "What? You're taking her side?" He shook his head regretfully.

Taking advantage of the tense situation between Kaitlin and Matt, A.C. brushed past them. "I'll be in touch," she called out.

Whirling around to confront Kaitlin, Matt demanded, "How could you do that?"

"You were not going to talk her out of anything," Kaitlin answered thickly. "A.C.'s got her mind made up. Couldn't you see that?"

Shoulders in a slump, Matt gave an audible sigh. "You're probably right. I just wish she would've stayed for a few more days. Maybe it would have cleared her mind some." Wrapping an arm around Kaitlin, he held on to her for strength.

She decided it was best to change the subject. Kaitlin decided to broach the subject of them going away. It had been on her mind since the night of the shooting. "You know, I've been thinking. Now would be a good time to get away. I think it's something we both need."

He gazed down at her with clear, observant eyes. "I know what you're doing. You're scared."

"I am. I'm sure the shooter had to be Elian or someone he hired. He's not just going to give up like that. Not until you're dead. I'm not going to wait around and let that happen."

Matt appeared to be thinking over her suggestion.

"Well, what do you think?" Kaitlin pushed.

"Let's do it. Let's go as far away as we can."

"As soon as we can," she threw in.

"All right. I'll make some calls. In the meantime, try to talk your mother into going somewhere, too."

"Okay." Kaitlin placed a hand on Matt's cheek. "I am so sorry about Gennai."

"He died a hero's death. Gennai pushed me out of the way and took the hit."

"Oh, Lord." Kaitlin put a hand to her chest. "I didn't know that. It could have been you." She started to tremble all over.

Matt pulled her closer. "But it wasn't, baby. It wasn't." They still had a chance for a future. He didn't want to miss a minute of it.

Kaitlin called Matt early the next morning, saying, "I talked Mama into going to Michigan. She's going to spend a couple of weeks with Preston. Then she's going to Baton Rouge to visit Aunt Clarice."

"Good. I'm glad she decided to take your advice."

"Me too. It's a load off of my mind."

"I've been on the phone most of the morning. Preacher has arranged for us to leave tonight on a private plane."

"Where are we going?"

"I'll tell you when I see you."

She understood his hesitancy. "Okay. So, what time should I be ready?"

"Preacher will give you all the details when he sees you."

Again, Kaitlin understood. He was making sure their plans stayed a secret in the event someone was listening in. His house and hers had been swept for bugs, but one couldn't be too careful.

Six hours later, Kaitlin was escorted by Preacher and another associate to a private hangar at LAX. She was met a few minutes later by Matt.

"Did your mother get off okay?" he asked.

Kaitlin nodded. "Ray picked her up around four to

take her to the airport. He insisted on flying with her to Michigan."

"That's good." Matt escorted Kaitlin to the plane.

Preacher and Matt walked off to the side, talking in a hushed whisper.

A few minutes later, he was back on the plane, and they were rolling toward the runway.

"So, are you going to tell me where we're going?"

Matt shook his head. "I think I'll just surprise you."

Kaitlin gave him a quick jab in the side. "Oh, no you don't. Tell me."

"Do you still want to see Greece?"

She was thunderstruck. "You're kidding, right?"

He chuckled. "I'm serious. When we first went out, that was one of the places you talked about visiting."

"I can't believe we're going to Greece."

"First we're going to make a stop in New York. From there, we'll head to Greece."

"On a commercial plane, I hope." Kaitlin still didn't feel comfortable in the smaller planes. But she had to admit that the bigger ones didn't make her feel too much better. It was all due to the Flight 805 crash. Even though she hadn't been on the plane, she easily could have been.

"How're you holding up?" Matt's question intruded on her musings.

"Okay. Planes make me a little nervous these days."

Matt handed her a pillow. "Why don't you try and get some rest?"

"Maybe I will." Kaitlin pulled a blanket up over her.

They didn't arrive in Greece until three days later. Kaitlin wanted to do some sight-seeing in New York.

Matt had chosen Lemnos for the first leg of their vacation. From the air, the island looked like a giant butterfly resting on the water. Kaitlin admired the variety of flowers and plants.

They were staying at the Akti Myrina Hotel. Nestled into forty-one rolling acres filled with flowers and fruit trees, the resort in its sheer natural beauty fulfilled Kaitlin's dreams of what a Greek island should be. Upon their arrival, she had fallen in love with the area.

The bungalows climbed up a small hill from the beach, connected by stone walls, walkways, and flower-filled courtyards. Along the path, there were terra-cotta pots filled with flowers sitting on walls.

"What do you think?" Matt questioned. "Are you glad you came?"

Kaitlin nodded enthusiastically. "It's just the way I envisioned it."

When they arrived at their room, they found it spacious, with native stone walls and floors. Twin beds sat in the middle of the room.

"I just about burst out laughing when the lady at the front desk said we could push the beds together to make it a king."

Matt strode over to the veranda. Kaitlin followed.

"I feel so safe here, Matt."

He gave her a sidelong glance. "I'm glad."

He seemed so solemn. Kaitlin knew he was thinking about Gennai. She put her hand in his. "I'm so sorry, honey. I hate seeing you hurting like this. I wish there was something I could say or do for you."

"I appreciate the thought, but I'll be okay. It's going to take some time, I guess." Wearing a sad smile, he suggested, "Let's change and get this vacation started."

Kaitlin placed the camera to her face. She snapped pictures of the harbor village in Myrina, the capital and main town. She also took pictures of one of the archaeological sites—the prehistoric Poliochni, a Minoan civilization, and the ruins of Pelagian walls, which dated back to 551 B.C. At one time, Kaitlin had wanted to become an archaeologist, but being a romantic at heart, she opted to work in the wedding industry.

"This is an architectural masterpiece," Matt murmured. "I have a picture postcard of the Pelagian ruins. I have always wanted to visit Greece, just to see it in person."

"I've always been fond of the Porch of Maidens and the Tomb of the King in Athens."

"We'll stay here for a week, then fly to Athens and spend some time there."

"Sounds like a plan."

He was eyeing her. "I can't remember seeing you this relaxed in a long time."

"It's been a while," Kaitlin agreed.

They retired early because of the long day they'd had. Matt allowed Kaitlin the first use of the bathroom. She showered and changed into a pair of silk pajama shorts with a matching top. Slipping on a silk robe, Kaitlin stepped into the room.

The light from the candles played provocatively across her skin, highlighting the contours of her body.

Matt could only stare.

Running a hand through her short hair, she grinned. "What?"

"You look beautiful."

His voice caressed her, touching her all over.

He moved off the bed and came toward her. Sweeping her into his arms, he lay on the sheets.

Leaning over her, he said, "I just want one kiss." Matt reached for her, pulling her.

"Sure you can handle it?" she questioned brazenly.

"I can handle anything you have to give." His eyes challenged her.

"Uh-huh," Kaitlin murmured softly.

Matt lowered his head, kissing her gently. Lifting her

arms, Kaitlin pulled him closer. Enveloped in desire, she returned his kiss hungrily. Her hands stroked his bare chest through the thin shirt he wore. His body's reaction was evident to them both.

It was Matt who finally broke the kiss. "Okay, you win."

She couldn't help but grin. Bouncing out of bed, she strode over to the table to retrieve her novel. "I guess it'll be a cold shower you're taking."

Matt swatted her on the behind. "No thanks to you." He left her standing in the middle of the room.

As soon as he closed the bathroom door, Kaitlin's legs gave out, and she dropped to the floor in a heap. Crawling, she managed to climb back into the bed. When Matt came out, she pretended to be reading instead of lying there staring at his muscled body. He was only wearing black pajama bottoms. The man was fine. . . .

Kaitlin lowered her eyes when he glanced her way.

"Enjoying your book?" Matt asked her.

"Uh-huh," she mumbled.

"You're a woman of many talents, I see."

"What are you talking about?"

"You can read a book upside down."

Kaitlin tossed a pillow at him.

As they lay in a tangle a couple of hours later, Kaitlin watched the shadows dance across the walls of the candle lit room. They were good together. More than good, she told herself. Only with Matt had sex been so moving—so thorough and so utterly complete.

She could feel Matt's talented fingers working their magic once more. Kaitlin fought for sanity as the nerves along the surface of her skin tingled.

She felt his fingers against her spine. Shifting her position until she faced him, Kaitlin stared at Matt. Her passion had returned in all its full and amazing force.

They soon joined for the second time that night, rapture touching their souls.

The next week was spent taking a tour of modern Athens. They stayed near the beach in Glyfada.

"I love it here. The sand's so white and pure." Kaitlin scooped up a handful. "Look how fine it is."

Matt fingered a few grains.

"Look at the water. It's almost the color of an emerald."

He agreed. They dove into the sun-warmed water and swam out thirty or forty yards. They treaded water, facing each other. Matt's handsome face glistened in the sunlight. Kaitlin moved closer to him. She reached out and placed a palm against his chest.

The waves were high, and it was windy, so they swam parallel to the beach. Thirty minutes later, they felt as though they'd had a good workout. Matt and Kaitlin trudged back to shore.

Back inside their room, Kaitlin showered and changed first. While she waited for Matt to dress, she lay on her back, staring up as the huge blades from the ceiling fan rotated in slow motion.

It had been a good idea to come to this island with Matt. He was slowly becoming his usual self again.

Matt stuck his head in the doorway. "I hope you're thinking about me."

She sat up. "Always."

He entered the room and strolled toward the bed. Kaitlin swung her feet off the side and sat up, making room for Matt to sit beside her. She was grateful they did not have to worry about pushing beds together like the one in Lemnos.

She was still very guilt-ridden over the secret she carried, but how could she turn Matt's world upside down once again. How much more grief could one man stand?

Kaitlin tried to rationalize that she was doing the right

thing by keeping quiet but she could not avoid the sense of guilt that always followed her reasoning. No one in her family knew her secret.

"Honey, are you okay?" Matt asked. "You've got this look of pure panic on your face."

"No, it's nothing really. I'm fine."

Matt didn't let up. "Is there something you want to tell me? You know we can talk about everything."

Kaitlin pasted on a smile. "The last thing I want to do right now is talk." She stood up and started to unbutton her dress.

"What about dinner?"

"Order room service," Kaitlin stated as the dress fell to the floor.

FOURTEEN

Preacher put away his phone when Sabrina walked into the room carrying a plate of sandwiches and a tall glass of lemonade. "Don't let me interrupt," she said. "I just wanted to bring you something to eat."

Smiling his appreciation, Preacher patted the space beside him. "I hope you're planning to join me."

"There's something I've been meaning to ask. How did you get into this kind of business?"

Preacher took a bite of his sandwich and chewed thoughtfully. "My dad was a cop with the Jacksonville Police Department. He was my role model up until the day he died. I wanted to be just like him."

Feeling his angst, she sought to comfort him. "I'm sure he was very proud of you."

Preacher nodded. "He died shortly after I joined the vice squad."

"Weren't you in the military also? I think I heard you mention that once."

"Yeah. I was a Marine for eight years. Just like my dad."

"Are you still a part of whatever it is?"

"Would it matter if I said yes?"

"I have to admit that I'm a little fearful. I'm beginning to care a great deal for you, Preacher. I have to know where you are or whether or not you're okay. I don't function well on secrets. I have to be honest with you."

"I appreciate your honesty, but you don't have to worry, Sabrina. I'm out of the business now. I've missed ten years of normal life and being around my family. I had a wife once, but she couldn't handle the pressure. With the help of the good Lord above, I am still the same man I was before I went deep undercover. I didn't have a problem giving up the role. Now I can move forward without having to look back. The only reason I'm here now is because a friend needed my help. Once I know that everything is fine, I'm out for good."

"What do you do now?"

"I have a little business in Houston. I guess you might call it a detective agency."

"You call that a little business? Selling ice cream out of a truck in the neighborhood is a little business. That's something that'll get you killed."

"I don't do divorce cases or anything like that. I track down missing persons. I mainly take on cases that have to do with children. Runaways and stuff like that."

"That must really work on your emotions."

"It does. But I'm happy to report that so far I have found ninety-eight percent of my cases."

"That's a blessing."

Preacher downed the last of his lemonade. "Thank the Lord for that."

Sabrina raised her eyes to find him watching her. "What?"

"I was just thinking. I might be able to use your help sometimes. You can go with me to visit the parents—see if you pick up any vibes or something."

She considered his words. "Do you think I could really help?"

"It can't hurt. My old precinct worked with a psychic once on a case. She was able to lead us to the killer."

"Really?"

Preacher bobbed his head. "She came to us because she saw the murder in her mind. At first, my captain was against it, but when the second murder occurred just as she said it would, he changed his tune quickly."

"If there's anything I can do to help you, I will."

"Right now I need a little loving. Think you can help me out?"

Pushing him down on the sofa, Sabrina drawled, "I sure can, darling."

The Japanese man was dead. Elian placed his hand on the scar on his face. But Jaguar was still alive. The man actually had nine lives, it seemed. But the biggest shock of it all had been seeing Kaitlin with Jaguar. At first he thought his eyes were playing tricks on him. Now it all made sense. A.C. watching over Kaitlin like a hawk. They were all in this together.

This revelation did not bode well for Elian, however. From that moment on, everything had gone wrong. It had only been two days since he was tipped off about the hit that had been ordered on his life. Because of the threat on his life, Elian had to avoid all of his regular spots until he could catch a plane to Colombia. From there, he planned to go to Brazil.

As a result of all this, Elian was hiding in a run-down hotel in Santa Monica. The walls in the room were no longer white, just some filthy-looking tan color. The carpet was threadbare and hideous. He kept the paisley-print curtains closed for two reasons: one, he couldn't stand the sight of the cheap furniture, and two, he didn't want to be taken out by a hit man's bullet.

His stomach growled in protest. He hadn't eaten since the previous night, and he was hungry. Elian dialed the front desk.

When the call was answered, he growled, "Get me room service."

"We don't have no room service. There's a Burger King right across the street." She sounded bored and disinterested.

"I don't want Burger King."

"Then I'm sorry. Can't help you."

The woman hung up.

Muttering a curse, Elian knocked the phone off the nightstand. He couldn't take another night in this dump. He was used to the luxury of five-star hotels, but because he was on the run, Elian wanted to avoid the norm. Before leaving, Elian loaded twenty rounds into a Beretta 93R automatic. Feeling a little more secure, he grabbed his keys, then headed to the door and peeked out.

Ever observant, Elian surveyed the area. When his stomach complained loudly, he stepped outside, glancing left and right.

He paused for a moment before strolling over to the car confidently. Elian stole a peek at the floor in the backseat of the rented automobile. He held back his sigh of relief. Just as he opened the car door, the hair on the back of his neck stood up. A frisson of something he couldn't identify traveled through him. His eyes never stopped moving around as he searched his surroundings.

In his world, anyone could be law enforcement or a criminal with an axe to grind. Elian studied everyone he saw in the vicinity. The man peddling ice cream on the sidewalk; the woman who seemed to be engrossed in the magazine she was reading; and the man across the street with the dark glasses. He looked as if he were waiting for the bus or something.

Inside the car, Elian sat just watching the three people whom he felt could cause him trouble. None of them seemed remotely interested in him. Finally he was satisfied.

As soon as he settled the long-overdue score with Jaguar, he would be leaving town. He was in hiding now, but Elian would be patient. He would stick around as long as necessary. His fingers itched to strangle the life out of the one man he hated more than Hector. Even Kaitlin would not escape death this time.

Just as Elian turned the ignition, he glimpsed the face of the woman. Recognition came too late. He was swallowed by the huge fiery blast that followed.

Matt escorted Kaitlin onto the veranda. The air had cooled, a million stars were sprinkled across the dark sky, and the moon was full and bright. Athens was beautiful at night. It all seemed perfect for what he had in mind. Feeling for the tiny ring box in his pocket, Matt decided this was exactly the right moment to propose.

"Kaitlin, will you marry me?"

She clapped her hands in delight. "Yes. Oh, yes!"

Matt laughed. "Sure you don't want to take a second or two to think about this?"

"I've waited so long to hear those words. You can bet I'm not going to wait a moment longer."

Matt's lips touched hers, and she quivered. Her body was pressed tight to the contours of his. A hot yearning raged deep in his soul, desire pounded through his brain, and it was all he could do not to pick her up and carry her inside to bed.

Kaitlin gasped, and pushed her tongue into his mouth. Her hands were everywhere, her breathing as ragged as his own.

He recalled the last time they'd made love. It had been wonderful and intense. Matt lifted his head. "Let's take a walk. It might help cool us off."

"If you say so," Kaitlin murmured softly.

Matt took her hand and helped her down the steps,

keeping hold of her fingers as they walked. Following a path of crushed rock, he led her close to the ocean's edge.

He folded her hand over his arm as they walked the strip of beach beneath the watchful eye of the moon. While they walked, they discussed possible wedding dates.

Kaitlin shivered, rubbing her bare arms.

"Are you cold?" Matt asked.

"A little," she confessed. "But it's not unbearable. I can manage."

"We can turn around now."

"I'm fine, Matt." Kaitlin shivered again, giving Matt an innocent smile.

"No, you're not. Let's head back, sweetheart."

Walking briskly, they strolled to the villa.

Matt ordered a bottle of champagne. When it arrived, he said, "This is a special night. We should celebrate."

After the champagne arrived, Kaitlin and Matt spent the evening holding each other.

Downing the last of the champagne in his flute, he excused himself. Matt returned a few minutes later with another box.

"What's this?" Kaitlin asked while tearing open the gift. Her breath caught in her throat as she gazed at the most exquisite pearl and diamond necklace and earring set. "They're beautiful."

"I want you to wear them on our wedding day."

"Wow! I can't believe this." Hugging him, Kaitlin murmured, "I really love them, Matt."

"They hold special meaning for me. They once belonged to my mother, and her mother before that."

Kaitlin's eyes filled with unshed tears. "I am so very honored that you chose me to be your wife. I'm going to make sure you never regret it."

Matt hugged her. "I know that, sweetheart. There is nothing on earth that will ever tear us apart. We don' have to hide anything from each other. I want you to know that you can always come to me. You can tell me any and all things."

Kaitlin could only manage a tight smile.

The next morning, while Kaitlin was in the bathroom, Preacher called.

"Has anyone found Elian?" Matt asked quickly.

"No need to," Preacher replied. "He's been blown to bits in a car bombing. And back in Mexico, two of his men were found shot to death near Cancun."

"What?"

"Yeah. It happened two days ago. Somebody's taking out Cortez's men right and left. Looks to me like there's going to be a reorganization of some sort."

"Or A.C.'s getting to them," Matt suggested quietly. He glanced over his shoulder to see if Kaitlin had come out of the bathroom.

"Do you really think A.C.'s behind all the killings?"

"She could be. Losing Gennai was really hard on her."

"Yeah."

Neither one spoke.

Preacher was the first to break the silence. "Well, whenever you're ready, you can bring Kaitlin home."

"I want to be sure this is over before I do. What about Hector's daughter? Did you run a check on her?"

"Marta's whistle-clean."

"And her husband?"

"Nothing's come up. But we're still checking."

"Let me know if you come up with something. We're going to stay here for a few more days. I'll check back then." Matt hung up the phone.

"Who were you talking to?" Kaitlin asked from behind him.

Matt hadn't known she'd come into the room. "That was Preacher. Elian was the victim of a car bombing."

"Oh, dear Lord. How dreadful."

"You're upset over the man's death?"

Kaitlin shook her head furiously. "It's just such a horrible way to die."

"Better than he deserved." Matt fell into reflective silence.

Kaitlin eyed him, wondering what he could be thinking about. Although he'd been very attentive to her during their little vacation, she couldn't help but sense that there was something he was hiding from her. Touching his arm lightly, she asked, "You think A.C. did this, don't you?"

"She's an expert with explosives. But this . . ."

"She wanted revenge for Gennai's death."

"I know." Matt covered her hand with his. "I just find it a little hard to believe she's gone this far. Crossing the line like that. Maybe she spent too long undercover."

"Well, I have to admit that I'm not upset in the least over Elian's death. Especially if he murdered all those people. And then he murdered Hector."

Matt wisely held his tongue. He couldn't see the connection. Gennai was a friend. Hector had been a murderer. He deserved to die.

"I've been so worried about Marta—" She stopped short, seeing the expression on Matt's face. "I'm sorry. Let's talk about something else."

"Honey, I know you care for Marta, but you can't forget who she is. Who her father was." Matt didn't want to vocalize his suspicions until he had proof.

"It has no bearing on her," Kaitlin stated flatly. "She and I have been friends for a long time. I don't think I should make her pay for what her father was. It's not fair."

"I don't want to argue about this, Kaitlin."

"We're not arguing. I'm just telling you that I don't abandon my friends—just like you don't. In a sense your friends are no better than killers. At least Marta isn't like that."

Matt stiffened at her comment. "I don't think you're being fair, Kaitlin."

"I'm not saying your friends are criminals, Matt. But even you have to admit that the line between good and evil is a thin one. Even now you're wondering which side of the law A.C. is on. You're scared that your friend might be a murderer."

Matt couldn't refute her statement. What she was saying was true. He believed A.C. had killed Elian.

FIFTEEN

Matt was surprised to find A.C. in his house when he arrived.

"Welcome home," she said with a slight smile. "I trust you and Kaitlin enjoyed your little vacation." A.C. looked past him. "Where is Kaitlin?"

"She's on her way home. Ray picked her up. We had a good time." Matt dropped his luggage. "What are you doing here?"

"I know you, Matt. I knew you'd think I was responsible when you heard about Elian's death. I wanted you to hear it from me that I didn't kill him."

He stared into her eyes.

She leaned against the mantel over the fireplace. "Yeah, I wanted Elian dead, but I didn't do it. I realized that my killing him wouldn't make me grieve for Gennai any less. His death doesn't diminish the pain I feel."

Matt heaved a sigh of relief. He knew A.C. well enough to know that she was telling the truth. But the question remained: Who killed Elian? "Any ideas who might have done it?"

A.C. shook her head. "It could have been anybody. Things are crazy right now in Mexico. Marta is the head of the cartel."

"She took over?"

"Yeah."

Putting a hand to his mouth, Matt contemplated what this could mean. "Kaitlin doesn't know anything about this."

"She probably doesn't. Are you going to tell her?"

"She needs to know about the woman she thinks is her friend. I don't think Marta is to be trusted."

"Hector wanted her to take the cartel legit."

"But how do we know this is what Marta wanted? She could be the one who ordered the hit on her father. We really don't know."

A.C. had to agree.

The telephone rang. Matt answered.

"Hey, man. I'm glad you're home. I've been trying to reach you."

"What's up, Preacher?"

"On the day Elian was murdered, our friend was here in the city. In fact, A.C. was probably a witness to what happened."

Shock filtered through Matt. He cut his eyes to where she stood going through his collection of African-American literature. "Are you sure?"

"There were two other witnesses. They both told police about seeing a woman reading a magazine. By the time the police arrived, the woman had disappeared. The description fits A.C. to a tee. Down to that plait she's always wearing."

Matt felt sick inside. "Thanks."

When he hung up, A.C. asked, "Why didn't you tell Preacher I was here?"

He responded by asking, "Where were you on the day Elian was killed?"

Matt's question stunned her. A.C. blinked twice before she replied, "Excuse me?"

"Were you in Los Angeles?"

They stood almost toe-to-toe, glaring at each other.

"Elian was blown to bits in Santa Monica, Matt."

"And you were in the area, weren't you?"

A.C.'s eyes flashed in her anger. "I *told* you, I had nothing to do with his death."

"Just answer me. I want the truth."

"You are no longer my superior, Matt, so you can just go straight to hell!" A.C. snatched up her backpack. "I'm out of here."

He moved quickly, blocking her path.

"Let's not go through this again. Get out of my way."

"A.C., I want to help you if I can. Please don't leave."

"I thought we were friends, Matt."

She sounded hurt, and Matt felt like a heel. "Honey, I'm your friend—you know that." He took her by the hand and led her over to a chair. Matt eased down beside her. "Please tell me what happened that day."

"I was there," she added quickly. "But I had nothing to do with his death."

"What were you doing in Santa Monica?"

"I had gotten a tip that Elian was staying in this fleabag hotel, so I decided to go there and wait for him to show up."

"You went there to kill him, didn't you?"

"Yeah. Only it was done for me. Elian got into his car and was history. But before he died, I think he recognized me." A.C. gave a slight shrug. "I wouldn't have killed him, Matt. I don't think I could have. Death would've been an easy way out for him. Jail would have been better."

"Why did you run away?"

"The explosion freaked me out. I'd never seen anyone blown up like that. It was a horrible experience."

Matt believed her, and told her so.

Holding up one finger, A.C. confessed, "I will admit that for one tiny moment, I took intense pleasure in the fact that my face was the last one Elian saw."

* * *

Kaitlin's head thrashed on her pillow from her nightmares. Visions of faceless men swirled in her head,
causing her to quickly come awake. Propelling herself
out of bed, Kaitlin slipped on her robe and went downstairs to the kitchen. Navigating to the refrigerator, she
poured herself a glass of water. Throwing the little white
pill in her mouth, she chased it with the cold water.

She had not had one nightmare during the entire time
she and Matt were in Greece. She'd only been home
for a few hours and now they were back.

Kaitlin was thankful for these tiny little pills. They
helped her sleep. She had wanted desperately to have
everything return to normal, but it hadn't. Kaitlin
thought that once she was home, things would get better. She'd hoped the ghosts would disappear. "Please
help me, Lord," she prayed. "I don't want to lose my
mind."

Seeing a man murdered and then Gennai's death had
done something to her. Kaitlin hadn't been able to forget
the strong scent of blood that followed the gunshot, nor
the way the body sat slumped in the chair. She could
even remember what the poor man had been wearing.
Back in the recesses of her mind, there was still something tugging at her memory and Kaitlin couldn't figure
out what it was. It came in fragments of light—even
this didn't make sense to her.

Elian was dead, but she still lived in perpetual fear, and
it was taking its toll on her. Kaitlin headed down the
dimly lit hallway to the bathroom. It was about one A.M.
and the house was quiet. Her mother had retired hours
ago.

After taking a sleep aid, she crawled back into bed
and lay down. Not too long after, she began to feel the
effects of the pill. Her eyelids grew heavy, and she

could barely stay awake. Kaitlin drifted off to a dreamless sleep.

On Sunday, Matt pulled his car into the driveway of Amanda Ransom's home. Kaitlin met him outside. "Everybody's here. I can't wait to tell them about our engagement."

He reached for her hand. "They have probably already guessed. Especially with the ring on your finger."

"I just put it on. I've been wearing it around my neck." She held up her hand. "Four carats is a little hard to hide."

"What's going on, dear heart?" Ivy asked. She had followed Kaitlin outside.

Grinning, Kaitlin held out her left hand.

Ivy beamed with pleasure, embracing her. "Oh, sweetie! You and Matt are finally engaged. Oh, I'm so happy."

"Ivy, please don't say anything," Kaitlin implored her. "We want to tell everyone."

"Girl, I'm sure everyone already suspects. I don't know why people in this family try to keep secrets."

"I know. All of you are so nosy."

Laughing, Matt shook his head.

Ivy tried to look offended. "I wouldn't say that. I would just say that we're all very close."

"Uh-huh," Kaitlin uttered. She brushed an errant curl away from Ivy's face. "Come on, let's go inside before everyone thinks the party's out here."

Just as soon as everyone had gathered around them, Matt and Kaitlin made their announcement.

Elle asked, "So have you two set a date yet?"

Matt nodded. "December thirty-first."

Amanda hugged them both. "That's going to be wonderful. The start of a new year and a new life together."

Shaking hands with Matt, Ray said, "I'm very happy for you both."

"Thanks, man. It means a lot to hear you say that."

"You're a good man, Matt. I know that."

"Take care of my little sister," Garrick stated. "She's special to all of us."

"I will always strive to make Kaitlin happy."

"With God as part of it, you definitely can't go wrong," Laine advised. "People always say that it takes two to make a marriage work. They're half right. It takes two plus the Lord. He has got to be as much a part of this as you and Kaitlin."

"Preach it, Laine," Garrick said.

When Kaitlin and Matt had a moment alone, he asked, "When did Laine get so spiritual?"

"When he was going through all that stuff with his low sperm count. We talked about it a few weeks ago. Laine said that when he rededicated his life to Christ, things just turned around for him. The doctors are even saying it's a miracle."

"That's good. I know how much he wants more children."

Kaitlin nodded in agreement. "The sun rises and sets on Jonathan. Laine is crazy about his son. He's on fire for God, too."

Matt's eyes traveled to where Laine stood talking to his mother. "You know, I wouldn't be surprised if he's been called to the ministry."

Kaitlin's eyes followed his. "Laine? Preach?"

"I can see it."

Regis caught their eyes, and she moved toward them. "What is it?"

"Matt was just saying that he thinks Laine might be called to preach."

"Really? Now that's very interesting."

"What do you think, Regis?" Kaitlin asked. She had

a feeling there was something her sister-in-law wasn't saying.

"I'll support him no matter what."

During dinner, Ray stood and gave a toast to the newly engaged couple.

In a surprise move, Matt planted a kiss on Kaitlin's lips, to the delight of the children. He rose to his feet. "I would like to toast the love of my life. Kaitlin, we've been through a lot just to get here. But we are finally here, and I thank God for it. We will still have to climb mountains, and there will be times we may travel separate paths to get to the top. However, our love is strong—strong enough to conquer any problem. We can agree to disagree on certain issues, it's okay."

Matt's ice-green eyes grew bright. "I guess I'm trying to say that I love you, Kaitlin. I am honored that you have chosen me as your mate for life. Cheers."

Across from them, Jillian and Elle wiped at their tears.

Kaitlin stood beside him. "Matt, you have managed to make me feel so loved. I never thought it possible because growing up in a family this size and this close, well, I thought I had more love than I would ever need. Lord knows I'm blessed." She looked around the table at her mother and her siblings. "While I was away, I would sit and just imagine what you guys were doing." Kaitlin wiped away a lone tear.

"I wondered if I had new nieces and nephews to love . . . new in-laws . . ." She paused for a heartbeat before continuing. "But there were only a few rare moments that I imagined you with someone else. My heart wouldn't let me believe that you could love another woman the way you loved me. Matt, I will strive to walk with you—whatever path you take. We may not always agree, but we will find a way to compromise. Thank you for loving me."

"Please, no more toasts. My contacts can't take it," Ivy complained. She dabbed at her eyes.

"I'm with Ivy. I'm the only person here who doesn't have anybody. I'm getting tired of all this lovey-dovey stuff." Elle pushed away from the table and rushed out of the room.

Jillian and Ivy were both preparing to get up, but Kaitlin stopped them. "I'll check on her."

She found Elle in the bedroom they once shared. She was crying. Kaitlin sat down beside her, wrapping an arm around her.

Elle laid her head on Kaitlin's shoulder. "I'm so sorry, sis. I didn't mean to ruin this for you. I've just had it up to here with all this love and happiness. I want to announce my engagement or that I'm having a baby. I want all that, too."

"I understand." She turned Elle so that her sister faced her. "Listen to me. You are just sitting around waiting for Brennan Cunningham to come knocking on your door. The man is rich, and probably has women chasing him all across the world. If you want him, you'd better throw your hat into the ring."

Elle wiped her tears with the back of her hand. "You think I should just go after him? Just like that?"

"Yeah. Either that, or start dating. There are guys out there who are so crazy about you, but you pay them no mind."

"I am crazy about Brennan. I don't want anybody but him."

"Well, you won't get him by sitting here crying. Go after the man."

Elle laughed. "Jillian would say that, too. Ivy would just tell me that I should move on. She would say that I should face the fact that Brennan may not be interested."

"Yeah, she would." Kaitlin chuckled. "When you want a cold dose of realism thrown in your face, see Ivy."

"Allura's in her own world. She would probably just tell me to follow my heart. That's her advice for everything. And Mama . . . she would say—"

"Pray on it," they finished in unison.

The two sisters burst into giggles.

"Feel better?" Kaitlin asked.

"Yes, I do."

Grabbing Elle by the hand, she pulled her off the bed. "Then come on. I'm starving, and my food is getting cold."

SIXTEEN

Sabrina handed Preacher a computer printout. "Matt and Kaitlin are engaged finally. I think it's wonderful, don't you?"

Accepting the report, he replied, "Yeah. I've never seen Matt happier." Preacher quickly scanned the numbers before handing the report back to her. "These look great."

"Those two people really love each other." She sat down across from him.

"I happen to know of two other people who are just as much in love."

Smiling, Sabrina asked, "Who?"

"Us."

Her smile got even wider. "I do love you, Thaddeus Jacob Watson."

"Sabrina, I've been thinking about something. And since Gennai's death, it's been on my mind a lot."

"What is it, sweetie?"

Preacher cleared his throat nervously. "I think we should get married. I'm not much on long-distance relationships. Long ones period. When I see something I want, I go right after it. In this case, it's you. I'm not trying to scare you off or nothing."

"You're not scaring me."

"Good." Preacher pulled out a tiny box and opened it. "I bought a ring last night."

Sabrina stared at the exquisite emerald-cut diamond surrounded by sapphires. "You really want us to get married? You don't have to marry me to get me to move to Houston."

"Yeah. Girl, I love you to pieces. I don't have much sweet talk for a woman. So don't expect any. But I'll give you my heart. So are we getting married?"

"Yes," Sabrina replied without thinking. She loved Preacher, and she knew without a doubt that she wanted to spend her life with him.

Leaning forward, Preacher grinned. "I am humbled by your acceptance of me. I pray that God will bless our marriage."

Sabrina took his hands in hers. "He will. You have been such a blessing to me. And I'm very thankful for you and your love."

Over lunch, Preacher and Sabrina discussed a wedding date. He left an hour later, leaving her to start plans for their wedding.

He didn't want a big wedding, but he changed his mind when Sabrina cited her reasons for wanting one. She was touched by his thoughtfulness.

They decided to hold off telling anyone for right now. Preacher and Sabrina wanted to revel in their happiness, keeping out the rest of the world. Sabrina reached for the phone. The first person on her list was her minister. She and Preacher both wanted to attend the marriage classes at her church. They believed that under the guidance of Rev. Massey, these classes would help lay the foundation for their marriage.

Sabrina looked forward to getting married again. When her first husband died, she thought she would never be able to love anyone else. Then Preacher walked into her life and changed everything.

Her recollections of Marcus were still very vivid. Sabrina still missed him dearly, but it was time to move on. Marcus would have wanted that for her. Crossing the room in quick strides, Sabrina picked up one of the silver-framed photographs. It was her favorite one of Marcus.

He had been a very handsome man. Tall and fine. Marcus had been all that. An ex-basketball player for the NBA, he had his whole life in front of him. Then one night it had been taken away. Sabrina wiped away a lone tear.

"Marcus, I'll always love you, baby. I want you to know that. You were my first boyfriend. My first lover . . . everything. I'll never forget you or what we shared. I know that you would want me to move on. Preacher makes me happy. Marcus, I'm in love again. But you don't have to worry. You are in my heart, and I will always have our memories." Sabrina held on to the photo as if it were her lifeline. In a short time, she would be starting a new life with a new man. She wasn't scared or nervous about it. It was hard to avoid feeling a small sense of betrayal where Marcus was concerned.

Losing a loved one wasn't easy at all. Then there was the task of meeting someone new. Falling in love was difficult enough, but in situations like this, one had to question whether or not she was in love or just tired of being alone. Sabrina had asked herself this question over and over. The answer was always the same. She loved Preacher.

Laying the picture beside her, Sabrina picked up a brand-new photograph album. She spent the rest of the afternoon putting away her pictures of Marcus.

Kaitlin and the other Ransom women were gathered all over the family room in her mother's house with bridal catalogs and magazines spread out on the floor.

"I thought I'd never see the day when you and Matt would get married."

Thumbing through a copy of *Modern Bride* magazine, Kaitlin burst into laughter. "Leave it to you, Allura. You've said what everyone in this room is thinking. Me included. I have to admit there were times I thought I'd never even get to see Matt again. Or any of you."

"Can we change the subject?" Jillian asked. "I don't want to think about all that. It was hard on all of us, so let's just get past it."

"I understand how you feel, Jillian, but maybe Kaitlin needs to talk about it," Regis suggested.

Jillian glanced over at her sister. "I'm sorry. If you want to talk about anything, we'll listen."

Kaitlin shrugged nonchalantly. It was hard to miss the purplish circles of fatigue under big brown eyes that had always been her best feature. Her family was worried about her, but Kaitlin sought to reassure them. "I think I need to focus on my future. Matt and I are getting married in a few months, so let's just work on the wedding."

Carrie didn't look convinced. "Are you sure?"

"I'm sure." Kaitlin didn't want to dwell on what happened in Mexico, but seeing that man getting his head blown off still haunted her. Although she had no clue as to his identity, Kaitlin knew she would never forget him. Her hands trembled so, that she couldn't hold the scissors. They fell in her lap.

She rose to her feet. "I need some air. Excuse me for a minute." Kaitlin rushed through the house and headed outside.

Carrie had followed her. "Are you okay?"

Kaitlin glanced over her shoulder. "I'm sorry. I just needed to get out of there."

"I understand."

"I'm going to be fine, Carrie."

"Okay. I'll leave you for now. Just remember that I'm here for you."

"I know."

A few minutes later, Kaitlin eased inside. When she entered the family room, everyone grew silent.

Kaitlin gave in to nervous laughter. "I don't believe you all. I've told you already that I'm going to be fine."

Later on that evening, Regis pulled Kaitlin off to the side. "Honey, if you need to talk to someone, feel free to call me anytime."

"I'm fine, but thank you," Kaitlin repeated for the fifth time that day. "I appreciate it."

That night Kaitlin was restless. She lay still, listening in the dark. For what? She had no idea. Every time she closed her eyes, she dreamed of Elian. Every now and then she would hear the sound of a baby crying. She put a hand to her ears to shut out the sound.

Throwing back the covers, she gave up. She needed to take a pill. Otherwise she would get no sleep.

Kaitlin descended the stairs as quietly as she could. In the kitchen, she poured her water and took her pill.

"Hon, what are you doing up?" Amanda questioned from the doorway.

Startled, Kaitlin pressed a hand to her chest. "Oh, Mama, you scared me."

"I'm sorry, baby. I went to the bathroom, and I saw the light downstairs. What are you doing up so late?"

"I just needed to get something to drink."

"What do you have in your hand?"

"Just something to make me sleep."

"Kaitlin, child. What in the world is going on? You're not one for pills."

"I know. And I don't take them often. Just on those nights I can't sleep."

"Baby, talk to me. Tell me what happened over there."

Kaitlin's eyes filled with tears. "Mama, I was so scared. I have never been that scared in my entire life."

Amanda embraced her. "I'm so sorry, baby."

"I never should have gone to Mexico. But I was trying to help out a friend. It was supposed to be three or four days at the most. That's all."

"Matt and I were planning to talk and try to work out our relationship. I shouldn't have run away to Phoenix in the first place . . ."

Amanda stilled Kaitlin's trembling hands. "Honey, slow down. You're losing me."

Kaitlin took a deep breath. "Okay. I shouldn't have moved to Phoenix when Matt and I broke up. I found out shortly after I left that I was pregnant."

Amanda gasped.

"I knew I was pregnant when I came home for Bridget's christening and that's why I gave Carrie the okay to give Matt my phone number."

"The baby . . ."

She held up a hand. "Mama, I went to Mexico and that's when things went wrong. I walked into a room and saw a man murdered."

Her mother paled. "You saw someone murdered?"

She nodded. "That's how all this mess started. I walked into the wrong room. Elian had a gun pointed at this man and just shot him in the head." Kaitlin put her hands to her face. "It was so horrible, Mama. His brains . . . the blood . . ."

"All I could think about was that I was carrying Matt's baby and we were going to die. But then A.C. promised to keep me safe. I told her about the baby. When Hector asked me to marry him, I immediately accepted. I wanted to keep my child safe."

"Then what happened? Where is the baby?"

"I went into premature labor at the beginning of my sixth month. My son was born dead." Tears slipped from Kaitlin's eyes. "I did everything I could to keep him safe, but he died anyway." She cried harder.

"Ssssh, sweetie. It's going to be okay."

"I won't ever forget it. Lord knows I've tried. But I can't. I don't ever want to forget my baby, but everything else can go. I've never been so miserable. Living there and pretending. And the men . . . Hector was so paranoid that he changed bodyguards almost daily. On more than one occasion, I caught a guard leering at me." Kaitlin placed a hand to her mouth. "And then there were the stories these men would tell each other. Talk about your sick puppies." Kaitlin started to claw at herself, feeling dirty.

"Oh, my baby . . ." Amanda said, reaching for her daughter and holding her close.

"I just wish I could feel clean again. I feel so dirty, Mama."

Holding Kaitlin's face in her hands, she stated firmly, "You're not responsible, honey. You're nothing like those monsters."

"What should I do, Mama? Everyone is starting to ask questions—I can't tell them about the baby. The pain is still too fresh."

"Does Ray know about this?" Amanda asked.

"No. Matt doesn't either. Unless A.C. told him, but I don't think she'll say anything. He's lost so many people, I just can't lay this on him, too. Not yet."

"Why not?"

"I already told you. Matt's had so many people die on him."

"You're scared," Amanda threw in. "You're scared Matt will blame you."

Kaitlin nodded.

"It's my fault, Mama. I left Matt and took off to Phoenix. When I found out about the baby, I never said a word. He has every right to blame me. I put our baby in danger."

"Honey, I understand. I really do, but I think you should talk to Matt. I'm sure you two can work through the pain of losing a child together."

"I'm not willing to lose him over this."

"Maybe you won't have to. We won't know anything for sure until you talk to Matt."

"Just let me think about it some more, Mama. Then I'll know what I want to do."

Amanda nodded. "Sure, baby."

Back in her room, Kaitlin sat on the window seat, agonizing over what to do. She couldn't live like this much longer. It was beginning to affect her physically.

Spring was gone and the day announced the first day of summer It was also Matt's birthday. The first thing he did was drive out to the cemetery. His first stop was his twin brother's grave.

"Martin, happy birthday. I pray that you have found some peace finally. You've hurt so many people . . .' He hung his head. "It didn't have to be that way."

Feeling the hair on the back of his neck stand up Matt glanced over his shoulder. A.C. was standing there

"How did you know I would be here?"

"I took a guess." She kneeled down beside him "Happy birthday, Martin." To him, she said, "Happy birthday to you, too."

"You never met my brother."

"No, I didn't. You couldn't have saved him, Matt. No unless he wanted saving."

"I know." He stood and picked up the other bouquet he'd brought with him. A.C. rose. They walked a few feet away, laying flowers on the graves of his parents

Three hundred yards away, Matt laid flowers on

huge gravestone. He placed two similar bouquets on the other three graves. A.C. did the same.

"It's still hard to believe they're gone and not coming back. I keep expecting Gennai to pop up . . ." Matt's voice died. "Ted, too."

"I know how much you loved them both," A.C. murmured.

"Martin and I were twins, but it was Ted who seemed more like my brother. I'll never forget the day Gennai introduced him to Kyoko. It was love at first sight for them." His hands curled into fists. "I've buried almost everybody I have ever loved. I'm tired. Man, I'm tired."

A.C. hugged him. "It's going to be okay, Matt. You and Kaitlin have a beautiful future together. For now, focus on that. Ted, Kyoko, and Gennai are all up there in heaven smiling down at us."

"That whole organization should have blown up with Elian."

"Even death is too good for them, I think." A.C. wiped at a lone tear on Matt's face.

On the Fourth of July weekend, Ray and Carrie hosted family barbecue. When the doorbell rang, Ray went to answer it. Bending down, he greeted the two children standing at the door. He stood up to speak to the parents. "Brandeis, it's so good to see you again. Hello, Jackson."

The couple entered behind a little boy and girl.

Carrie made her way to the door, her eyes traveling to Brandeis's round belly. "Honey chile, why didn't you tell me you were expecting? When are you due?"

"We wanted to surprise you." Brandeis placed a gentle hand on Carrie's protruding belly. "We're due four days apart."

With Jackson's assistance, Brandeis limped over to the sofa.

Mikey burst into the living room. "Y'all made it! Auntie Bran, I missed you like crazy." He was about to leap into her lap but stopped when he saw her stomach. Pointing to her belly, he announced, "We're sure having lots of babies around here."

Everyone laughed.

The kids ran off to play on the patio while most of the adults gathered in the living room and family room.

Sabrina and Preacher arrived a few minutes later.

Dinner was served around two o'clock. Regis, who'd been watching her sister since her arrival, said, "Sabrina, I haven't seen you grin like that in a long time. What's up with you? You sure been acting strange lately. You're not pregnant, are you?"

"No, I'm not pregnant, but I do have something to share with all of you."

Overhearing them, Allura said, "Well, let's hear it." In a loud voice, she called everyone into the den. "Sabrina has an announcement to make."

Kaitlin whispered to Matt, "I bet I know what it is. They're engaged."

A few minutes later, Sabrina said, "Preacher and are getting married. After the wedding, we're going to live in Houston."

Regis's mouth dropped wide open.

Sabrina bubbled with laughter. "Close your mouth, sis."

"When did this happen?"

"Last night. Preacher proposed after dinner."

"I'm so happy for you."

"I'm glad. I know you had your doubts about Preacher, but he's really a good man, Regis."

"Honey, it don't matter what anybody thinks. Just follow your heart," Allura advised.

Kaitlin's eyes found Elle's and held. The two women smiled in amusement.

"You were right. There's going to be another wedding in this family. Sabrina and Preacher are getting married." Matt stood and congratulated his friend.

"So you're going to finally settle down?"

Preacher nodded. "I've finally found someone who makes settling down look real good."

Sabrina awarded him with a kiss.

Ten minutes later, Kaitlin and Matt eased away to one of the other rooms.

"Are you happy for them?" she asked.

Matt nodded. "Why did you ask me that?"

"Well, you looked a little funny in there. I was just wondering at the cause."

"I think they're good together. I was just thinking about Gennai and A.C. They had made plans to spend their lives together. Now she's alone."

"I'm praying that she'll find love again. She's such a beautiful and caring woman. A.C. risked her whole life when she saved my life. She has been through so much herself. I hope she will find happiness."

"Me too. She deserves it."

While Matt was outside playing basketball with her brothers, Kaitlin spent a few minutes with her mother.

"Have you spoken to Ray about those nightmares you've been having?"

"No, Mama. There's nothing he can do about them, so what's the point?"

"I think it'll be better than taking those pills all the time. Talking to Matt will help you, too."

Kaitlin was offended. "I'm not taking medication all the time. Just on those nights I really can't sleep."

"I don't think it's a good idea. They may be addictive."

She struggled to keep her temper in check. "Mama, don't worry about me. I'm fine."

"If that were true, you certainly wouldn't need pills to help you fall asleep."

Kaitlin rushed to her feet. "I'm going outside." She needed some fresh air. Her chest was beginning to hurt, and she felt like she couldn't breathe. Kaitlin regretted confiding in her mother.

Amanda would not let this rest. She would keep pushing at Kaitlin until she pushed her over the edge. She had to find a way to make her mother see what she was doing.

Kaitlin found peaceful solitude on the front porch. Everyone was out in the back. She was still a little upset with her mother, but even that was waning. Swinging on the swing was calming.

Ray broke her moment of blissful serenity by asking, "Hey, sis, can we talk?"

She stopped swinging, allowing him to sit down beside her.

"Sure. What's going on?"

"I wanted to talk about Hector Rosales."

"Did Mama ask you to talk to me?"

Ray shook his head. "No. Why would she ask me to do that?"

Kaitlin looked down at her hands. "I don't know. Just thought she might have."

"You've been inside of the Rosales home for more than two years. Do you remember hearing anything that may have struck you as strange or odd?"

"No, not really. Look, Ray, I didn't attend his meetings or anything like that."

"We know that he had a big bookmaking operation an extortion ring, and several chop shops. We also know that he owned a couple of bars, five restaurants, and candy store. He—"

"I don't know anything about any of that," Kaitli

interrupted. "A.C. is the one you should be talking to. She would know more about this stuff."

"I just wondered if maybe you heard something in passing."

"I can't help you, Ray. And anyway, what difference does it make? Why are the U.S. Marshals so interested?"

"It might clear up some unsolved murder cases and a few disappearances." Ray surveyed her. "What's going on, Kaitlin? Why are you giving me all this attitude?"

Matt joined them. Noting the look of distress on Kaitlin's face, he inquired, "What's wrong?"

"I was asking her some questions about Hector, and she's getting upset."

"I'm tired of talking about life with Hector. Why can't you understand that?" She stared ahead at the house in front of her.

"Kaitlin, it's no big deal. I just had a few questions, and I thought I'd ask. I don't see any harm in that."

"Why don't you just leave me alone." She stormed off the porch.

Ray and Matt exchanged puzzled glances.

"What in the world was that about?"

Shrugging, Matt answered, "I was just about to ask you the same question."

SEVENTEEN

Matt entered the living room. Kaitlin turned around in her chair. When she saw who it was, she said, "I didn't know you were still here."

He sat down on the love seat, facing her.

"I wanted to talk to you."

"About what?"

"Hector Rosales."

Her temper flared. "Not you, too. Matt, why can't you and Ray drop this? The man is dead!"

"Why are you so defensive?"

"I'm just tired of this. I want to move on with my life."

"So do I. But before I can do that, I have to know the truth."

Stunned, Kaitlin asked, "What are you talking about?"

"Why are you so loyal to Rosales? Did you have feelings for the old man?"

"Yes, I did care for him, but not like you're thinking. Hector saved my life, Matt. He was very good to me. I wish you could see past your hatred for him."

Matt looked disgusted. "I will never forgive him for what he did to Ted and his family. *Never.*"

"The man that I came to know was not at all like the one you've described. Hector was kind and he wanted—"

"Don't you try to sing his praises to me," Matt said.

His tone unnerved Kaitlin. She'd never heard him sound like that.

His eyes cold, he stated, "I'm not sure I know you anymore."

"What is that supposed to mean?"

"You left me because I didn't tell you of my connection to Carrie and Mikey. Remember that?"

"Matt . . ."

"No, let me finish. You left me. That's how all this started. Then you go off to Mexico and marry this . . . this murdering bas—" He stopped short. Putting his hand to his mouth, Matt shook his head. "How could you be so forgiving?"

She took a deep breath and sighed. "You don't understand."

Kaitlin opened her mouth to tell Matt about the baby, but she couldn't.

"You're right about that," Matt shot back. "I don't think I can ever understand how you can be so self-righteous about certain situations and defend a cancer-ridden murderer in another."

Kaitlin thought they were past this, but apparently she had been wrong. "I am well aware of what Hector was. All I thought about for the last two years was coming home to you and my family. Matt, we have to find a way to get past this. I don't want to keep having this same argument over and over."

"Neither do I."

"Maybe we should have agreed to just disagree on the subject of Hector Rosales."

Matt wore a strange expression, prompting Kaitlin to ask, "What now?"

"Kaitlin, I think we should put the marriage off for a while. This is really messing with me and I don—"

She cut him off. "You don't want to marry me?"

"I didn't say that. I just need some time to work through my issues. Can you give me that?"

Hurt and anger welled up within her, overflowing. "I'm so sick and tired of your complaining about what you can't deal with. You don't have a clue of what I've had to go through. I don't even think you care. You're so caught up in revenge." Kaitlin was furious now.

"Kaitlin—" he began.

She wouldn't let him finish. "You know what? You can have all the time you need, Matt. The marriage is off permanently. Now get out and don't bother looking back."

"This is not what I want," he shouted.

Laine stuck his head into the room. "What in the world is going on in here? We could hear Kaitlin yelling all the way in the den."

"Matt was just leaving."

"We need to talk about this."

"She wants you to leave, Matt. Why don't you let her cool off for a bit?"

"I don't want to leave her like this."

"She'll be fine. Just give her some time to calm down, okay?"

"Is he gone?" Kaitlin asked from behind Laine.

He turned around to face her. "You want to tell me what just happened here?"

"Matt and I aren't getting married. We broke up."

Laine was clearly surprised. "I can't believe this. Kaitlin, you and Matt have been through so much together. What in the world happened?"

"I think our relationship was endangered from the first, but I have to admit, I never thought it would end."

Laine ran a hand over his face. "Baby, you and Matt have got to work through your difficulties. You can't just walk out every time there's a problem."

"I know that, Laine. It's not me. Matt can't seem to let go of the past."

"Kaitlin, I think you and Matt share this problem."

"What do you mean by that?" she snapped.

"Sis, listen to me. Something happened to you, and you are still dealing with whatever it is. You won't let any of us in. Not even Matt. Maybe if you tell him everything, he'll understand better." Laine shrugged. "I don't know, but it might help."

"I don't believe this," Kaitlin whispered. Did everyone feel this way? she wondered.

"Honey, I'm not trying to hurt you, or upset you. I have a feeling that if you and Matt go your separate ways, you're going to regret it for the rest of your days."

Laine moved closer, stopping in front of her. Planting a kiss on her forehead, he said, "Think about what I've said. Okay?"

Kaitlin promised she would. Her arms crossed, she rubbed them up and down. Maybe Laine was right. For the time being, she just wanted some time to herself. She couldn't take on Matt's issues along with her own.

Matt didn't immediately drive away, instead he sat outside of Ray's house in his car. He wasn't so sure leaving Kaitlin in the state she was in had been such a good idea. He muttered a curse over his selfishness. All of the evidence was right in front of him. Kaitlin's irritability and her need to not talk about Mexico.

He could kick himself for not noticing before. Kaitlin was clearly suffering from some kind of post-traumatic stress syndrome.

Matt arrived home forty minutes later and immediately sat down with his computer. Logging on to the Internet, he searched for everything he could find on the subject.

Kaitlin was hiding something. He was sure of it. But what? What had happened in Mexico and why was it such a secret?

Sitting cross-legged in the middle of the bed, Kaitlin picked up one of the bridal magazines and was about to toss it into her wastebasket. The dress on the cover caught her attention. It was similar to one of the dresses that had been designed by Sara Mendelssohn's daughter, Barbara.

It was too bad she was selling the stores. The woman was a phenomenal designer, but she hated the business end of it. She was willing to stay on as in-house designer . . . .

An idea raged through her. Kaitlin reached for the phone.

When she was done with her phone call, Kaitlin jumped off her bed and headed into the kitchen. "Mama, guess what?"

Amanda looked up. "You and Matt have made up and the wedding's back on. I knew the two of you would work things out."

The smile disappeared from Kaitlin's face. "I haven't spoken to Matt. Things haven't changed between us."

"Oh. Then what news are you talking about?"

"I'm going to buy the stores. That is, if I can get some backing."

"It sounds like a good idea. Sara always talked about making you a partner one day. And you deserve it, too. You've been with that company since you were fifteen years old."

"I remember when Sara was running the first bridal shop from her converted garage space right here in Riverside."

Amanda nodded. "She was just three houses down. Right there on the corner."

"I went down there and asked for a job as soon as I got my work permit."

"She was a good lady. I didn't think she'd hire you, but she did." She frowned. "You're not going to move back to Phoenix, are you?"

Kaitlin shook her head. "No. Actually I'm going to move the home office here."

"Where are you going to get the money?"

"I'm thinking about asking Laine and Garrick."

Amanda nodded her agreement. "They'll help you. Preston will, too."

The rest of Kaitlin's afternoon was spent at the library, working on a business proposal.

Two days later, she met with Laine, Garrick, Regis, and Garrick's wife, Daisi, over lunch.

Laine went over her proposal once more. "This looks wonderful, sis." Closing the folder, he said, "Regis and I talked about this last night. After reviewing everything, we decided it would be a good investment."

"I think it's a wonderful idea, so we don't have any problem lending you the money," Regis announced.

"I can't thank you both enough. I won't let you down." She glanced over at Garrick.

He smiled. Taking the hand of his wife, he said, "You have Daisi's and my full support. She and I both agree that this is a very lucrative venture."

"Thanks so much. All of you. Laine, you'll draw up the contracts for me, won't you?" When he started to object, she added, "No, I want this to be all professional and legal. This is business. I'm going to pay you guys back every cent."

Regis gestured for the waiter. "I think this calls for a celebration."

"What's wrong, sweetie?" Laine asked Kaitlin. "Why are you looking so sad?"

"I was just thinking this would be perfect if Matt were here."

"You and Matt will work everything out," he tried to reassure her. "Just remember what I told you."

"I don't think so, Laine. I don't want to work anything out with him. I won't marry a man who—"

Garrick cut her off. "Hector killed his best friend, Kaitlin. I'll be honest with you. I don't know if I would be so charitable either."

"But, Garrick, he won't even try to understand why I did what I did. I wanted to stay alive. And if it weren't for Hector covering me with his body that day when we were ambushed . . ." Her eyes filled with tears. "I could have been shot, too."

Without a word, Daisi handed Kaitlin a napkin.

Laine covered her hand with his own, squeezing it. "Honey, it's going to be okay. What you and Matt share . . . well, let's just say that you two will work it out. Believe me, I know what I'm talking about."

Matt stood outside the reception area of Dr. Daphne Butler's office. She was the psychiatrist Sasha had seen after Martin raped her. He still was uneasy about seeing the shrink.

He started to leave. Maybe this wasn't such a good idea. The door opened. "Mr. St. Charles?"

Matt turned around. "Yes."

"Won't you come inside?"

"I'm not so sure I'm doing the right thing."

"Why don't we go inside my office and talk. Then if you still feel the same way, you're free to leave."

Nodding, Matt agreed. He followed Dr. Butler into her office.

"This is about my fiancée." Matt went into the details of what Kaitlin had gone through. ". . . Now she's not able to sleep at night. At least not without a pill."

He spent the next hour discussing what he could do to help Kaitlin through her ordeal. Matt learned that a lot of it depended on him changing his attitude. Kaitlin was worth it, he decided. He didn't want a life without her.

EIGHTEEN

A.C. was back in Los Angeles in time for Labor Day. For the past couple of months, she'd been in Philadelphia with her father. Matt opened the door to let her in. "Hey, it's good to see you. Come on in."

They sat down in the den.

"How are you doing, A.C.?"

"Some days are better than others. I miss him so much."

"I wish I could tell you that it gets easier over time."

"My dad said the exact same thing. He's still mourning my mom. In a way it's kind of romantic."

Matt eyed her.

"I'm going to be fine," she assured him. "I will."

"A.C., I worry about you. You try to hide your feelings, and it's not always healthy."

"I've always had to look out for myself. It's hard to put myself into someone else's hands just like that."

"You loved him very much."

A.C. looked him straight in the eye. "I did. I do." She suddenly burst into heartrending sobs. "I don't know how I'm going to make it without him. Gennai and I made so many plans, Matt. We even talked about having children."

"You wanted to have a child?"

"Don't seem so surprised. I love children, and I wanted to be a mother. That's all changed now."

"It doesn't have to. Maybe in time—"

She shook her head sadly. "There won't be another person. I have loved two men with all of my heart and soul. I've lost them both. I can't take another one. I can't."

Matt embraced her.

After a moment, A.C. pulled away. "I need to wash my face." She excused herself and walked the short distance to the bathroom. When she came back, she was her old self once more.

Dropping down in her chair, she said, "I can't believe you and Preacher both are engaged. I never thought I'd see the day when the two of you decided to settle down."

"Preacher's wedding is in a few months, but for me, it'll be a while before that day comes."

A.C. sat forward. "What are you talking about, Matt? You and Kaitlin aren't going to wait that long before you get married, are you?"

"You might as well know. Kaitlin and I aren't going to get married. The wedding's off."

"Who called it off?"

"I wanted to postpone it but things got out of hand," he replied. "Maybe it's for the best right now. Kaitlin's mom told me that she was taking pills to help her sleep at night. She's afraid Kaitlin might get addicted to them. She's been under a lot of stress, and I didn't realize just how bad it was."

A.C.'s expression changed. "Matt, have you lost your mind? Why would you leave her at a time like this?"

"It wasn't my intention. We got into an argument over Hector. Kaitlin has feelings for the man, and it really got to me."

"The man is dead, Matt. What does it matter?"

"A.C., that man . . . you don't understand either."

She was angry now. "How can you say something like that to me? I understand exactly how you feel, Matt. I wanted Elian dead, remember? I'll tell you what kept me from killing Elian. Gennai used to always talk about Grandmaster Takamatsu. He once said that you should reflect on all the progress in your life and allow the positive, creative, and joyous thoughts to outshine and overwhelm any sorrow or grief that may be lingering in the recesses of your mind.

"He was right, Matt. Love is waiting right there in front of you. It's up to you whether you decide to choose it or living the rest of your life filled with regret."

Before she left, A.C. paused in the doorway. "I'm just passing through. I've got to fly to Mexico City tonight. Take all we've said to heart, my friend."

"A.C., do you think you can ever forget what happened?"

"No. I can never forget. I will never forget how the man I loved was shot down right before my eyes and how some of my friends were destroyed. However, I will not be eaten up by hatred."

Half an hour after A.C. had gone, Matt received another visitor. He stepped back to allow Laine entrance into his house. "Hello, Laine."

"I hope you don't mind my stopping by without an invitation, but I was out this way, and you've been on my mind."

"It's fine." Matt gestured toward a chair. "Have a seat."

"No need to. I won't be here long. I came to talk to you about my sister."

His arms folded across his chest, Matt replied, "I figured as much."

"Matt, she loves you very much."

"I love her too, Laine. That won't ever change."

"But you don't want to marry her?"

"It's not that I don't want to marry her. It's just very difficult right now. I think we have a lot to work through before we finally tie the knot."

"I don't know about difficult, but it's stupid." Now that he had Matt's full attention, Laine asked, "Do you remember what you said to me when Regis was pregnant?"

Matt nodded.

"Take your own advice, man. Just think about it. Kaitlin would be dead if she had taken that plane to Phoenix."

"There were a few survivors," Matt countered.

"And she might not have been one of them. My sister was gone two and a half years. Man, you suffered terribly. We all did. Are you sure you want to lose her all over again? And for good this time?"

Kaitlin waited for her plane to Phoenix. Although she tried not to think about it, the crash was prominent in her mind.

It wasn't until the plane began taxiing on the runway that Kaitlin felt a tightness in her chest. It was becoming increasingly difficult for her to breathe. At the moment, all she wanted to do was get off the plane. Kaitlin was in the throes of a panic attack. Instead of things getting better, they seemed to be getting worse.

Feeling dizzy and nauseated, she lay back against the seat with her eyes closed, praying fervently. She soon started to feel better, but she was still shaken.

Barbara met Kaitlin's plane and drove her over to the store. She gave Kaitlin a quick tour. Nothing much had changed, she noted.

"I've never had a head for business. And since Mother's death, I haven't felt much like designing wedding gowns."

"I loved it here."

"Mother would want you to have the stores. So do I."

Over the next couple of days, Kaitlin and Barbara pored over the details of the sale with the Mendelssohn attorney.

Exhausted, Kaitlin practically had to drag herself into her hotel room that evening. She had to stifle a yawn.

The message light on her phone was on. She walked slowly toward it, hoping all the while that Matt had called. Kaitlin picked up the receiver and began to retrieve her voice mail. Disappointment welled up inside her. There was only one message, and it was from her mother.

Kaitlin took a shower and changed into a pair of pajamas. Tonight she planned to order room service, since she didn't feel much like going out. Barbara had invited her over again for dinner, but Kaitlin didn't want to intrude. She'd already spent the last two evenings with Barbara and her family.

Kaitlin stared at the telephone, willing it to ring. She really wanted to talk to Matt. She missed him. Kaitlin burst into tears.

Two days later, Kaitlin returned home. Greeting her mother with a kiss, she asked, "Did Matt call while I was gone?"

"No, dear. I'm afraid he didn't."

"Oh." Kaitlin tried to hide her disappointment.

"Why don't you give him a call?" Amanda suggested. "It's a shame the way you two are behaving. You've been through too much to have it end up this way."

"Maybe you're right." She picked up the phone and called the restaurant. Sasha answered.

"Hi, Sasha. I was trying to reach Matt. I tried him at home but there was no answer. I'm hoping he's there with you."

"I'm sorry, Kaitlin. He's not here at the moment."

"Oh."

"I know where you can find him. He's at Rose Lawn cemetery. He goes by there every other week to put flowers on the graves."

"Oh. He's probably not going to feel up to company when he gets back." Kaitlin knew that Matt was still reeling from Gennai's death. And then there were the others. His parents, Martin, Ted and Kyoko. All of them were buried out there.

"Matt will probably be a basket case when he returns, Kaitlin."

"What do you think I should do?"

"I think you should get your butt over here and straighten out your man. Lord knows I've tried to talk some sense into him. He won't listen to me."

Kaitlin broke into a short laugh. "He may not listen to me either, Sasha."

"Matt loves you. He'll listen."

Kaitlin and Sasha said their good-byes. Opening her laptop on the kitchen table, she sat down to work on a sales forecast.

When she looked up again, it was two hours later. Kaitlin shut off her computer and ran up the stairs to her room. Looking in her closet, she selected a pair of black jeans and a UCLA sweatshirt to put on.

She drove into Los Angeles in heavy Friday afternoon traffic, praying that Matt would be home when she arrived. An hour later, she pulled into his driveway and parked behind the Lincoln Navigator he'd bought at her suggestion.

Kaitlin rapped loudly on his front door. When Matt answered, she stated, "Since it's apparent that you're not going to make the first move, I thought I would."

* * *

"Come in, Kaitlin." Matt stepped back enough to let her enter. He closed the door behind her. They stood facing each other in the middle of the living room.

Kaitlin folded her arms across her chest and said, "Matt, we should talk. We love each other, and I think we really need to communicate better. We haven't even encountered any real trouble yet and we're already calling it quits. I don't know about you, but I'm ashamed of myself."

Matt considered what she said. "Maybe you're right. I've been thinking along those same lines myself." He gestured toward the leather sofa. "Why don't we talk over here?"

Kaitlin followed him to the sectional sofa. They sat down side by side.

Matt took her hand in his. "Honey, I owe you an apology. I have been really selfish."

She was confused by his comment. "What are you talking about? Selfish how?"

"I've been pushing you to relive everything that happened to you in Mexico by talking about your marriage to Hector. It was wrong of me to do so. It didn't occur to me that you were suffering. You weren't sleeping and, I don't know. . . . I just lost it every time I heard you mention Hector's name. Your loving nature is one of the reasons I fell in love with you."

"I fell in love with your forgiving nature, Matt. Your brother was a horrible man. But it didn't stop you from loving him. He was still your brother. You tried to help him. You even tried to make amends for all the wrongs he committed. Carrie clued me in about Sasha. Martin raped her."

"I blame myself for your leaving and ending up in Mexico. I went to see a shrink about helping you and this is what came out. I'm dealing with my hatred of

Hector. I want you to know that I understand why you married him. You were afraid. I'm so sorry, baby."

"I was deathly afraid, Matt. I appreciate your apology. And I guess I owe you some type of explanation, so here it is . . .

"I have been blaming myself for a lot of things."

Matt looked puzzled. "What do you mean?"

"There's something I should have told you a long time ago. I found out I was pregnant shortly after I moved to Phoenix. You had gone to Europe and I . . . I decided that it was over between us."

"You weren't going to tell me about the baby?"

Kaitlin had never seen Matt look so hurt. "I wasn't in the beginning because I was still so angry." Her voice grew tender. "But when I went home for Bridget's christening, I realized how very much I missed you and wanted you to be a part of our child's life."

"You were carrying our child . . . Kaitlin, how could you keep this from me?"

"Please let me finish."

Matt stood up. "Where is the child?"

"Honey, please sit down."

"Kaitlin, tell me."

She sighed heavily. "He was stillborn. I went into early labor."

Matt's eyes became tear bright. "We had a son?"

Kaitlin nodded. "I'm so sorry, Matt. I'd planned to tell you but I ended up going to Mexico. It was supposed to only be a three- or four-day trip at the most."

Matt wore a pained expression on his face. "Did you name him?"

"Yes. His name is Matthew. I named him after you."

Tears rolled down Matt's face, wetting the collarless silk shirt he wore.

"Please forgive me, Matt. I married Hector because

I thought I could keep my baby safe from harm. He promised to protect us by giving us his name."

"My son is a Rosales?"

"He is still your son, Matt. No matter what his name may be."

"Did you see him?" When Kaitlin nodded, he asked, "Did you hold him?"

"Yes. He was such a beautiful baby, Matt. It was love at first sight for me." She choked up. "He looked like he was just sleeping. All I wanted was for him to open his eyes."

Matt reached out, taking her hand in his. "Tell me everything. I want the image of my little boy forever stamped in my mind."

Kaitlin told him everything. How easy the labor had been up until the devastating news that her little boy was dead. She told him about seeing Elian murder a man. ". . . I just can't seem to forget it. It haunts me."

Matt wrapped an arm around her. "Honey, I'm so sorry. I truly am."

"I feel so bad for that man's family because I don't know if they even have a clue what happened to him. But on the other hand, I don't want to have to go to the police or to court. I don't want to have to live my life in hiding. I'm being selfish, too."

"Honey, Elian is dead. So is Hector. They can't hurt you."

Something in Kaitlin's expression prompted him to ask, "Honey, are you okay?"

"Yeah. I'm fine. It's just that I can't seem to . . ." Her voice died. She raised her eyes to Matt. "You know how you remember something but you have no idea what it is, well, that's what I'm feeling now. There's something I should remember. I still feel as if there's something or someone out there waiting to hurt me."

"And you don't have a clue as to what it is? Does it have anything to do with the baby?"

Kaitlin shook her head. "There are times when it seems as if I'm getting close to remembering, but then it just slips away." She chewed on a fingernail.

"Stop that," Matt said gently. He held her closer to him. "I want you to think about some counseling. It may help you."

"I've been considering it. Mama's been after me about it for a while now." Kaitlin sat up straight. "Matt, I'm going over to Ray's. Will you come with me?"

"Sure. Are you ready to tell him everything?"

"Yeah. I think I'll feel better if I do."

They drove the short distance to Ray's house in Westwood. Kaitlin took several deep, calming breaths before ringing the doorbell.

The door opened a few seconds later.

Kaitlin pasted on a smile. "Hello, Ray."

"I didn't expect to see you two. Come on in."

They stepped inside. Matt spoke up. "Ray, Kaitlin needs to talk to you."

He looked from Matt to his sister. "Okay. Sure. Carrie and the kids aren't here. They're over at Ivy's."

With Matt by her side, Kaitlin told her story to Ray. He listened without saying a word. When she was done, he said, "A.C. told me about the murder, but she didn't tell me you witnessed it. With Elian dead, there's nothing we can do." He paused before adding, "I'm sorry about the baby."

"Will I have to testify?" Kaitlin questioned.

Ray shook his head. "The case is closed."

"Do you know who he was? The man that was murdered."

"He was an FBI agent working out of the L.A. office. He was following up on a lead."

"What was his name?"

"Adrian Williamson. Why?"

"I just wanted to know. I feel kind of responsible for him. It might sound kind of dumb to you."

"I understand." Ray lifted her face with his hand. "Sis, why couldn't you tell me this before?"

"I just couldn't." Kaitlin realized her eyes were wet. "Could you do me a favor, Ray?"

"What is it?"

"Could you find out where Adrian Williamson's buried?"

Ray and Matt exchanged puzzled looks.

"I need to do this. Please help me."

"Whatever you need, sis. I'll find out what I can."

Two days later, Matt and Kaitlin traveled to Forest Lawn cemetery. When he parked the car, he turned to face her. "Are you sure you want to do this alone?"

Kaitlin nodded.

"I'll be right here."

She climbed out of the car and walked up the grassy knoll. Kaitlin stopped at the first grave, reading the words engraved on the headstone. The man was the same age as her. She dropped to her knees.

"Hello, Adrian. I . . ." Her voice broke. "I-I was th-there that day." Kaitlin had no idea what to say, but she kept talking. "I'm sorry. I'm so sorry I couldn't do anything to save you. He's dead, you know. Your murderer is dead. I hope this will give you some peace."

Kaitlin placed the flowers she'd brought with her near the headstone before getting up. "May your soul rest with God, Adrian Williamson."

She made her way slowly along the narrow path back to the car. Matt stood with his back against the door on the driver side. He met her gaze. Kaitlin gave him a tiny smile.

When she reached him, Malt held out his arms to her.

She practically rushed into them, needing to feel the security of his embrace.

"I love you," he whispered.

"I love you, too."

"I've been thinking about something."

Kaitlin stepped away from him. "What?"

"I want to bring our son here. I want to move his body here."

She was quiet a moment before responding. "I'm not sure about all the red tape that would be involved. I want Matthew to rest in peace."

"Then I need to go to Mexico to visit his grave."

The look on his face pained her. "I'm so sorry I never told you. I never should have kept my pregnancy a secret."

Matt embraced her once more. "Marry me, Kaitlin. In fact, let's just get married today."

She laughed. "The thought's very tempting, but I really have my heart set on a wedding."

He kissed her. "Then I won't take that from you. We'll have our wedding. And this time nothing will come between us."

NINETEEN

Matt and Kaitlin attended church together the Sunday before Halloween. After the service, she escorted him up to the front to meet her minister.

"Pastor Kenneth, this is Matthew St. Charles. My fiancé."

"It's nice to meet you, brother. I've been looking forward to meeting the man blessed enough to marry Miss Ransom here. She's a wonderful young lady."

"Yes, she is," Matt agreed.

"Will you two excuse me? I need to catch Mrs. Thatcher." Kaitlin rushed off.

Taking advantage of their time alone, Matt spoke with the minister about joining the church and attending new member classes. It was time he found a church home. For the last ten years or so, he'd gone from church to church, looking for one that would shout, *I'm it*. He had come to realize that that wasn't about to happen.

"What were you two talking about?" Kaitlin asked when she joined Matt near the car.

"About my joining the church. I really liked it here."

She seemed a little surprised. "Really?"

He nodded. "I think it's important to make some changes in my life. One of those changes is finding a good church."

They were joined by Laine and his family. "Didn't know you guys were in church today."

Kaitlin gave a short laugh. "That's because you all got there late."

"Jonathan had a little accident on the way out, so we had to turn around and go back home," Regis explained. She glanced around. "Where's Mama Ransom?"

"She's still in the church somewhere. Probably talking to Mother Dunbar." Taking Matt by the hand, she asked, "Are you all heading back home now, or are you coming over for dinner? We were thinking about taking Mama to a restaurant."

"That sounds fine to me," Laine acknowledged. He looked to his wife for confirmation.

Regis agreed.

Late that afternoon, Matt and Kaitlin decided to check out a movie. Amanda had gone straight home after dinner and decided to lie down. Laine and Regis were on their way back to Santa Monica.

"I feel like it's been ages since I've been to a theater."

"Me, too." Matt stuck his hand into the popcorn.

After the movie, Matt drove her back home. At the door, Kaitlin wrapped her arms around him lovingly "Thanks for everything, Matt. This was a wonderful day."

He softly stroked her cheek. "Anything for you sweetheart." Matt's eyes scanned her face. "How have you been sleeping lately?"

"Fine. Since I went to Adrian's grave and have started counseling, I haven't had any nightmares. I threw away the pills."

"Good. That's exactly what I wanted to hear. Honey you're finally safe. Nobody is going to hurt you."

"I know that. You're my black knight."

Matt burst into laughter.

* * *

"Where were you?" Matt inquired when Kaitlin answered the phone. "I've been trying to reach you all day."

"Carrie went into labor early this morning. I went to the hospital with Mama. She had another little girl—a little Halloween baby."

Matt smiled. "That's great. I'm sure they're thrilled."

"Ray's on cloud nine. He wanted another daughter. Mikey is a little peeved, however. He wanted to go to a Halloween party."

"He can still go, can't he?"

"You know everybody's at the hospital. He says they're going to stay there all night."

"I'll try and get by to see Carrie later on tonight and then I'll take Mikey to the party. Think Carrie will be up to some company?"

"Matt, she's got no choice. She's a Ransom. There are so many of us, and we have to be in the middle of everything. You know births and weddings are major events in our lives. We can't miss them."

He tossed back his head and laughed. "Honey, I'll see you later."

"Call Ray at the hospital and tell him that you're taking Mikey to the party."

"Will do. I'll see you on Friday." Matt hung up the phone. Staring at the photo of Kaitlin on his desk, he couldn't hold back his smile. She was smiling back at him, with her beautiful brown eyes and that smooth complexion. His eyes traveled to the mole right above her mouth.

Glancing down at the calendar, Matt counted. Eight and a half more weeks to their wedding. He was looking forward to starting their life together as man and wife.

* * *

Sabrina and Preacher's wedding was the following Saturday. In a medium-sized room near the front of the church, the bridal party readied for the ceremony.

Regis applied the finishing touches to her sister's hair. "You look beautiful, Sabrina. And so happy."

"I am. This is the beginning of a new life for me."

"It shouldn't be boring. Not with a man like Preacher."

"He's a very nice and gentle man, Regis. I'm actually looking forward to being a partner in his detective agency."

"You're very excited about this project, aren't you?"

"I am."

Marc knocked on the door before sticking his head inside. "Sabrina, you ready to get married?"

"I sure am," she replied.

Regis attached her veil. "Okay, you're all set. Let me take off this robe and put on my gloves and then we're ready."

They could hear the music. Regis planted a kiss on her sister's check. "I love you, Sabrina." She took her place in line as the matron of honor.

Marc escorted Sabrina to the altar.

The ceremony was over thirty minutes later.

During the reception, Sabrina and Preacher greeted their friends and family. When Matt and Kaitlin came up to congratulate the happy couple, Sabrina said, "I want you all to meet a very good friend of mine, Khalil Sanford, and his wife, Blythe."

"It's nice to meet you both," Kaitlin stated. She admired the rich African fabric that Khalil wore. They were soon joined by another couple. Kaitlin recognized Sheldon Turner immediately. She used to be a fan of his when he played basketball for the NBA. The two little boys with them looked just like Sheldon.

"Preacher's got celebs turning out for this event," Kaitlin noted. "Boy, he's in the big leagues now."

"You're talking about Sheldon Turner?" Matt asked.

"Yeah. I saw a few other NBA players here as well."

"Sabrina's ex-husband was a basketball player. I remember when he was killed in that car accident."

She snapped her fingers. "That's right. I remember that now. I never got the connection before. She doesn't go by her married name."

"Preacher's a far cry from a professional basketball player. He'll be good to her, though. She won't have to worry about that."

"Matt, it's obvious that Sabrina loves him to death. I don't think he'll have any problems living up to her expectations."

"You're probably right. He's happy, too, In fact, I don't think I've ever seen him happier.

TWENTY

Kaitlin and the other women burst into laughter. The television show was hilarious. The telephone rang, and she reached to answer it, never taking her eyes off the TV. "Hello."

"Kaitlin, it's Marta."

Her smile disappeared.

"Kaitlin, are you still there?"

"What do you want?" she asked in a low voice. When Elle glanced over in her direction, Kaitlin plastered on a smile.

"I need to see you."

"Why?"

"Can we meet somewhere?"

"Why don't you just come to Los Angeles?"

"I'd rather not. I'm sure you understand."

"Actually, I'm not sure I do."

"I'll explain everything to you in person. Meet me in Phoenix. Can you do that?"

"Why Phoenix?"

"I know you bought the Mendelssohn bridal stores." Anger filled her. "Do you have someone watching me?"

"Kaitlin, I'll explain everything to you. I promise. Do me a favor and please come alone."

"Why?"

"Kaitlin, don't worry. There is nothing to fear. I give you my word as your friend. We are still friends, aren't we?"

When she hung up, Ivy asked, "Who was that on the phone?"

"Nobody important."

"Are you sure? You look kind of strange."

"Ivy, mind your own business," Kaitlin snapped, returning her attention to the television. She chewed on her bottom lip nervously. Matt would have a fit if she went to Phoenix to see Marta. It was not an easy decision. Marta was her friend. She really sounded as if she needed to talk.

By the time Kaitlin climbed into bed, she was still undecided. Her mind told her to be careful but the sadness she heard in Marta's voice called to her.

Before she fell asleep, Kaitlin had decided to make the trip to Phoenix.

Kaitlin met Matt over at La Maison. Together they selected the menu for the wedding reception. Afterward, Kaitlin announced, "Honey, I'm leaving tomorrow for Phoenix. I need to check on the final arrangements for the store."

Putting aside his notes, Matt raised his eyes to hers. "I'll go with you."

"You don't have to do that," Kaitlin said quickly. "You've missed so much time at the restaurant. I think you should stay here."

"My restaurant is in capable hands."

"Honey, I still think you should stay here. We're planning a huge wedding in a few months and there are still details that need to be taken care of."

"Okay. Just leave me a list of what needs to be done."

Kaitlin handed him a sheet of paper. "I've already contacted the florist. You can scratch that off the list."

"Okay." Matt glanced up. "When are you coming back?"

"In a day or so. I just want to make sure things are going well. I won't be gone long."

"A few minutes is much too long, baby. Sure you don't want me to come with you?"

"I'm positive." She hated keeping the real reason behind her trip a secret, but Kaitlin knew exactly how he would react. Matt didn't trust Marta. He'd made that clear on several occasions. She could not just walk away from her friend. This talk was long overdue.

Something about Kaitlin's trip to Phoenix bothered Matt. There was more to it than just checking on the store. He was sure of it.

Matt left the restaurant early. As soon as he arrived home, he headed straight to the bedroom. Laying out a garment bag, Matt started pulling underwear out of the drawer. Snatching a couple of shirts out of the closet, he threw them on the bed.

He was going to Phoenix. He'd had Sasha make the arrangements before he left La Maison.

After Kaitlin was done with her business in Phoenix, they would travel to Mexico to visit the grave of their son. He would call the agency and make arrangements for them to enter and leave Mexico without worry.

Matt grieved for the little boy he would never come to know. It still bothered him that his son was buried in Mexico and given the name Rosales. But he was determined to do whatever was necessary to move the baby's body to Los Angeles. Matt made a mental note to have the agency aid him in this as well.

He wanted Matthew buried in the empty grave site

bearing Kaitlin's name. Matt also made a note to call Garrick and have the headstone changed.

Picking up the suitcase, Matt rushed out the house and to the car. He didn't want to miss his flight.

TWENTY-ONE

Marta was already at the restaurant when Kaitlin arrived. They were seated immediately.

"Muchas gracias," Marta murmured to the hostess.

"I'm glad you agreed to see me. After everything that happened, I wasn't sure we would ever see each other again."

Kaitlin's expression was guarded. "What do you want, Marta?"

"I thought we should talk, no?"

"Okay. About what?"

"Can we please order?"

Kaitlin glanced around the restaurant, spotting what she was looking for: Marta's bodyguards. Kaitlin wondered if she was in danger.

"They will not harm you," she said in response to Kaitlin's silent question.

"You said that once before."

"I am so sorry, Kaitlin. I truly mean it."

Her eyes flashed angrily. "Yet you did nothing to help me return home. Marta, I really thought you were my friend."

"And I thought you were mine," Marta shot back. "I actually believed you had amnesia. I even believed that you'd fallen in love with my father. I hadn't seen my father that happy in a very long time."

"I cared for Hector, but I never claimed to love him. I was as honest with him as I could be."

"I suppose it was a matter of survival."

"It was."

Marta surveyed her. "How are you, Kaitlin? Really?"

"What do you think, Marta?" she snapped. "I lost my baby and I saw a man murdered. My life was in danger. How do you think I am?"

"Do you think I'm anesthetized from something like murder? I hate the person my father used to be. I really do. I lost all of my friends because of who he was. All except you." Marta leaned forward. "I hope I haven't lost you, too."

"You put my life in danger, Marta."

"It was an accident. You walked into the wrong room. But it was because of me and my father that you were able to stay alive." Her voice softened. "There was nothing we could do to save the baby."

"Only because you thought I had amnesia. What if I hadn't pretended? Would you or your father have allowed me to live?"

Marta was quiet.

Hurt, Kaitlin stood up. "I've got to go."

Holding out her hands, Marta pleaded with her. "Wait! Please."

She sat back down slowly. "What is it, Marta?"

"I love you like a sister, Kaitlin. I would not allow anything to ever happen to you. I swear it on my own life. I am sorry about what happened. And I hope you can forgive me."

"I don't know, Marta. I just don't know." She was really trying not to hold a grudge, but Kaitlin was finding it hard. Matt had told her that Marta now headed the cartel. In a way, Kaitlin felt a little betrayed. She had always assumed that Marta would stay as far away from the business as possible.

"Please." Her eyes filled with tears.

Seeing the pain on Marta's face softened Kaitlin's heart. She didn't want to hurt her friend. "I want you to know something, Marta. I'm never ever coming to visit you again in Mexico. Never."

"I understand. I hope you will call me every now and then, however."

Kaitlin had to be honest. "I really don't know about that, Marta. Maybe in time . . ."

Matt caught sight of Kaitlin in the restaurant with a woman. Further inspection proved that the woman was none other than Marta Rosales-Guerra.

"So this is why she wanted to come alone," he whispered. She had lied to him.

Disappointment swept through him. Matt had assumed that they were done with the whole Rosales mess. Apparently he had been wrong in his assumption.

He didn't believe for a minute that Kaitlin and Marta had run into each other by accident. This had been a planned meeting.

A part of him wanted to confront Kaitlin, but Matt decided against it. This wasn't the time or the place. He worried about her safety, though. Not seated too far from them were Marta's bodyguards.

He eased into the restaurant and took a seat near the back. The hostess came over.

"Sir, you can't just—"

"I'm here on business. I need you to stay near a phone in the event you have to call the police." Matt never took his eyes off the two women—or off the men in their immediate area. He had to find a way to get Kaitlin out of there.

* * *

Marta's eyes met Matt's. Her mouth dropped open in her surprise. "Jaguar! I thought he was dead."

Kaitlin glanced over her shoulder. It was Matt. *I wonder what in the world he is doing here.* Marta recognized him as Jaguar. Kaitlin warily eyed the men surrounding them. Did they recognize him as well? She was suddenly afraid for him.

Marta returned her eyes to Kaitlin. "Do you know him?"

"He's my fiancé. Excuse me, Marta . . ." Kaitlin rushed to her feet and headed in his direction. She could tell he was furious with her. Kaitlin noted something else in his eyes. Concern. He was worried about her.

"When did you get here, Matt?"

"About an hour ago." Nodding toward Marta, he asked, "Why didn't you tell me you were coming to see her?"

"Because I knew you'd be upset."

"You can't trust her, Kaitlin."

"She and I were once close friends. She wanted to talk to me, that's all."

"Kaitlin, you could have walked into a trap, can't you see that? You are surrounded by thugs."

Kaitlin took Matt by the hand. "I'm sick and tired of this! Come with me right now. We're going to straighten this mess out once and for all."

"Jaguar, I have to admit this is quite a surprise. I'd heard rumors of your demise."

Sitting across from her, Matt replied, "Obviously, they were wrong."

"You and Kaitlin are engaged. I think that's wonderful."

He eyed her. "Do you?"

"*Sí.* Kaitlin is beautiful, she's intelligent and will make you a good wife."

"Why did you want to see her?"

"I felt we needed to talk. We needed to clear the air, Jaguar—"

"Leave Kaitlin alone," Matt demanded. "She doesn't belong in that sick world of yours."

Kaitlin gasped. "Matt . . ."

Marta was a little taken aback. "There is no need for hostility. Jaguar, I am well aware of your feelings for my father."

"Your father murdered a friend of mine and his family."

"I am so sorry for that. I truly am."

"It won't undo what happened."

"You're right, it won't," Marta acknowledged. "Jaguar, I would like to tell you about the last three years of my father's life."

"It won't matter to me."

"Hear me out, please. When he found out about the cancer . . . well, it changed him. He started to have lots of regrets. He made his petitions to God for forgiveness before he died. I'm not trying to excuse what he did—"

"Then don't," Matt quickly interjected.

"Honey . . ." Kaitlin touched his hand. "Just listen to what she has to say."

"Kaitlin, I'm sorry, but I don't care about Hector, or the fact that he had cancer. He was a vicious murderer and the head of a large drug cartel."

Marta became visibly upset by Matt's comment. Huge tears rolled down her cheek. "I understand how you feel, but please understand me. Hector Rosales was my father. I loved him. Much in the same way you loved your brother, Martin. He was the one who died in that car a few years ago."

Matt was a little taken aback. "How do you know about Martin?"

"I know many things about you. Including the fact that

your real name is Matthew St. Charles. I also know that you fathered the child Kaitlin lost. She called for you during her labor. I'm sure you know that I am now the head of the Rosales operations. I promised my father that I would continue what he started. All of the businesses owned by my father will be legitimate within the next two years."

Matt said nothing.

"I want you to know something else. Kaitlin has nothing to fear from the Rosales organization. She and everyone near and dear to her will be safe. You have my word on that. I have taken all the necessary means to guarantee that she will be safe from now on."

Matt met her gaze with his own. "Tell me something, Marta. Did you give the order for Elian's death?"

Marta merely smiled.

"Are you still mad at me?" Kaitlin asked, during their plane ride home. Matt hadn't said much since they left Mexico yesterday. For a while at the cemetery, she and Matt were able to connect, but now he had retreated back into his silent shell. Kaitlin decided not to push. He had every right to be mad, she reasoned.

"I'm hurt that you didn't feel you could share this with me."

"I didn't want to fight with you, Matt. You and I disagree when it comes to Marta."

Giving her a sidelong glance, he said, "I hope she knows what a good friend she has in you."

"I think she does. Marta knows I'll be there for her. No matter what."

"Honey, I really hope this doesn't mean that she'll be coming to our house."

"No, Matt. You don't have to worry about that. After yesterday, Marta and I made our peace, and we kind of said our good-byes. We live in two different worlds, and I don't think the two will ever mesh."

"At least we agree on that," Matt muttered.

Laughing, Kaitlin gave him a jab in the arm.

TWENTY-TWO

Everyone gathered at Laine's house for Thanksgiving dinner.

Amanda stood at the head of the table, saying, "We have much to be thankful for this year. God has blessed us with two new beautiful additions to our family tree. Trevor and Allura's son, Anderson. Ray and Carrie's daughter, Janelle." Amanda's eyes grew bright. "And the return of Kaitlin. Oh, I just praise God for his blessings." Her hands clasped together, she continued, "God is a good God. He never turned his eyes off our Kaitlin. He protected her, even when we had given up hope. I just thank him today and every day. . . ."

"Yes, Lord," Laine murmured. "Thank you, Jesus."

"I think this year we should just take a few minutes and just speak on his blessings. Oftentimes we forget to say thank you."

Laine spoke up. "Mama's right. I want to start by saying that I thank the good Lord above for each and every one of you. I have been truly blessed by having such a wonderful and loving family. I thank him for my wife and my son. I thank him for never turning his back on me even when I turned mine on Him."

"Speak, brother," Preston shouted.

One by one, everyone gave thanks to God. When it was Kaitlin's turn, she said, "I have so much to be thankful for." Her eyes filled with tears. "Answered prayer is powerful."

Everyone murmured their agreement.

She continued. "I thank God for my life. For giving me two loving parents. Wonderful role models in my brothers and sisters. The person who comes into this world without ever knowing what it's like to be loved . . . my heart aches for them. But in being loved, I have learned that one has to love and be able to accept love. In order to have that kind of love, one has to love God. I'm grateful for God-loving parents." Kaitlin paused for a moment. "Thank you, Mama, for teaching me about God's love. You taught us that God was not to be feared but to be loved. It's that love that helped me through all the rough times in my life."

Matt wrapped an arm around Kaitlin. "I thank God for giving me the loving family that I used to dream about as a child. My parents were not the best, but they gave me life. God was never a part of my life as a child. My father was not a believer, and he would beat my mother if she ever mentioned God or church. But I guess God had other plans. He brought Bob into my life. Bob made sure I went to church." He gave a small laugh. "Although I was pretty mad with you on Sundays, thanks, man."

He and Bob embraced.

Matt continued, "I'm thankful that in a few short weeks Kaitlin and I will be man and wife. Lord knows it's been a long road getting there."

Dinner was served and conversation was minimal as everyone ate. After dessert, Kaitlin and Elle volunteered to do the dishes.

"Elle, where have you been? I've been trying to reach you for a week now."

Grinning, she replied, "I was in Hawaii with Brennan." Elle lowered her voice. "I've been seeing him for about two months now."

"And you went to Hawaii with him? Elle . . . I didn't mean for you to—"

"Calm down. I was there on business for Jupiter Records, and Brennan offered the use of his private plane."

"Did the two of you . . . you know?"

Fanning away a curl, Elle nodded. "We did." She burst into a wide grin.

Kaitlin giggled. "Really? Oh, my goodness!"

"He's already told me that he cares for me. Kaitlin, I'm in love."

Embracing her, Kaitlin said, "Girl, I'm so happy for you. See, I told you. Sometimes you have to go after what you want."

A week after Thanksgiving, Amanda handed Kaitlin an envelope. "This came for you earlier by messenger. I guess it was pretty important."

She could tell it was from Marta by the handwriting on the envelope. She opened it and read the note. Marta needed to see her again.

"What's going on with you, girl?" Kaitlin whispered. At least she was in Los Angeles. In the note it said that she'd discovered something about Armando.

Grabbing her keys, she called out to her mother, "I'll be back in a little bit."

Kaitlin pulled out of the driveway and headed toward the freeway. She stuck in a CD. Might as well listen to music, because she was in for a long ride into Los Angeles with the Friday afternoon traffic.

She was relieved when she finally arrived at the Sunshine Bagel Shoppe. Kaitlin and Marta used to eat here all the time when they attended college.

She was barely out of her car when an iron hand grasped Kaitlin by the arm and dragged her out of the door. She resisted as much as she could. Kaitlin fell, scraping her knee. The two men then picked her up and carried her to a waiting car. The driver waited for the simultaneous closing of both doors before speeding away.

Kaitlin sat in the middle of the backseat, with a man on either side. The noises from the street sounded muted, so she could only assume that the windows in the Mercedes had to be bulletproof. She felt the familiar tightening in her chest and it was difficult to breathe. Kaitlin was in the throes of a severe panic attack.

The man sitting on her left became aware of her agitation and tried to calm her. In Spanish, he instructed her to breathe in and out slowly.

Kaitlin noted that the man addressed her as Señora Rosales. Was he one of Hector's men? She didn't recognize him. Kaitlin took a deep breath, and exhaled slowly through her mouth.

The two men on either side were arguing. The one on her right wanted a black bag placed over her head while the other one argued that she was already in distress. Eventually the argument was settled and the black hood was thrown to the floor.

From what she could tell, they were taking her somewhere near Brentwood.

Some time later, they pulled into the driveway of a huge estate. Kaitlin was taken to a room with floor-to-ceiling windows and left there to sit and wait for whoever. She didn't have long to wait. She was soon joined by Armando.

"Kaitlin. It's good to see you again. I knew if I waited long enough, Marta would lead me to you."

"Where is Marta?" From where she sat, Kaitlin assessed him. Marta had been right about Armando being good-looking. He had a blatant sexuality that was apparent in the way he moved and the way he stood. But he had something else, too. He had a presence that spelled dangerous. It was in the coldness of his dark eyes. Kaitlin didn't know why she hadn't noticed it before.

"I thought we should talk. We have a lot to talk about, you and I."

"*We* have nothing to talk about."

"I wish that were true. You, my beautiful Kaitlin, are a liability. I have worked much too hard to let you get in my way." He stared at her, undressing her with his eyes. "It is unfortunate."

"What are you talking abou—" Kaitlin stopped short. In the sunlight, the glint of silver on Armando's boots triggered something in her mind. Suddenly, she had a clear recollection. The hidden memory of that day had been stashed away in the recesses of her brain. Elian wasn't the only man in that room that day. There had been someone else there, too. In the ensuing madness all she'd glimpsed that day was the toe of his boots.

"What is it?"

Kaitlin raised her eyes to meet his, boldly. "You were in the room with Elian that day."

"You act surprised."

"I am. Until now, I didn't remember. It was the way the sunlight hit your boot that brought it all back to me."

"Your timing is awful, no?"

Kaitlin glowered at him. Her hands were trembling so much that she slipped them under her thighs to keep Armando from seeing just how frightened she really was.

"Elian said you were faking your amnesia. I didn't believe him. I merely thought he was being his usual paranoid self."

"Please let me go. I swear I haven't told anyone anything, Armando. And besides that, I wouldn't do anything to hurt Marta. We have already talked."

"Marta has nothing to do with this. I will deal with her later. She and Hector are such pathetic people."

Kaitlin was stunned by the hatred in his voice. "It was you, wasn't it. You were the one who wanted Hector dead."

"Elian and I both wanted him dead."

"Why?"

"He should have died that day instead of Salvador Cortez. *My uncle.*"

Kaitlin was stunned. Armando and Elian were related.

"I went to Hector and told him that I had a friend in Los Angeles. He was the president of a bank, and was willing to allow us to filter money through the bank. Everything had been arranged."

"But he wanted nothing to do with money laundering."

"The man actually looked down his nose at me—as if he were a saint. My uncle died defending Hector. And for what? To see everything he'd worked for crumble to the ground because the old man suddenly got a conscience."

"Hector was dying, Armando. He wanted to make things right before he died. Lord knows he had a lot to make up for, and in the end his heart was in the right place."

"Hector was a fool!" Armando spat. "Right before he died, he wanted to see me. To tell me that Marta would become head of the Rosales Cartel. He said that she would honor his wishes. He wanted my word that I would stand behind her. Hector didn't know it, but that's when he sealed Marta's fate."

"You never loved her, did you?" Kaitlin queried. "You only married Marta because you thought you would become the head of the cartel. You used her."

"It was never personal. Just necessary." He laughed harshly. "And she was so easy."

She was disgusted by Armando.

"How can you be so horrible? Marta is devoted to you."

"And she will die devoted to me."

Kaitlin swallowed hard.

"There were so many times I told Marta how lucky she was to have a man like you. Dear Lord, what does that say about me? But I should have figured it out. Around her, you and Elian acted as if you hated each other. However, I was always finding the two of you in a huddle somewhere. The two of you were arguing that day in the garden." Kaitlin snapped her finger. "I thought Elian was the one in charge, but he wasn't." Her eyes met his and held. *"You were the one.* You ordered the hit on that man, didn't you?"

Armando shrugged nonchalantly. "What does it matter?"

"You also ordered the hit on Elian. You had him taken out. I knew Marta couldn't have done something so vile."

"You should be thanking me."

"Don't hold your breath, Armando. I have nothing to be thankful for when it comes to you."

He placed a hand over his heart. "I am hurt by your words."

Kaitlin scanned the room, searching for something she could use as a weapon.

Armando inched closer to her. She turned her attention back to him.

"You know, I like your haircut. You are a very attractive woman. I've always thought so."

Kaitlin glared at him.

"Come on. Don't tell me you've never thought of us."

"Excuse me?"

"Of us. Making love. You have wondered about it just as I have." He stroked the side of her face. "Very beautiful."

"Don't delude yourself, Armando. You are definitely not my type. On top of that, Marta is my friend."

"Such loyalty." He inched closer to her. "I wonder if you will still feel this way in a little while."

"Stay away from me."

"Kaitlin, I know about Jaguar. He is not man enough for you."

Her laugh was harsh. "And you think you are?"

"Why are you still denying your attraction to me?"

Kaitlin couldn't hide her disgust. "Why can't you see the truth? I despise you, Armando!"

Matt picked up the phone. It was A.C.

"Matt, I've been following a lead on Marta's husband. I'm here in Brentwood, and they just brought some woman here. I wasn't close enough to get a good look at her, but it looked like Kaitlin."

"What?" He tried to quiet his loudly beating heart. "A.C., are you sure?"

"Sure enough to be making this call."

"How long ago?"

"About an hour ago."

"Give me the address. I'm on my way over there."

Matt ran to his room and threw open the doors to his closet. He quickly loaded a gun he kept hidden there. A few minutes later, Matt was running out the door.

On the car phone, he called Preacher and updated him.

"I'll be right there."

"No," Matt argued. "You stay home with Sabrina. A.C. and I will take care of Armando."

"Be careful."

"We will." Before he hung up, he said, "Preacher, say a prayer for all of us. And call Ray."

A.C. met Matt on a deserted road near the estate. "I don't know why I never made the connection. Elian was about as paranoid as Hector was when it came to trust

He was pretty much a loner, but I've seen him several times with Armando in the past."

"What do you know about Armando Guerra?"

"Not much, really. He grew up in Texas. Had a list of arrests as long as his arm, but no prior convictions. Moved to Mexico about six months before he and Marta became engaged."

"Sounds like it was a whirlwind relationship."

"It was. And an even quicker marriage. Kaitlin and Marta had the wedding planned in a matter of weeks. Matt, you're not going to believe this. Armando is really Jose Armando Cortez. His father was Salvador's brother. He and Elian were cousins."

"Why did he bring her here?"

"This house was a wedding gift from Hector to Marta and Armando."

A black Mercedes pulled into the driveway. They couldn't glimpse the driver because of the dark windows.

"Who is that?"

"I don't have a clue," A.C. muttered.

They took pains to avoid being seen as they crawled closer to the huge mansion. Hiding behind a group of bushes, they sat waiting for the driver to get out of the car.

A tall woman dressed in black climbed out. Wearing dark glasses, she glanced around before opening the front door. She seemed to hesitate a moment before easing inside.

A.C. and Matt exchanged looks.

"We've got to get Kaitlin out of there." Matt drew his gun.

"Keep your hands off me!"

"Pretty soon you will be crying out your pleasure." Armando ripped the buttons off Kaitlin's top.

She tried to pull away from him, but his grip was like a steel vise.

Throwing her down on the bed, Armando pulled her skirt up. With one hand holding her down, he tried to unzip his pants with the other.

Kaitlin heard a blast—a loud explosion as three shots rang out in quick succession. Kaitlin saw the look of utter incredulity on Armando's face as he looked down, then back up at Kaitlin before dropping to the floor.

Scrambling away from him, she pulled herself up and made her way to where Marta was standing.

"Marta . . . are you okay?" Kaitlin asked.

Staring in a daze, she replied, "I suppose I should feel guilty or sad, but oddly enough, I don't. Armando betrayed me, and he had my father murdered. He would have killed me, as well. I think that I am entitled to hate him." Suddenly, Marta burst into tears.

Embracing her, Kaitlin said, "I'm so sorry."

"I should be the one apologizing to you. You wouldn't have ever been involved if it hadn't been for me."

"You had no idea of the kind of man you married."

"As it turns out, I didn't know anything about Armando. I didn't even know his heart." She looked woefully at Kaitlin. "His real name is Jose Cortez. He and Elian were cousins."

"He told me."

"I guess it was his plan to have me murdered so he could head the Rosales cartel. No one wanted the organization to go legit."

"What happened here?" Matt demanded as he burst through the door.

"Armando was trying to . . . he attacked me. Marta came in . . ." Kaitlin took in a slow breath. "She shot him."

Kneeling, A.C. checked Armando's pulse. "He's dead."

A gunman burst through the door, waving an automatic in one hand and a badge in the other.

"Freeze! Federal agents."

There were agents everywhere. DEA, U.S. Marshals Fugitive Unit, FBI, and local police. They wandered about the room, mumbling to one another.

Kaitlin looked up at Matt in confusion.

"It's going to be okay," he mouthed.

The adrenaline that had flooded her bloodstream earlier was now dissolving. Fatigue washed over her from head to toe. Kaitlin stole a peek at Marta. She was still standing there wearing a dazed look on her face.

"Marta?" she whispered. "Honey, can you hear me? It's Kaitlin."

Marta did not respond.

"I think she needs a doctor," Kaitlin whispered to Matt. "Look at her. She's in shock or something."

A.C. stood beside them. "I'll take care of her." She grabbed Marta by the arm. "Come on. Let's get you out of here."

Marta offered no resistance.

"Where are you taking her?"

"To the hospital."

"I think I should go with her. I want to go with her."

Matt wasn't sure about this. "Kaitlin, you've been through enough—"

"She's my friend," she countered. "I'm going to be there in case she needs me."

Matt nodded in resignation. "I'm going with you."

TWENTY-THREE

All of the Ransom women gathered at Jillian's house for Kaitlin's last night as a single woman.

"Tomorrow is your wedding day, Kaitlin. Yet you seem so calm."

"Yeah, she sure does," Allura observed. "I was a nervous wreck."

Ivy agreed. "You nearly drove us insane, dear heart."

"I just wanted everything to be perfect."

"And it was," Carrie stated. "Your wedding was beautiful. And it was so sweet of you to include Mikey and me."

"I knew you were the one for Ray."

"All of you had such pretty weddings. Not me—Ray and I got married in the hospital. With matching gowns."

Laughter rang out around the room.

Kaitlin handed a bottle of nail polish to Elle.

"Regis, I'm sorry I missed your wedding to Laine. I saw the pictures."

"Huh, you mean both of their weddings, don't you?" Elle asked.

Julian broke into laughter.

"Well, we all missed the first one."

Laughing, Regis held up her hands. "All right, ladies. Enough about me. Tonight we are here for Kaitlin."

Kaitlin held out her right hand for Elle to polish. "I hope it's perfect. I've worked so hard on everything. It's got to turn out perfect."

"It will, sis," Jillian assured her. "After everything you and Matt have gone through . . . well, let's just say that you're owed this much."

"I imagine it might be a little hard to just settle down into a little boring life after all the excitement you've had in yours lately." Regis reached for a carrot stick and stuck it in her mouth.

"Wrong. Boring is just what I need. The secret-agent life is definitely not for me."

"What do you think our men are doing?" Ivy asked.

Allura and Kaitlin burst into mischievous laughter.

Looking perplexed, Ivy stared at her sisters. "What? What's funny?"

Between giggles, Kaitlin told her what she had done to Matt.

Ivy was clearly not amused. "Mind you, dear heart. It might just backfire on you."

"I'm not worried," Kaitlin shot back.

"Me either," Allura stated. "Trevor isn't crazy."

Silence filled the room as the women stared at one another.

"Okay, Ivy. You stay here with the children and Mama. We're going to Matt's bachelor party," Jillian announced.

Standing a few feet away from a woman garbed in a tiger-print catsuit, Matt demanded, "Who hired the stripper? I said no strippers."

"I didn't do it," Ray announced.

"I didn't," Laine and Garrick chorused.

"Aw . . . come on now. Somebody hired her." Matt had been explicit in his instructions. He didn't want a stripper because he'd promised Kaitlin there wouldn't be one.

Garrick crossed the room in quick strides. "Matt, you're not gonna believe this, but Kaitlin's here. And she's rounded up all of our wives."

"What?" Matt groaned. The night couldn't get any worse.

Nyle burst into laughter. "Some of y'all will be in the dog house tonight."

Matt and Ray exchanged looks.

"Hide her in the back somewhere for now," someone suggested.

Scratching his chin, Matt uttered, "I don't know . . ."

"Would you rather your bride-to-be walk in here and find a half-naked woman dancing on a table?"

"Send her to the kitchen."

Matt did as he was told. It was just in the nick of time, he thought, because when he turned around, Kaitlin was coming toward him. Plastering on a smile, he met her halfway.

"Hi, honey."

"What are you doing here, Kaitlin?"

"I thought I'd come out and see if you were telling me the truth. We did agree there would be no strippers, right?"

Matt could only nod.

She surveyed the room. "Well, it certainly *looks* as if you kept your end of the bargain."

He honestly didn't know how to respond. Kaitlin would kill him if she found that woman in the kitchen.

"Honey, what's wrong? You look as if you're not feeling well."

"I'm fine," Matt croaked.

The women were cracking up with laughter. Tears were trailing down her face, Kaitlin laughed so hard.

"What's so funny?" Laine asked.

Jillian's eyes sparkled with her laughter. "You guys look so guilty. It's hysterical."

Matt tried to appear puzzled. "What are you talking about?"

"My hubby's over there sweating bullets." She asked John, "Anything you want to share with us, sweetie?"

He glanced at the other men before shaking his head.

Kaitlin burst out in another bout of laughter. "Matt, what did you do with her?"

"W-Who?"

"The stripper. Don't tell me you have her hiding in the kitchen."

Laughter rang out through the restaurant.

Matt was floored. "How did you know? Did Sabrina get some kind of psychic vibe or something?"

"No. I'm afraid she had nothing to do with this. I know about the woman because I paid her to come."

"You did what?" Laine asked in shock.

"I arranged for her to come. Tomorrow, Matt and I will become man and wife. I don't see why he shouldn't have some fun tonight." Kaitlin turned to look at Matt. "Just make sure it's the right kind of fun."

He chuckled under his breath. "You are crazy, sweetheart. And you're very thoughtful. However, I don't need a half-dressed stranger over here dancing for me. In fact, now that you ladies are here, let's have a real party."

"I've never heard of this before," Daisi muttered. "We should be home getting our rest for the big day tomorrow. Especially you, Kaitlin."

"I'm fine. Now stop being a mother hen and go over there and dance with Garrick. If you don't, I'll call Tiger Lily out and let her entertain my brother—"

"You'll do no such thing," Daisi snapped. "I'll be the only one stripping for my husband." Realizing what she'd said, Daisi clamped a hand over her mouth, her tawny complexion flushed bright red.

With a yelp, the usually conservative Garrick stated, "Baby, I can't wait to get home tonight."

Everyone cracked up with laughter.

Moving to the beat, Kaitlin followed Matt to the dance floor.

Kaitlin had never been one for tradition. She'd sent out wedding invitations in plastic champagne bottles, had the wedding cake decorated with festive sparklers and chose a wedding dress in a splendid silver color.

She stood beside Preston, oblivious to the chattering going on around her. Her mind was consumed with thoughts of Matt. In a short while, they would become man and wife. Briefly, Kaitlin's gaze settled over her bridesmaids. They were regal and stunning in the forest green gowns they wore. She had chosen the color to complement Matt's incredible green eyes.

Kaitlin felt a slight nudge as Preston whispered, "It's time, sis. I've waited a long time for this wedding to happen."

Smiling, she took his arm and nodded. "I'm ready." It was true. Kaitlin had been dreaming of this moment her whole life. The time when she would marry her soul mate, her best friend and the man who gave her life meaning.

Matt was not prepared for the vision of beauty floating toward him. Kaitlin was exquisite in the form-fitting beaded gown she wore. She had chosen not to wear a veil and Matt decided it was a wise decision. Tiny seed pearls had been arranged throughout her short hairstyle.

As she and Preston made their way up the aisle, Matt smiled.

Moving quickly, he met them halfway. Taking Kaitlin's

hand in his, he kissed her cheek and whispered, "Right at this moment you don't know how happy you've made me. I love you."

With a gloved hand, Kaitlin gently wiped a lone tear that had slipped from Matt's eye. Her own eyes tear bright, she whispered back, "Let's get married."

Together, they moved to stand before the minister.

TWENTY-FOUR

Precisely at the stroke of midnight, newlyweds Matt and Kaitlin St. Charles ate twelve grapes. One for each stroke of the clock, to ensure good luck in the New Year. Kaitlin had come across this custom that originated in Spain while she was researching New Year's Eve traditions for her wedding.

The guests were asked for their New Year's resolutions by the videographer. Personalized wine stoppers were given to the adult guests while tiny top hats filled with candy were handed out to the children. Parents and babysitters had taken the children home hours earlier.

Their reception was an all-night affair, so Matt had engaged his chef to prepare a special sunrise breakfast of pancakes, omelets, croissants, ham, bacon and sausage along with plenty of coffee and juice.

"We should have given out sunglasses as favors," Kaitlin commented. "To cover up the I-partied-all-night look."

Laughing, Matt agreed. He dug into the ham-and-cheese omelet on his plate.

Jillian and her husband had gone home shortly after midnight, but had recently returned for the breakfast buffet. She sat down next to Kaitlin.

"You two couldn't hang, huh?"

"I admit it. We couldn't. By the time we got home

last night, I was dead tired." Jillian reached for her juice. "John fell asleep on the couch." She glanced around the room. "When did Carrie and Ray leave?"

"I think it was about an hour after you left. I knew they weren't going to make it back this morning—"

"They just arrived," Matt cut in. He pointed toward the door with his fork. "They made it."

After she and Matt greeted more arriving guests and ensured that everyone had whatever they needed, they returned their attention to their own plates.

Every now and then Kaitlin would glance over at Matt and smile. He was more than ready to leave. She could see it in his eyes.

Right after breakfast, Matt and Kaitlin made their getaway.

Stifling a yawn, Elle stated, "Instead of riding off into the sunset—I guess you could say Matt and Kaitlin rode into the sunrise."

Putting on her sunglasses, A.C. spared Elle a look. "Honey, you really are tired, aren't you?"

Hidden away in a seaside villa on the island of St. Thomas, Kaitlin lay in Matt's arms.

Staring up at the ceiling fan, she said, "We've been here two days and it's done nothing but rain."

"What does it matter? We haven't really spent any time out of bed."

Planting a kiss on his neck, Kaitlin snuggled closer. "I know, but I'm assuming you're going to want to see something of the island. When Laine was here, he and Regis took some great pictures."

Pulling the covers away, Matt raised himself up. "I'm going to have to give this some serious thought. Taking pictures of paradise or experiencing paradise . . . yeah, I'm going to have to think about this."

Laughing, Kaitlin reached for her husband.

The next ten days went by quickly for the two lovers. They had spent all of their time on the island wrapped in a cocoon of euphoria. St. Thomas had proven to be a lover's paradise.

The night before they were to leave, Matt sat Kaitlin down. "There's something I want to tell you, sweetheart."

"You look so serious," she observed. "What is it?"

"While you were in the shower, there was a new bulletin. Marta . . ." Matt didn't know how to break the news to her.

"She's dead, isn't she?"

He nodded. "She killed herself."

Kaitlin put a hand to her mouth. "She was supposed to be guarded. How could this happen?"

"I don't know all the details."

She shook her head. "Marta didn't kill herself. She was murdered. I don't know how but I know she didn't kill herself."

"She was distraught after Armando's betrayal, honey. Remember how she was after she killed him."

"Still, Marta wouldn't have killed herself. I know her, Matt."

"I'm sorry, baby."

Kaitlin nodded. For a moment she couldn't speak.

"Honey, I arranged for little Matthew to be moved to Los Angeles. He's been buried in the . . . in the empty grave that bore your name." Matt scanned her face. "I hope you're not upset. I just think we should sever our ties to Mexico completely."

Her tears were flowing freely now. "I'm not upset. I just . . . how did you manage this?"

"I contacted the agency and called in a few favors. Garrick changed the headstone to read: Matthew Rosales St. Charles. That's about as charitable as I can be to Hector."

Kaitlin reached for him. "Now Matthew will be close to us. We can visit with him often." She hugged Matt. "I love you so much."

EPILOGUE

Nine months later

Kaitlin squirmed in her chair.

"What's the matter, honey?" Matt whispered. "You've been moving around in that chair all evening. Don't you like the movie?"

"I would enjoy it more if my back didn't hurt so much," she whispered back. "It's been killing me all day long."

He glanced over at her. "Your back has been hurting all day?"

Kaitlin nodded.

"Honey, do you think you're in labor?"

Shrugging, she answered, "I don't know. I don't think so. I've just got a terrible backache, that's all."

"Let's go. I think you're in labor."

"Don't you want to finish the movie? You've been wanting to see this movie for a while now."

"Come on here, girl." Taking her by the hand, Matt ed her out of the theater.

Ten minutes later, when the first hard contraction hit, aitlin knew without a doubt that she was in the throes f labor.

Matt pulled out of the parking lot and headed to the

hospital. When he heard Kaitlin groan, he asked, "Are you having another contraction?"

"Y-Yes."

Matt checked his watch, making a mental note of the time.

"Did you call Mama?"

He nodded. "I called her while you were in the bathroom. I told her I was taking you to the hospital."

"She's not going to try and drive into L.A. tonight, is she?"

"No. Nyle and Chandra were there. They are bringing her to the hospital."

"That's good." Kaitlin settled against the cushions of the front seat and tried to make herself comfortable. Her back protested every move she made. Even the seat belt irritated her. Kaitlin finally unbuckled it and just held it across her.

Matt glanced over, but said nothing. She was grateful, because he was a stickler for people wearing seat belts. Only he would never have to worry about a protruding belly.

As soon as they arrived at the hospital, Kaitlin was taken to a room. While she changed into an unfashionable hospital gown, Matt took care of the insurance information.

She was settled into bed with monitors strapped to her by the time he joined her. "Matt, where's Mama? Is she here yet?"

"Not yet. But Jillian's here. Do you want to see her?"

"Yeah."

Matt crossed the room and stuck his head out the door. "Jillian, she wants you."

Kaitlin was so glad to see her sister, she could have kissed her.

Placing a gentle hand on her cheek, Jillian asked, "How're you doing, sis?"

Before Kaitlin could respond, a great pain overtook her. She squeezed her eyes shut.

"Breathe, Kaitlin. Breathe in and out slowly. The contraction will pass," Jillian advised. "Try to remember what you were taught in Lamaze class."

"I try, but as soon as the pain hits, girl, I feel like I'm losing my mind."

"Focus on the clock or the television when you begin to feel the contraction. Remain as calm as you can. Don't try to fight the pain, just accept it."

Kaitlin looked at Jillian as if she were crazy.

An hour later, Kaitlin was near delirium. Moaning softly, she repeated over and over, "I want Mama. I need my mama."

"Honey, as soon as she gets here, I'll bring her in," Matt said.

As the contractions grew closer, Kaitlin's lack of patience increased. "I don't like this, Matt. I really don't."

All Matt could say was, "I'm sorry, baby."

Seeing the hurt look on his face, Kaitlin instantly regretted her comment. "I didn't mean it like that. It's the pain. I don't like the pain. Why won't the baby come out? Maybe something's wrong."

Matt tried to soothe away her fears.

"Why can't I just have a C-section?" Kaitlin asked her doctor as soon as the woman entered the room.

"You're doing fine, Kaitlin. There is no need for a cesarean."

"Just thought I'd ask anyway." Kaitlin made a face. "I'm really not into this pain thing. I don't think anybody ever hurt like this."

Trying to hide her amusement, the doctor stated, "I think we have all felt that way at one point in time."

"No, I'm serious. I think God has it in for me."

* * *

Thirty-two hours later, Travaile Bevin St. Charles was born. She burst into the world screaming her tiny little head off. Matt was thrilled to death, but also a little worried. Each time he looked over at his wife, Kaitlin scowled. Her expression dared him to come close.

Jillian spied him standing near the window. She walked over to him. "Don't worry, Matt. Once some of the soreness wears off, she'll be back to her old self," she assured him. "It was a long labor and very trying for her, I'm sure."

"I guess now is not the time to mention that I'd like to try again in a couple of years. I would like our children close in age, so they can grow up together."

Overhearing them, Laine said, "I don't know if I'd do that right now. For a long time I couldn't get Regis to even talk about another baby. She's just now considering it." Laine chuckled. "If I were you, I wouldn't mention it to Kaitlin until your daughter's at least a year old. My sister's been known to hold a grudge or two for months on end."

Matt nodded in agreement. "Don't I know it."

Jillian burst into laughter. "Kaitlin's not that bad. Childbirth is hard on a woman. But if we didn't love you guys so much, there probably wouldn't be any children in this family."

The next day, Matt arrived at the hospital carrying a huge teddy bear and an armload of roses. He stuck his head into the room. "Hi, honey."

Kaitlin looked over at him. "Hey, Matt."

She looked so sad, he felt his heart constrict. Was she unhappy over becoming a mother? Matt moved inside the room and took a seat in one of the visitor's chairs near the bed. "You okay?"

She nodded.

This wasn't good, Matt worried. Kaitlin wasn't acting normal at all. He couldn't even get her to look at him.

Suddenly she burst into tears.

"What's wrong?"

Kaitlin didn't respond.

"You don't want the baby?" he asked softly.

The tears stopped. Anger flashed in her dark brown eyes. "Have you lost your mind, Matt? Of course I want our baby. She's my little girl. I'm just so scared I won't be a good mother."

Relief swept through him.

"Honey, you're going to be a great mother. You're so good with all of your nieces and nephews."

"But they're not mine. Travaile is mine. Ours," she quickly amended. "I want to be the sort of mother that Mama is."

"And you will be," he assured her.

"You really think so?"

Matt kissed her. "I know it."

One month later, Kaitlin climbed out of their car and carried the baby's bag while Matt carried Travaile into Amanda's house. This was their first outing since the baby was born.

As was their usual custom, everyone gathered in the family room for announcements. This time, Laine was standing in the center of the room. "Regis and I have an announcement to make. We're going to have another baby."

The room exploded in applause.

"I'm afraid you aren't the only one with baby news," Sabrina remarked. "Preacher and I are expecting, too. In fact, Regis and I are due exactly two days apart."

Again, the applause and good wishes thundered throughout the room.

When Nyle and Chandra stood up, everyone shouted, "You're getting married."

The surprise came when Elle stood up. Even Amanda looked a little puzzled.

"I have some news too." She took a deep breath, then exhaled loudly. "I've been seeing someone. Brennan Cunningham III."

A low murmur snaked around the room.

"That's not all. I'm going to have a baby."

The room was deathly quiet.

"Brennan doesn't know about this baby, and I don't want him to. Please don't ask me why, because I don't want to discuss this beyond today. I'm going to have my baby alone."

After dinner, Kaitlin and Matt took a walk together. Travaile was sleeping, and they decided to spend a few moments alone.

"There were a lot of announcements today," she said. "This family has seen a lot happen over the past few years. We've lost family and close friends . . . it's been a lot."

Matt agreed. "In the interim we've also found love. Brandeis was able to overcome the pain my brother caused her. She's got a loving husband and two point five kids. She's happy."

"My brother was given a second chance with the love of his life. Ray and Carrie are so much in love, and she's a very devoted mother. Then Jillian and John got married. I'm still not over the shock of that. I don't know why I'm so surprised, because they have always loved each other." Kaitlin placed her hand in Matt's. "I'm so glad Laine found Regis. She's so good for him. My family has been truly blessed in the love department. You are my blessing, Matt."

"I'm glad you feel that way. There has been no greater love for me since my heart found yours. I grieve for little Matt but I'm so thankful for Travaile. I'm saddened when I see A.C.—I'm so happy, and I know she's hurting. We've got to do whatever we can to help Elle through her pregnancy."

Holding Matt's arm, she leaned against him. "I feel so bad for my sister and A.C. They deserve so much more. My prayer is for everyone to have at least one chance to experience real love. A love that makes you want to shout about it. It fills you up so that you can't eat sometimes. All you need is that one special look from the person."

"Every time I look at our daughter, I see in her the love we share. There are times, Kaitlin, when I'm holding her, that I am overwhelmed. Love is all around us, baby. In our children, our family, and our friends. We just can't abuse it."

Wrapping her arms around him, Kaitlin said, "I will never take you or our children for granted. Our time together in this life is so precious, and I don't want to lose a minute of it fighting. I want you to know that even though we may not always see things eye to eye, undeniably my heart is yours."

Dear Readers:

Well, here it is: the long-awaited story of Kaitlin and Matt. I truly hope you have enjoyed this one and found it worth waiting for. I really loved working on this project, but not as much as I liked all of your letters and E-mails requesting this story. Thank you so much for your support and words of encouragement.

Please note that I have a new mailing address: PO Box 99374, Raleigh, NC 27624-9374. You can continue to send your E-mails to jacquelinthomas@usa.net, and be sure to visit my Web site at www.jacquelinthomas.com.

Blessings,
Jacquelin

ABOUT THE AUTHOR

Jacquelin Thomas is a multipublished author of African-American romance. While completing her ninth project for BET Arabesque Books, she recently made the move from California, and currently resides in North Carolina.